CONNECT THE STARS

by Marisa de los Santos and David Teague

SCHOLASTIC INC.

ISBN 978-1-338-05226-8

Published by Scholastic Inc., 557 Broadway, New York, NY 10012, by arrangement with HarperCollins Children's Books, a division of HarperCollins Publishers.

12 11 10 9 8 7 6 5 4 3 2 1 16 17 18 19 20 21

Printed in the U.S.A. 40

First Scholastic printing, March 2016

Typography by Sarah Creech

For Susan Cooper and Elizabeth Enright,
whose books we love

CHAPTER ONE

Audrey Alcott

Harriet Tubman Middle School

Greenwood, Delaware

I WAS THIRTEEN YEARS OLD, and I could have written a book on lying. *A Field Guide to Lies and Liars* by Audrey Alcott. I never actually wrote it because that would have been just too depressing, but if such a book existed, it would include little facts like this:

Drive-By Liars shoot out of nowhere and keep talking like it never happened. Red Carpet Liars dress up their lies in sparkles and accessories. Charity Liars are sure they're doing you a favor. Auctioneer Liars talk fast. Helium Liars squeak. Poison Ivy Liars scratch. Sitcom Liars joke. Library Liars whisper. Toothache Liars wince. Underwater Liars take a deep breath first. Fishhook Liars like to watch you squirm. Lost Quarter Liars keep their eyes on the ground. Birdwatcher Liars keep their eyes on the skies.

These examples are just the tip of the iceberg.

Yes, I was an expert, possibly the world's leading. Not because I did it, because I hadn't lied in years. Not because I'd conducted a scientific study of it. I repeat: I was thirteen years old, a seventh grader; I barely had time to finish my homework, much less conduct scientific studies. I was just born with a gift, I guess you could call it. My parents, the only people besides me who knew about it, called it a superpower, but that was mostly just to make me laugh, and let me tell you, there was nothing super about it.

I could tell when someone was lying.

Not just someone. Anyone. *To* anyone. All the time. Every time. Without trying at all. I could tell if someone was lying the way your typical person can tell if someone is laughing or doing jumping jacks. And I'm talking about every kind of lie. Big, small, planned, spur-of-the-moment. White lies, half-truths, false compliments, faked emotions. I'm sure there are plenty of people out there who think a gift like that would be awesome. How cool would it be to be a walking lie detector? Not cool at all. Especially if you happen to think it's nice to like people, trust people, have friends.

I mean, think about it: I knew *every single time* someone was lying. Sometimes I didn't even have to see the person's face. Sometimes I could be so far away that I couldn't even hear the lie. I could just tell. I just knew. And for some reason, once we all hit middle school, kids seemed to lie ten times more than they ever had before.

"I love your haircut."

"I got an A on my social studies test without even studying."

"I tried to call you, but my dumb phone wouldn't work."

"Nice job on your presentation!"

"I wanted to go, but my mom wouldn't let me."

"Oops! I didn't see you there!"

"I love your sweater. Wish I had one just like it."

"Oh my gosh, I totally forgot it was due today!"

"I would never say that about you."

"I am so sorry."

"I promise."

"I *swear.*"

Most of these would slip right by the average person, but none of them slipped by me. I don't even know how many I'd hear in a single school day, but if lies were rotten tomatoes splatting against me, I would have gone home stained every day. On especially bad days, I would have walked out of that school drenched, head to toe, in red. It's why, once I was old enough to make resolutions and stick to them, I decided never to lie myself. It's just too icky for everyone involved. I can't say it was always easy to stick to this, especially when it came to white lies, but when a friend asked something like "Do these pants look bad on me?" I got pretty good at saying things like, "You should wear whatever makes you happy," or "I wish I had hair like yours," or, in especially desperate situations, "Whoa, look at that orange car over there! It's like a giant tangerine!" I got some funny looks, along with some hurt ones; some people got downright insulted. But I knew that lying to your friends was the biggest insult of all.

Then a day came that felt like a miracle, a day when I thought I might actually be doing it: getting through an entire day of school without witnessing or being told a single lie. A lie-free getaway! Just the thought of it filled me with hope. I flew breathlessly out of my last class to my locker and shoved my books into my backpack as fast as I could shove, and victory was just starting to well up inside me like trumpet music, when I slammed my locker door, and there was Lyza Turnbill where she must have been waiting for who knows how long, all moon-bright teeth and eyelashes.

Lyza's eyelashes were her trademark. She'd been fairly popular all along, but December of sixth grade, when she got a tube of mascara in her Christmas stocking, she hit new, dizzying, unforeseen heights of popularity. With a few expert sweeps of the mascara wand, she officially became *That* Girl. But as she stood there next to my locker, the thing I noticed most was not, for once, her lashes. It was her aura. Because Lyza Turnbill was a Migraine Liar.

Ever since I could remember, my mom had gotten migraines, horrible, throbbing headaches that she swore she wouldn't wish on her worst enemy, even though I'm pretty sure she didn't have even one enemy, much less a worst one. Sometimes, before an especially bad migraine hit, her senses sent her signals that it was coming. Weird flashing lights. The smell of rotten eggs. My mom called these signals an "aura."

Lyza's aura didn't smell like rotten eggs, although there would have been a kind of poetic justice in that, and I didn't get a headache after hearing her lie, although I did feel pretty rotten. Lyza's aura was just a feeling: tiny, electric prickles that ran, antlike, up and down my arms. *Oh, come on,* I thought, shivering, *no, no, no, not today. Not when I was so close.*

"Audrey," said Lyza with a moan, "I have some unbelievably bad news."

I didn't say, "Oh, no, what?" The truth was that I had a pretty good idea of what Lyza was about to say, the gist of it anyway. I'd even kind of been expecting it.

I had the crazy urge to yank the locker door back open and climb inside. My second favorite hermit, the poet Emily Dickinson, refused to speak with visitors to her home, unless it was through a closed door, and this suddenly struck me as a brilliant idea. Unfortunately, the lockers at Harriet Tubman Middle School were too small to hold even the tiniest sixth grader. In fact, they'd probably been designed to keep tiny sixth graders from getting shut inside. Which was reasonable, even kind. But right then, I wasn't in a reasonable or kind mood. Right then, I silently cursed the locker designers for callously disregarding the needs of normal-sized seventh-grade girls who wanted to climb in on purpose.

With regret, I turned away from my locker, sighed, and said, "Okay," even though nothing was especially okay.

"So you won't believe this," Lyza began.

Hah. I already didn't.

"But my mom is making me cancel *my birthday party* because my grandmother from California decided *at the very last minute* to come visit me. God, she's *so* annoying!"

For a second I was so distracted by the fact that Lyza had not just lied but *grandmother* lied—it took a very special, extra-cold-blooded kind of liar to drag in a grandmother—that I almost didn't notice that she was doing exactly what I'd suspected: uninviting me to her party.

"She wants to surprise me," said Lyza, rolling her eyes and waving her hands in the air in a mockery of happy surprise. "Except it's obviously not a surprise anymore because my mom had to tell me so I could cancel my party."

How did I know she was lying? How did I know anyone was lying? How could I be so sure? It wasn't something I could break into pieces and explain. I just knew, naturally, automatically. When Lyza lied, the lie was so much a part of her that it *was* her, in every breath, syllable, swallow, finger twitch. It went all the way through, from her invisible pores to her delicate bones. Like she'd been soaking in it. Like she was a lie pickle.

I didn't say anything, just looked at her with a gaze that I hoped was intimidating, an I-know-you're-lying-but-I-don't-really-care stare. Lyza didn't seem to notice.

"Leave it to my grandmother," Lyza said, shaking her head in disgust, "to come all the way from *California*. California is just so far away."

"Yes, it is," I said, because it was the first true thing she'd said.

Then, like something melting, Lyza's face went sad, her mouth pulling down at the corners, her eyes drooping with sorrow. She reached out and squeezed my arm. "I am so sorry. I was so looking forward to hanging out with you, Auds."

That's when I felt a flash of anger. Because saying this to me was so *extra*, so totally unnecessary, so blatantly, stomach-souringly fake. She'd done what she came to do;

she should have just walked away. I was so mad I almost blurted out, "News flash: I wasn't going to go to your party anyway. I'd rather face a pack of wild hyenas than your stupid friends."

The first sentence would have been true. Lyza and I weren't close. We weren't anything close to close, and I was sure she'd only invited me because her mom had made her, which would have been the only reason I'd have invited her to my party, if I were still a person who had parties, which I wasn't. Being at her birthday party when I didn't even like her would have felt like a lie all by itself. Honestly, I wasn't even especially upset that she'd uninvited me. I got it. I mean, the way she did it stank, but the act of uninviting was at least sincere. If she'd just come up and said, "Audrey, I didn't really want to invite you to my party, and I would appreciate it if you didn't show up," I might even have been impressed.

But anyway, the second sentence—"I'd rather face a pack of wild hyenas than your stupid friends"—that one would have been a lie. Not because of the hyenas. I mean, the hyena part wasn't technically accurate, because I'd done a report on hyenas in fourth grade and knew that the spotted ones, at least, were scary and had no problem eating the occasional human, but the hyena part was so obviously hyperbole that it didn't count as lying. It was the rest of the sentence that was a lie. I didn't really think Lyza's friends were stupid. Most of them were my friends too—or had been, before I decided to give up friends the way people give up smoking or chocolate (except for Janie, of course, my best friend in the world. I'd never give up Janie). But most of them were smart or funny or both. So I didn't say that second sentence because, as I mentioned earlier, I never lie, and in the end, I didn't say the first one either, because by the time I'd considered all of this, the angry feeling was gone. All I felt was tired and a little sad, because lies are exhausting and, yeah, a little sad.

Quietly I said, "Well, if the party's canceled, at least Boo-Dog will be happy. He won't have to spend the whole night hiding under the dining room table."

I'm not sure why I said it. Maybe just to make the moment less awkward. Or to remind us both that we hadn't always been who we were right then, the Liar and the Lied To; we'd been more. And then I saw it, so slight but unmistakable: a glimpse of the old, pre-mascara, pre-Y Liza Turnbill, the one who used to play on my and Janie's soccer team when we were seven; who had, almost every day of the summer before third grade, split a blue raspberry Italian ice with me at the pool; and who owned a sweet, shy, slightly overweight pug named Boo-Dog.

"Good old Boo-Dog," said Lyza softly, and for a second,

she sounded so much like Liza that I could almost see her blue-stained teeth.

But then she straightened up, shrugged, and the real Lyza was back.

"See ya, Audrey," she said. And with a swing of her blond ponytail, she was gone.

"Yeah. See ya, Lyza," I said. I tugged my backpack onto my back and slid both straps over my shoulders, like I was going on a journey instead of just out to the bus line.

I walked down the hallway and out the front doors of the school where the buses were waiting. But I didn't get on mine. If I cut through the woods, my house was only a couple of miles away. I'd walked that way before, a lot actually. I knew that no one would be there, except trees, squirrels, and birds, chutes of sunlight slanting through the branches, bright sky overhead, and I knew all these things would be exactly what they seemed to be.

A squirrel wouldn't squeeze my arm and pretend to be my friend. A bird wouldn't lie about its grandmother. The trees would stand tall and straight and honest. The sky would be one long, blue stretch of truth.

Here are some bad things that might happen if you built a tiny cottage next to a pond in the middle of the woods and went to live in it all by yourself, like my first favorite hermit, Henry David Thoreau, did: blisters from hoeing your tiny, just-enough-beans-for-one-person bean field, beestings, sunburn, loneliness, Twizzlers withdrawal.

Here are some bad things that would never happen.

You wouldn't come back to school the Monday after Lyza Turnbill's party and have to listen to people blabbing their heads off about how fun it was, right in front of people who hadn't been invited—or who had been invited and then uninvited, *unnecessarily* uninvited, since they wouldn't have gone anyway, not if you paid them a thousand bucks.

Lyza would not realize that you must have heard about the party, and she wouldn't therefore feel the need to come up to you and say, "Oh, my gosh, Audrey! My grandmother got double pneumonia right before she was supposed to get on her airplane, and her doctor wouldn't let her travel, so I had the party anyway, and I completely forgot to call you to tell you it was still happening, and I, like, didn't even realize I forgot until right this second when I saw you, and I am *so so so* sorry!"

If you were living in a house by a pond, you wouldn't have an English project partner named Xander Fishburne who, just *two minutes* before Lyza told you this lie, handed you the copy of *To Kill a Mockingbird* you'd lent him, damp, bloated to twice its normal size, and totally destroyed, and lied to you (his eyes swiveled upward in perfect Birdwatcher Liar fashion) about how his "stupid little brother" had dropped it in the bathtub.

And this lie would not have put you in a very bad, lie-intolerant mood, so that when Lyza told you *her* lie, you didn't just walk away like you should have but instead stopped dead in the middle of the hallway and said, "You gave your grandmother double pneumonia? *Double?* Wow. That's cold, even for you."

And Lyza would not have narrowed her eyes and said, "I didn't give it to her. She lives three thousand miles away from me, at *least*. She just got it."

And you would not have said, "Did you ever consider, even for a second, just telling me the truth? Just saying, 'Audrey, I uninvited you to my party because I didn't really want you there because we aren't really friends, and I thought that maybe you'd never find out I had it, but then everyone came back to school talking about how my dress matched the hot-pink icing on my three-tiered red velvet cake, and now you know I had the party, and I don't care that much, but it is just a little bit awkward, so I think we should both just forget about it and move on.' Did you ever think of just saying that? Instead of making up a lie about your grandmother having pneumonia in not one, but *both lungs*? Old people can die from that. Did you know that, Lyza?"

And if you were hoeing your bean field in your straw hat and old clothes, miles away from Harriet Tubman Middle School, Lyza would not have started waving her arms around, her big, shiny, obviously new silver bracelet with the rhinestone cursive L dangling from it would not have been practically blinding you, and she would not have started shrieking indignantly, "How dare you call me a liar? Yeah, we're not friends because—guess what?—you don't have any friends anymore because you think you're so great and no one can stand you!" so loudly that everyone in the entire school and possibly everyone in the entire town and possibly even Lyza's grandmother in California could hear.

And all of this is why I should have moved to that house in the woods before middle school even started.

Because I had made a vow never to lie, I couldn't say, even to myself, that what Lyza said to me didn't hurt. It hurt a lot, and part of the reason it did is that it was—at least partly—true. I had decided weeks ago to just stop having friends (except Janie) because if you didn't have any friends, you didn't have to walk around worrying that one of them was going to lie to you. I'd stopped answering texts, stopped asking people over, stopped accepting invitations, and people noticed. They thought I was pushing them away, which I guess I was. Still, it hurt like a kick to the shins to hear Lyza say that I didn't have friends. I stood there, pressing my books against my chest to keep from shaking as she stared at me triumphantly.

"That's not true," I said. My voice came out so small, it was almost a whisper. "Janie's my friend."

Lyza rolled her eyes and said, "Hah! Janie hardly ever even comes to school anymore, probably so she doesn't have to see *you*. And when she does come, she hardly ever talks anymore, probably because she doesn't want to talk to *you*."

"She's been sick a lot lately," I said.

"Sick of you," said Lyza.

That's when I did what I should have done from the beginning—turned my back on Lyza and walked away. A minor crowd had formed around us, and as I walked through it, I looked for Janie's face, but it wasn't there. I remembered her saying something about maybe coming in late that day.

As I made my way through the throng of onlookers, kids jumped back or turned sideways to let me pass, like actual contact with me might bring them bad luck, like friendlessness was contagious. I thought about striding straight past my classroom, out the door of the school, and into the woods. That's what Henry David Thoreau would have done. But Henry David Thoreau probably never had a last-period math test that was worth one-eighth of his grade. I walked to my class. I stayed.

And that turned out to be a big mistake.

CHAPTER TWO

Aaron Archer

Dolley Madison Middle School

West Chester County, Pennsylvania

I CAN REMEMBER ALMOST ANYTHING. When I run across a fact on Google, or in the pages of a history book, or pretty much anywhere else, it goes into a folder on my mental hard drive. If I need it later, I click the folder, and out pops the fact.

And sometimes facts pop out whether I need them or not.

If I hear a symphony, or overhear a conversation, I can play the whole thing back in my head, note for note, word for word, like it's streaming over the internet from a giant data server in rural Oregon. Except it's not in Oregon. It's in my brain.

Most people think it would be great to have an onboard computer like mine, and I can see how you might get that impression. Automatic hundreds on every test, and no pesky studying, right?

If only things were that simple.

Not that I'm complaining. My brain *does* come in handy. If you need to know all the vice presidents in chronological order, or the definition of onomatopoeia, or what the fourteenth element on the periodic table is, then I'm your man. In first grade, when Hardy Gillooly picked me to be on his football team at recess, I dropped six straight passes, and he got sort of mad, but after I recited every single Heisman Trophy winner since 1932 at lunch, he forgot all about it, and we've been best friends ever since.

On the other hand, if you want to know something that's not written down anywhere, like how a king feels about his kingdom, or the true meaning of a poem—well, I'm coming to that.

When I got to seventh grade, my English teacher, Mrs. Dunaway, who was also the Quiz Masters coach, told me I should join the team. Which turned out to be a good idea. My teammates elected me captain, and we swept all our matches leading up to the state finals, where we were favored to win the Pennsylvania State Quiz Masters Championship. For six straight years, the Dolley Madison Destroyers of West Chester County (that's us) had been runners-up to the Philbrick Philosophers of Pittsburgh, but this season, that was going to change.

All the pieces were in place. The sixth grade had thrown a car wash to buy us uniforms with our names on the back. The student council had held a bake sale to raise money for a nutritious lunch at the Spaghetti Factory before the competition started. The volunteer fire department had made a donation so we could ride to Harrisburg in a limo, a yellow stretch Hummer.

The *West Chester Watchman* did an article on us and put our picture on the front page: Hardy Gillooly, Jimmy Stell, Andrea Lark, and me. The reporter made it official. In letters two inches high, she declared DESTROYERS DOMINATE: THIS IS DOLLEY MADISON'S YEAR!

On the ride to Harrisburg for state finals, Mrs. Dunaway ran the team through one last set of drills. To simulate actual game-time conditions, she sat us in a row on the backseat of the Hummer, set a bell on the little table bolted to the floor, and barked questions at us.

"History," she began. "The Smoot-Hawley Tariff was signed in what year?"

Ding. "Nineteen thirty," I said.

"Geography. The nation bordered by Ethiopia, Somalia, and Eritrea is—"

Ding. "Djibouti," I said.

"Wild Card," said Mrs. Dunaway.

I liked Wild Card. It could get interesting.

"Of the two most famous T.E.s in history, one is Thomas Ernest 'T. E.' Hulme, noted British poet, and the other is—"

Ding. "Thomas Edward 'T. E.' Lawrence, 1888 to 1935, also known as Lawrence of Arabia," I said. Of course, there was also T. E. Newell, who played one game at shortstop for the St. Louis Brownstockings in 1877, got zero hits in three at-bats, and disappeared before anybody could find out what his T. E. stood for, but no way was he up there with Lawrence of Arabia, so I kept him to myself.

"Correct," said Mrs. Dunaway. "Geology. The temperature at the Earth's core is—" began Mrs. Dunaway.

Ding. "Ten thousand eight hundred degrees Fahrenheit, or six thousand Celsius," I said.

"So," said Mrs. Dunaway, setting down her notecards, "the team strategy is to depend on Aaron for all the answers?"

"Exactly!" replied Hardy.

"Yes, ma'am!" said Jimmy.

"I guess," sighed Andrea.

"Andrea?" said Mrs. Dunaway.

"It's just that sometimes—" began Andrea.

"Yes?" prodded Mrs. Dunaway.

"I feel kind of awkward," said Andrea. "I wish the rest

of us had more to do. I mean, I know Aaron is just doing what he's good at, and he's the whole reason we've gotten this far, but he answers ninety-eight percent of the questions."

She was right. That number was pretty much smack on the money, based on our successful run through the city, county, and regional championships. Since everything is stored so conveniently in my brain, it usually comes out really fast. So ninety-eight percent of the time, I hit the buzzer before anybody, even my own teammates. Who were actually pretty good, when they got a chance to answer.

"What should we do, team?" asked Mrs. Dunaway, sitting back in her seat with a thoughtful look on her face. She did this kind of thing in class too. She was one of those teachers who let students have a crack at problems before she weighs in. Which I always appreciated, even though it makes more work for us.

Andrea just shook her head. Hardy scratched his ear. Jimmy shrugged.

"Aaron?" said Mrs. Dunaway. "You're the team captain."

See, this was the kind of question I was talking about before, when I said sometimes things are not so simple.

Figuring out what to tell Andrea wasn't like remembering nineteen digits of π or the capital of Kazakhstan. Which is Astana. I could see how she felt, but what should I say? I had no idea. Then a thought came to me. "Rafael Belliard of the Atlanta Braves," I told Andrea, "had a batting average of .000 in the 1995 World Series, but the BRAVES STILL WON!"

That didn't sound quite like what I was after.

Andrea got a funny look on her face.

"Scott Pollard of the Boston Celtics won an NBA championship ring in 2008, even though he didn't play a single minute of a single game," I tried.

That didn't sound right either. What I was trying to get across was—I didn't *know* what I was trying to get across!

"Are you saying I'm Scott Pollard?" asked Andrea a little bit stiffly. "Is that supposed to make me—"

"We're a team, Andrea!" interrupted Jimmy. "We all worked hard this season. If we win, every one of us deserves the championship as much as the others, no matter how many questions we answer in the finals, or don't."

Yep. That was it. Jimmy had hit the nail on the head. Andrea seemed to feel better. Why couldn't I ever think of things like this?

"Thank you, Jimmy," said Mrs. Dunaway, shuffling her

notecards. "And now. More geology. The pressure at the center of the Earth is—"

Ding. "Three million six hundred thousand atmospheres," I said.

"While we're on the topic of geology," said Mrs. Dunaway, scanning through her cards, "what do you know about minerals? Just, I mean, a general overview, so we can go on to other topics?"

"The aforementioned pressure extremes have created many of the minerals valued by people of today," I began.

"Aforementioned!" cried Hardy.

"Examples include apatite, turquoise, gypsum, dolomite, quartz, talc, garnet, molybdenum, and moolooite," I added.

"Moolooite! Yeah!" hooted Jimmy giving me a high five.

"Not to mention diamonds," I concluded.

"We're gonna cream those guys!" added Andrea, perking up.

"You probably are," said Mrs. Dunaway quietly.

"Awesome!" said Principal DuPlessy, who was riding up front with the driver. He turned around to address us. "That kid is smart. Two thousand eight hundred degrees!"

"*Ten* thousand eight hundred degrees," I corrected. "Fahrenheit."

"Whatever," said the principal, digging out his cell phone. "I'm calling Knotts. And this time I'm betting him a—a—a head shave!" Mr. Knotts was the principal of Philbrick Middle School. Principal DuPlessy had bet Mr. Knotts something increasingly dire every year for the past six years, and lost, so he had to carry a teddy bear around school for a day, or wear pajamas, or dye his hair green or . . . now . . . possibly shave it all off—although there was no way that was going to happen.

"Plus," the principal went on, "when we win, the whole school gets a Tae-Kwon-Do-Gurt Fresh Yogurt and Toppings party! With all the toppings! Except peanut butter cups, of course, due to allergy concerns."

Hardy and Jimmy high-fived each other. "Tae-Kwon-Do-Gurt!" exclaimed Jimmy. "Aaron, you rock!"

"Now get out there and win!" thundered Principal DuPlessy, suddenly sounding just like General George S. Patton sending his troops off to battle in Europe. "Or else!" He narrowed his eyes at us. "Just kidding." He chuckled, and we all relaxed. "Not really," he added, his smile disappearing. "'Cause if we win, I've got a shot at Principal of the Year. But if we lose, I have to cut off all my hair." The limo pulled up to the Spaghetti Factory across the street from the convention center. The principal climbed out and stomped away across the parking lot.

"I guess we better win," observed Jimmy.

"Principal DuPlessy does seem kind of worked up," I said a little nervously.

Hardy said, quietly and sincerely, "Aaron, you've got a superpower. A *brain* superpower. Maybe one day you'll use it to do something great, like save a city, or the world. But today, we have some Philosophers to beat!" Hardy was something of a superpower aficionado. Sometimes he and I discussed how many strikeouts Superman might throw if he were drafted by the Phillies. Four million?

"Do you really think I'll do something great one day?" I mused.

Mrs. Dunaway answered. "It's certainly within reach," she said. "For all of you."

"In the meantime, Aaron," said Hardy, "I figured out we have a chance to break the state record. A hundred and four points. Set by the Philbrick Philosophers in 2011."

"Awesome!" said Jimmy. "Plus, get ready to win us a Tae-Kwon-Do-Gurt party!"

Alec LeBec, the famous game-show host, who had grown up in Harrisburg, drew the first Quiz Masters question out of the fishbowl. "Category: History. Name the opening battle of the American Revolution."

Zzzz! I buzzed in.

Hardy fist-bumped Jimmy, who fixed his tie and smiled for the photographer. Andrea watched me intently.

"The Battle of Lexington and Concord!" I said.

"Correct," said Alec LeBec. "More history. The treaty ending the Civil War was signed in what town?"

Zzzz! Me again.

"The treaty to end the Civil War was signed in Appomattox Court House, Virginia," I said.

"Category: Technology and Exploration. The first man to walk on the moon was . . ."

I could tell by the look on Andrea's face. She knew this one. I let my finger hover over the buzzer so she'd have a chance.

Zzzzzz.

Only.

It wasn't our buzzer that'd buzzed. It was Philbrick's. During my moment of hesitation, Sheryce Norman of the Philosophers had beat us to the punch.

"Neil Armstrong," said Sheryce. She looked a little baffled. She'd heard about our team. She was probably surprised she'd even gotten a chance to answer. Andrea shook her head. She looked upset with herself.

Alec LeBec checked his slip. "Correct," he said, and drew another slip. "Science," he intoned. "The boiling point of mer—"

Zzzz. That was me.

"Destroyers?"

"—cury is six hundred seventy-four point one degrees Fahrenheit, three hundred fifty-six point seven degrees Celsius," I answered.

"Literature," read Mr. LeBec from the next slip. "The author of—"

Zzzz.

"Dolley Madison Destroyers?"

The name that appeared most often on the bookshelves of my brain was . . . "William Shakespeare."

Principal DuPlessy began to applaud from the front row. Before he was principal, he used to be the basketball coach, and he liked winning. The crowd joined in.

I knew it was time to do my thing, and I did it, so the Destroyers went on a little bit of a roll after that. By the end of the preliminary round, we had fifty-six points and the Philosophers only had four.

"Now," said Mr. LeBec. "For the bonus round. Philosophers, how many points do you wager?"

"Um, well," mumbled Sheryce. "One, I guess. Since

there's no way we'll win anyway." The rest of her team nodded sadly.

Turning to us, Mr. LeBec said, "Destroyers?"

"Fifty-six!" called out Hardy.

"Wait!" I said. "I mean," I whispered to my team, "that's *all* of our points. We'll win even if we don't bet a thing!"

"Yeah," said Hardy. "But we need to bet a *bunch* to get the record!"

It was true. In the bonus round, if you answered your question right, you doubled your bet. On the other hand, if you got your question wrong, you lost your whole wager. The current high score was 104, achieved in 2011 by the Philbrick Philosophers. With Hardy's bet, we had a shot at scoring 112.

"Maybe we should just go with what we've got?" suggested Andrea.

"Aaron won't get our question wrong," Hardy said. "And we've got to set that record so high it will stay on the books forever! Think about it! A hundred and twelve points! This is your day to shine, Aaron. Knock it out of the park! Fifty-six points, Mr. LeBec!"

Alec LeBec said, "The Destroyers wager fifty-six points."

Sheryce and the rest of the Philbrick Philosophers sat very still. Mr. LeBec drew a slip of paper. "And the bonus question is—"

Zzzz.

Me again, making sure we got a jump on things.

"Could you just wait till I finish?" asked Mr. LeBec.

"Sorry," I said.

"Now," he began, "please answer the following multiple-choice history question . . ."

Piece of cake. Multiple choice. The answer is right there in the question!

"How did the King of England feel in 1776 when his American subjects declared their independence? A, like a father who is disappointed in his children. B, like a judge who must mete out justice to miscreants. C, like a teacher who must teach his students a lesson. D, all of the above."

Zzzz.

I had this.

And then . . . I thought—wait. How did the king *feel*? Was this written down somewhere?

I looked up to find Hardy, Jimmy, and Andrea gazing expectantly at me. Out in the audience, I could see Mrs. Dunaway's eyes swimming strangely behind her glasses.

I mean . . . I—I knew who the King of England was in 1776: George the Third. He imposed unpopular taxes and wore a powdered wig. For that matter, I knew who the King of England was in 802: King Egbert. In 839, King Ethelwulf ascended the throne. I felt myself shaking.

"Hardy? Andrea? Jimmy?" I pleaded with my look. But they couldn't help me. I'd buzzed in. I had to answer.

After King Ethelwulf came King Ethelbald. My palms were clammy. Then King Ethelbert, King Ethelred, and King Alfred the Great. I felt very cold.

How did he *feel*?

Mrs. Dunaway gazed at me sharply from the sidelines. Her pupils were as small as pinpricks. She seemed curious. She seemed concerned. She seemed interested to see what I was going to do next.

There was King Ethelstan and King Edmund the Magnificent. How did the King of England *feel* in 1776? King Edgar the Peaceable. The answer was hidden—underneath all the other answers. King Edward the Martyr and King Ethelred the Unready . . .

Wait—did I say that out loud?

"I'm sorry," replied Mr. LeBec, looking at me strangely. "'Unready' was not one of the choices. Your score is now zero." He turned to the other team. "Philosophers, would you like to attempt an answer?"

"What—the—" stammered Sheryce, staring at me.

"The correct answer is D," said Mr. LeBec. "You lose

one point. Final score: Philbrick Philosophers three, Dolley Madison Destroyers zero." He leaned back from his microphone, far enough so he thought nobody would hear, and he said, "This has got to be the worst Quiz Masters in history."

CHAPTER THREE

Audrey Alcott

Harriet Tubman Middle School

Greenwood, Delaware

AS SOON AS I HEARD Lyza's panicked shrieks in the gym locker room, even before they'd gone from high-pitched animal sounds—think giant, terrified guinea pig—to actual words, I knew I was doomed. I knew not because of any borderline supernatural ability, but just because that was the kind of day I was having. Someone might think that a day that begins with the most popular girl in the seventh grade screeching at you in the hallway in front of everyone about how you have no friends can't possibly get any worse, but I knew it could. I'd spent the day bracing myself for the next hit. Even so, when it came, it was worse than I ever thought it would be.

Somebody stole Lyza's bracelet.

And since, in the middle of gym class, my hair band had broken and I'd had to run back to the locker room for another one, and since half the gym locker doors were so beat-up and bent that they didn't shut properly so that no one even bothered to lock them, and since by that point in the day, the story of my dustup with Lyza the Lyar had bounced around the school long enough to have been embellished and twisted into something way more dramatic and awful than it was (and it was pretty dramatic and awful to begin with), everyone thought I'd taken it. As soon as the girls in the locker room figured out what exactly Lyza was screeching about, every head swiveled, meerkat style, in my direction.

And because Lyza had spent the past eight months unabashedly flattering and sucking up to Coach Prouty, mainly to get out of doing anything in gym that might make her sweat (while the rest of us played volleyball or ran laps until we were half dead, Lyza recorded soccer stats or graded Coach Prouty's health quizzes or stood around fluttering her lashes), when Lyza pointed her manicured finger at me, Coach Prouty believed her right away.

It didn't help that in the face of her accusation, I got a little surly. There was Lyza crying her saucer-sized eyes out in front of the entire gym class and saying, "Audrey and I had a misunderstanding this morning, but I honestly thought we were friends again. I thought we'd both risen above it. We used to play soccer together, and she's always been a nice girl, I mean mostly, and just the thought that she would stoop to *stealing*—wah wah wah, blah blah blah, sob sob sob," and there I was, arms crossed, eyebrows raised, lip curled—surly.

It was all so ridiculous. I had reason to believe that I was quite possibly, almost definitely, the most honest person in the room.

"She probably took it herself just to get Audrey in trouble," someone behind me mumbled, and I looked over my shoulder, hoping it was Janie, but it was Elinor Frack, one of the other non-invitees to Lyza's party. Even as I wished Elinor were right, I knew she wasn't. Lyza's shrieks over her missing bracelet had the unmistakable ring of truth.

When I turned back around, I did see Janie, though. She was in her regular clothes, leaning against a locker in the back of the room. She must have just gotten to school. Through the crowd of people, I caught her eye, and she gave me a quick half smile of moral support before she bent over to tie her shoe.

I was sent to Dean Amory's office. I'd been summoned to her office before, not because I was in trouble—because I never was—but because Dean Amory liked to keep an eye on the emotional and social well-being of her students, and she worried about me. She worried about my thin skin, my low tolerance for lying and deceit, my ever-shortening friend list, my increasing withdrawal from the Harriet Tubman social scene. I knew that she liked me, but still, most of our conversations in her office began with her sighing like a deflating balloon, and this conversation was no different.

"I didn't do it," I told her. "I have no criminal record. I've never even gotten detention. I shouldn't have to defend myself against this spurious accusation, but I will go on record as saying that I did not do it."

"She uninvited you to her party," said Dean Amory. "That must have hurt."

"How did you know that?" But I wasn't really surprised. Dean Amory knew everything that happened at our school. This was such an accepted fact that she didn't even bother to answer my question.

"She told you it was canceled when it wasn't," she said.

"Well, I was never going to go anyway."

Dean Amory frowned her concerned frown, an expression I'd seen many times before. "Why not, Audrey? Social experiences are so important. And parties are fun!"

"Hold on," I said, leaning against the back of my chair and eyeing her. "Do you think I stole Lyza's bracelet because she lied to me about her party?"

Dean Amory sighed again, her shoulders rising up and

up and then suddenly falling like someone had dropped something heavy on them, which, if I'd been in a better mood, might have struck me as sort of funny because her standard line to me was: "Don't carry the weight of the world on your shoulders, Audrey. It's not your job."

"I don't think you stole her bracelet," said Dean Amory evenly, "and I don't not think you stole her bracelet. I'm more interested in why she would accuse you, in what passed between you regarding the party that would make her think you took it. How did you get here, Audrey? Can you tell me?"

"You don't *not think* I stole it?"

"Look," said Dean Amory, opening her hands toward me. "I'm sure that if you did take it, it wasn't because you wanted it. And I'm also sure that if you took it, you will eventually give it back. Sometimes people do wrong things not because they're bad people, but because they feel helpless or lost. I certainly don't believe for a second that you're a common thief."

To my supreme irritation, tears stung my eyes. I stood up.

"I'm not an uncommon thief, either," I said. "I didn't steal it. Not for any reason. I am not a dishonest person."

"Oh, Audrey, we're all dishonest sometimes."

"I didn't steal it."

"Okay. Fine. But let's talk about the deeper issues at play here."

"Are you going to call the police? Suspend me? Throw me out of school?"

My voice trembled when I asked this, because even though I would have dearly loved to walk out of that place and never come back to it in my lifetime, I did not want to be *thrown* out.

Dean Amory gave me a long, drawn-out, searching look before she shook her head. "No."

"Then can I go?"

Wearily, she nodded. When my back was to her, before I could open her door, she said, "It gets better, you know."

Slowly I turned back around. "Are you sure? Because it seems like everything's gotten so much harder this past couple of years."

"For everyone, honey. Self-consciousness is a necessary step in growing up, but it can also be a little painful. Remember when you laughed at whatever you thought was funny without worrying about whether other people thought it was? Remember when you wore exactly what you wanted?"

I thought about it. "I had these rain boots with strawberries on them. I wore them even when it wasn't raining."

"And no one cared or probably even really noticed. Right now, everyone's trying to figure out who they are, where they fit, what their roles are. They don't always say what they mean. Sometimes they say things they don't mean. Maybe they aren't their best selves, but they're trying."

"I wish it could have stayed the way it used to be. People lied a lot less."

"I promise it gets better."

I could tell she wasn't just saying this; she honestly believed it. I felt a sob rise in my throat. "I really do want you to be right about that," I said.

"Good." She smiled. "Keep the faith, Audrey."

I shrugged, mostly because acting casual was the only hope I had of not bursting into tears.

"I'll try."

I did try, sort of. But it was a lot easier to believe that people were good and doing their best when I wasn't actually *with* them. In the three weeks before the end of the school year, I spent as much time as I could alone in the woods. Henry David Thoreau wrote, "I went to the woods because I wished to live deliberately, to front only the essential facts of life, and see if I could not learn what it had to teach, and not, when I came to die, discover that I had not lived." I'm sorry to say that my motives weren't quite so lofty. Mostly

I went to get away from life instead of confronting it, but after a few trips, since I was there anyway, I decided to pay attention and try to learn what the woods had to teach.

I didn't learn the meaning of life, but I did notice, for the first time, how the forest was a big world that contained smaller ones. A dead tree, the cool, damp ground under a rock, an anthill like a pile of brown sugar, a stand of blue flowers, a patch of emerald-green velvet moss: they were all tiny worlds alive with busy citizens, every creature moving around with purpose, like they knew just what to do and where to go. A bronzy centipede slinking through the dirt. Roly-poly bugs like miniature minivans. An army of black beetles, marching. A cloud of white moths rising spookily out of the grass.

I'm not especially a bug person, but I loved seeing these things, and sometimes I didn't even look at anything. I'd sit with my back against a tree and my eyes shut, and just the stalky, tree-barky, brown-dirt smell of the place would make me feel peaceful. I'd breathe it in and know that my world—Harriet Tubman Middle School—wasn't even close to being the only world there was.

Sometimes, though, I got lonely, especially for Janie. She'd been my best friend since she'd moved to Delaware from Oregon when we were five, but Janie and I hadn't been spending as much time together as we used to. As much as I hated to admit it, Lyza was right about that. But she was wrong about Janie being sick of me. Janie Franklin and I were friends the way moss is green, the way squirrels run up trees. We were a fact.

But a few months ago, we had just stopped hanging out as much. I guess I was caught up in the whole I-am-surrounded-by-people-who-lie thing, which seemed to get worse and worse as seventh grade went on, and she'd gotten strep and other more minor illnesses and started missing school, and I guess we both just got busy. My mom said that every friendship has its ups and downs, its natural fluctuations. When she put it that way, my friendship with Janie sounded like any natural part of life, like the ocean tides or the seasons, which is how it had always felt to me.

I'd called Janie a couple of times in those last few weeks of school, but she was bogged down with makeup work. Janie was as smart as anyone, but school wasn't always easy for her, and like I said, she'd missed a lot and was racing to get all the late work in and all the tests taken before the school year ended. I missed her. I'd even be in the woods, where I hardly ever thought about people, and I'd get this pang in the center of my chest, right where my ribs connected, and it would take me a second, but then I'd understand that the pang was missing Janie.

So on the day after the last day of school, I got up, got

dressed, and walked to her house. It was the hottest day of the season so far, as though even the sun had gotten word that it was our first day of summer vacation, and the sky was that true, deep summer blue. Under that sky, I suddenly felt like skipping, like the weight of the world Dean Amory was always talking about had fallen off my shoulders, or at least had gotten a lot smaller overnight.

As I stared up the sidewalk to Janie's front porch, I noticed that the big planters on either side of the porch steps were empty, which was weird because Mr. Franklin was a serious gardening guy, always pruning, and planting, and moving flower bulbs and bushes from one spot to another, and filling planters. By early June, they should have been overflowing, flowers flopping over the sides and vines trailing like kite tails. Everything else looked normal, though. Even the wind chimes hanging from Janie's porch sounded like summer.

But when Janie answered the door, she didn't look like summer at all, more like one of those days in late February that are so gray and dull you can't remember that spring is right around the corner; you can't remember spring at all. She looked rumpled, like she'd just gotten out of bed, which I knew couldn't be true. Janie was a morning person. Even at sleepovers, she'd be the first one up, and we'd all stumble sleepily downstairs hours after she did, to find her talking to the parents in the kitchen, bright-eyed as a robin.

"Hey!" I said.

Janie didn't smile, just reached up and twisted a piece of her red hair.

"Oh. Hey."

"You want to hang out?"

Janie glanced over her shoulder and lowered her voice. "I can't," she said. "Sorry. I still have some makeup work to finish."

She was telling the truth, but the nervous look on her face made me wonder if there was more going on than just homework. When she glanced over her shoulder again, I guessed that maybe she'd gotten into a fight with her mom. Janie's mom was really nice, but even the nicest moms could get mad at their kids, especially when their kids didn't want to do their homework on the first day of summer vacation. But what kid would? No wonder Janie looked like February.

"That stinks," I said.

From inside the house, I heard Mrs. Franklin's voice call out, "Who is it, Janie?"

"It's nothing, Mom," Janie called back. "I'll be right there."

I heard her mother's footsteps coming toward the door.

Janie stiffened and said, "Sorry, I have to go."

She started to shut the door, but her mom was already there. She was smiling at me and didn't look mad at all, just a little tired.

"Hey there, Audrey," she said. "Happy summer."

"Thanks!"

"Mom," said Janie, "just give us a minute, okay?"

Mrs. Franklin looked at Janie with surprise. "Oh. Sure," she said slowly. She smiled at me again, with worried eyes this time. Then she reached out and touched my cheek.

"Look at you," she said. "Already tan. Guess you've been spending some time outside."

"Yes," I said. "Just walking around in the woods, mostly."

"Well, that's nice."

It was when she pulled her hand back that I noticed it: the silver bracelet, that cursive L so sparkly in the sunlight, it threw tiny rainbows across the front of Janie's white T-shirt. I felt like an enormous hand had curled around me and was squeezing as hard as it could. Without meaning to, I made a sound, halfway between a grunt and a whimper. When I could tear my gaze away from that L, I looked at Janie. Her face had gone even paler, and her lips were pressing and twitching against each other, and her eyes looked round and scared.

"I bought it," Janie said. "L for Liana."

She was looking straight at the ground, a Lost Quarter Liar. I'd already known that from hearing Janie lie—not often, but a few times—to other people. But now she was lying to me.

Janie. Lying. *Janie. Lying. To me.*

My throat tightened and my chest ached. I'd never had an asthma attack, but I thought I might be having one now.

Mrs. Franklin had been staring from me to Janie like we were a puzzle she was trying to figure out, but now she lifted her wrist and looked at the bracelet.

"Oh, this," she said, smiling. "Janie gave it to me for my birthday last week."

"You," I said to Janie.

Janie shook her head. "No. Stop."

"Do you know?" My voice came out harsh and sandpapery. "Do you know how half the school stopped trusting me? Did you see the way people looked at me in the hallways? Did you hear them hiss 'thief' as soon as my back was turned? When I was nearby, people actually *covered up their locker doors* while they were opening them, so I wouldn't see their combinations!"

"I didn't steal it," said Janie, staring at the ground, the lie surrounding her like a cloud so thick that she looked blurry, not like Janie at all.

"Steal it?" whispered Mrs. Franklin.

"Even Dean Amory thinks I might be a thief!" I was almost shouting, my breath as ragged as sobbing. Maybe it was sobbing. "How could you do that? How could you take it and then let everyone think it was me?"

Janie started shivering like she was freezing. That's when Mrs. Franklin put her arm around Janie, pulled her backward against her chest, and kissed the top of her head, hard. When she raised her face to look at me, her eyes were full of something broken. Sorrowful is what she was. Mrs. Franklin—her eyes, her entire self—was full of sorrow. I took a step backward.

"Janie didn't steal it. I found it in a catalog, and she ordered it for me for my birthday," said Mrs. Franklin. She was making statements, but she didn't sound certain, more like she was pleading with me. I don't exactly know for what, but it didn't matter. What mattered was that she was lying.

Mrs. Franklin, an *adult*, and one who I could have sworn loved me, lying to my face. I couldn't breathe. I couldn't move. I can truly say that it was the worst moment of my entire life. Mrs. Franklin turned around and went into the house with Janie and shut the door, and I just stood there on the porch like I was glued. Then Janie yanked open the door. Her face was angry and red. She leaned toward me.

"You think you're so smart!" she hissed. "You think you see right into people! But you know what? You don't see anything!"

She hated me. She must have, to talk like that, to do what she'd done, to lie to my face. I'd thought nothing could hurt more than having people think I'd stolen Lyza's bracelet, but knowing that Janie—*my best friend, Janie*—hated me was a thousand times worse.

That night, after I'd cried myself to sleep and slept so hard I missed dinner, I told my parents that I wasn't going back to school in the fall.

"You can homeschool me," I said, "or I can do it myself, but I am never going back."

When I made this announcement, my parents were sitting on the couch, sifting through movies, trying to find one to watch. My mother and father exchanged one quick look, and then my dad brushed all the DVD boxes onto the rug and patted the space between him and my mom. Their faces were so worried and kind that I couldn't help it—I started to cry again. I curled between them and buried my face in my mom's shoulder.

"Honey, what happened?" she asked.

I'd come out of my room fully intending to tell them about Janie and her mom. My parents knew about my special little gift-that-wasn't-a-gift. They'd always known. And they knew about Lyza's bracelet too, because I'd told them right away. To my huge relief, they hadn't believed for one second that I'd taken it, and now it should have been so easy to tell them who had. Janie was lost and gone forever. She hated me. Why shouldn't I tell everyone the truth? But for some strange reason, I couldn't even tell my parents. It made me mad, that I was so stupidly loyal when Janie had lied to me in the worst possible way, but mad or not, I just could not tell on her.

But I couldn't lie to my parents either, so I said, "Someone lied to me, two people, in fact. Please don't ask me about it, but they were people I thought never would."

"Oh, sweetheart," said my mom into the side of my head, her voice muffled by my hair. "Everyone makes mistakes."

"Everyone *lies*," I said.

"Maybe so," said my dad, "but most people do a lot of good things, too. Don't give up on the human race, Ace." Because my first two initials were A.C., my dad had called me Ace ever since I was a little kid. Hearing him say it, that sweet old nickname, somehow made me cry harder.

When I could talk, I said, "That's why I have to stop going to school."

"What do you mean?" asked my mom. Gently she took my chin between her thumb and forefinger and lifted my face toward hers.

"I don't want to give up," I told her. "I want to keep the faith, like Dean Amory says. But if I keep going to school, I don't think I'll be able to do that."

"Staying home can't be the answer, though," said my mom. "You'd miss it. You've always loved school."

It was true. I was one of those possibly very annoying people who genuinely loved sitting in a classroom learning new things, surrounded by other people who were doing the same thing. And everything had been fine until sixth grade. I mean, kids had lied now and then, but mostly they were who they seemed to be.

"Things will get better," said my dad, sounding just like Dean Amory.

"When?" I asked.

"It doesn't happen all at once, but in a couple of years, when all those kids start to feel more at home with themselves, they'll start to be more straightforward, and it'll just keep getting better after that. And meanwhile, all the other things about them, the good, funny, interesting parts, will still be there, *more* there."

A couple of years. It sounded like eternity to me.

"Then I'll live in the woods for a couple of years," I said, burrowing my face back into my mother's arm, "and wait for things to get better, and *then* maybe I'll go back to school."

Five days later, at breakfast, they showed me the brochure.

"Let's put aside the question of school for now . . . ," began my father.

There was no question, only an answer: I wasn't going. But my parents were obviously so excited about what they were about to tell me that I decided not to say this out loud.

". . . and talk about this summer," my dad finished.

He handed me the brochure. It was glossy and colorful: cacti festooned with flowers, a wide, wide sky, mountains rising high in the background. Across the azure sky, in big letters, were the words THE JOURNEY TO CONFIDENCE!

"Wilderness camp," said my mother, grinning. "Six weeks in the great outdoors!"

"Oh," I said, blinking. "Wow."

I opened the brochure and read the camp description:

A six-week, two-hundred-mile trek tracing the historical route of the famous Marquesa de Baca expedition of 1532 through the gorgeous, unpopulated wildlands of West Texas, el Viaje a la Confianza, or the Journey to Confidence, will forever transform your child.

Days of cross-country hiking through stunningly beautiful but challenging desert terrain, interspersed with six specifically targeted wilderness team-building challenges, el Viaje a la Confianza is expertly led by accredited wilderness authority and former NCAA champion quarterback Jared Eastbrook. Fully stocked food, water, and first-aid checkpoints along the route ensure safety while preserving the isolated atmosphere essential to building the self-assurance of campers and to connecting them with the magical world around them!

Start your child on the Journey to Confidence today. After el Viaje a la Confianza, no challenge will be too great!

My dad said, "We think you could use a break, and since you love being outside so much . . . voilà!"

"Will there be other kids?" I asked, touching a finger to the photo of the bright-crimson cactus flowers. How cool that something so delicate could grow out of something so rough.

"Well, yeah," said my dad, "but you'll all be so busy surviving the wilderness that no one will have the time or occasion to lie."

I knew better. But the mountains on the brochure's cover looked like they'd been painted with a giant brush dipped straight into the liquid heart of a sunset. Wherever it was, it looked like no place I'd ever been, and that was exactly where I wanted to be.

CHAPTER FOUR

Aaron Archer

Dolley Madison Middle School

West Chester County, Pennsylvania

A FEW MORNINGS AFTER THE Great Quiz Masters Catastrophe, which is what people had started calling it when they thought I wasn't listening, Mrs. Dunaway peered at me through her glasses while she took attendance. After Xavier Zug answered "Present," she announced, "Poetry recitations!"

After the moaning died down, Mrs. Dunaway called, "Aaron Archer. Please present the poem I asked you to memorize."

I hadn't exactly memorized my poem the way everybody else memorizes poems, by sitting on the edge of my bed, saying it twenty times out loud, and hoping for the best, since, like I mentioned, every word I've ever laid eyes on has been automatically filed away on my hard drive. There are poems in there about lovely trees, and boys on burning decks, and clouds, and even one about vast and trunkless legs of stone. But out of all the poems in the world, the one Mrs. Dunaway had asked me to recite was one so crazy it hardly seemed like a poem at all.

The Red Wheelbarrow
by William Carlos Williams

so much depends
upon

a red wheel
barrow

glazed with rain
water

beside the white
chickens.

"Excellent," said Mrs. Dunaway after I was done. I told her thanks and headed for my seat. "Wait," said Mrs. Dunaway. "I've got a question."

"What is it, Mrs. Dunaway?" I asked.

"How much is *so* much?" she asked.

"*How* much is . . . ," I began. "I thought we were just supposed to *recite* a poem."

"Some of us are reciting," replied Mrs. Dunaway, "and some of us are reciting and then answering questions."

"Okay, Mrs. Dunaway," I said.

"How much is so much?" she repeated.

I mentally scanned the author biography underneath the poem. "William Carlos Williams has long been known as a revolutionary figure in American poetry," I read off the page in my mind. "Yet unlike other poets of his time who pursued exotic lives and difficult poetic themes, Williams lived in Rutherford, New Jersey—"

"No, Aaron," Mrs. Dunaway interrupted. "Perhaps you didn't understand the question."

I *didn't* understand the question. Or the chickens. I glanced around at the class. They didn't seem to understand any of it either. Hardy shrugged his shoulders at me, and Andrea had a little crease of confusion on her forehead.

Mrs. Dunaway's eyes focused on me like lasers. "I mean," she explained, "if William Carlos Williams thinks that *so* much depends on a red wheelbarrow, then *how* much does he think depends on a red wheelbarrow?"

"I get it," I said. I didn't get it.

"Close your eyes," Mrs. Dunaway suggested. She wore the same expression she'd had when I'd tanked in the Quiz

Masters final: concerned, but curious. "What is your red wheelbarrow? Where are your white chickens?"

"Uh—" I said.

Everybody in the whole room thought I knew everything in the world, with the possible exception of how King George felt about his American subjects in 1775.

The problem was, all I really knew was a ton of facts. Sure, I thought about other stuff, maybe not chickens or wheelbarrows, but once in a while I liked to think about what depends on what. Like—how my neighbor Mrs. Larson depends on her six cats, which is why I help her remember when it's time to give each individual one its worm pill.

Needless to say, though, I never got as far as old William Carlos Williams. I never got to chickens and wheelbarrows.

But since I had the feeling Mrs. Dunaway was trying to help, I tried to follow her advice about William Carlos. I closed my eyes.

"Look at the poem," she suggested. "Really look."

I looked.

"What do you see?" asked Mrs. Dunaway.

"Words," I said, "on a page." I could even visualize the numbers at the bottom and the fold in the corner of the dusty yellow paper where my mom had turned it down to mark her place in the poetry book.

"Focus," prodded Mrs. Dunaway, "on the colors in the poem. Red. And white. And why does the poet mention the rain? What does it all look like, Aaron?"

"Can you give me a hint, Mrs. Dunaway?" I asked. "What's the answer? Did William Carlos Williams ever tell anybody?"

"I'm not sure William Carlos Williams *knew* the answer," said Mrs. Dunaway. "But you do. You just don't know you know."

Slowly, I tried to visualize the water drops glistening on the red paint after a huge storm, and the clean white of the feathers, and somewhere, in a far corner of my mind, I started to understand that this wasn't about chickens and farm tools. William Carlos Williams was telling me something more than that. He'd hidden another idea under his words. William Carlos Williams was telling me that sometimes the plainest things can be very, very—

The sound of toe-tapping invaded my thoughts. I opened my eyes.

Principal DuPlessy loomed in the doorway, bald as a billiard ball, a FedEx box jammed under his arm. Unfortunately, a razor mishap had obliterated his eyebrows along with his hair.

Although Mrs. Dunaway and most of my friends had gotten over the Great Quiz Masters Catastrophe, he hadn't. Not even close. And when Principal DuPlessy fell into a bad mood—for instance, the kind of mood he might slip into after watching his Quiz Masters team blow its big chance at a state title, and subsequently seeing a bald head and missing eyebrows to remind him of this debacle every time he looked in the mirror—he took his frustrations out on the person he considered responsible: the coach. "Mrs. Dunaway?" he barked. "A word?"

"I'm teaching," replied Mrs. Dunaway without a glance in his direction.

"Mrs. Dunaway," he repeated. "A word." This time, it wasn't a request. Mrs. Dunaway joined him in the hall.

The principal didn't scream or throw things, like he used to when he was the basketball coach and somebody missed a layup, but he was still plenty mad. We could hear every word he said out there.

"Wheelbarrows? Chickens?" sputtered Principal DuPlessy.

"That's two words," pointed out Mrs. Dunaway.

"Whatever," muttered Principal DuPlessy. "They aren't what I came to talk about."

"What *did* you come to talk about?" asked Mrs. Dunaway.

"The Central Standards Exam!" exploded Principal DuPlessy.

"Four words," observed Mrs. Dunaway.

"Four very *important* words, when it comes to the reputation of Dolley Madison Middle School," replied Principal DuPlessy. "Which is in tatters right now, thanks to your Quiz Masters performance. How am I supposed to win Principal of the Year with performances like that?"

Mrs. Dunaway raised one eyebrow.

He pointed at a number on the floor in front of her door. He had painted numbers like this outside a few classrooms around the school. They showed everybody how deficient each homeroom teacher had been on the Central Standards Practice Exam, and on which part. Mrs. Dunaway was a –2, LANGUAGE ARTS. Which was kind of a problem, since she was supposed to be teaching us language arts in her homeroom.

"You've got two language arts deficiency points, and you're asking the one student in your class who's actually *good* at the Central Standards Exam about chickens!" cried Principal DuPlessy.

"I'm quite proud of that question," replied Mrs. Dunaway. "I thought it up just for Aaron."

"It's not the right kind of question!" spluttered the principal.

"What kind of question," asked Mrs. Dunaway, "is the right kind of question?"

"This kind!" snapped Principal DuPlessy. He yanked the FedEx box out from under his arm, ripped off the label that said DO NOT OPEN UNTIL JUNE 2, dug out a Central Standards Exam question booklet, sliced off the little round seal with his thumbnail—which I was pretty sure broke about a hundred rules—and opened it to page one. He read:

"Identify the coordinating conjunction in the following sentence: 'Whether I shall turn out to be the hero of my own life, or whether that station will be held by anybody else, these pages must show.' A, whether; B, or; C, to; D. held.

"Well?" he demanded, glaring at Mrs. Dunaway.

"Well what?" she shot back.

"Well, can your students identify the whatever in the whatever?" asked Principal DuPlessy.

"If any of my students ever read the most exquisite first sentence in the history of novels and started picking out the coordinating conjunctions, I'd slap a pointy hat on his head and stick him in the corner for a week!" retorted Mrs. Dunaway.

"Let me put it this way," seethed the principal. "Your students have been below standard on language arts for the past four years. YET YOU ARE THEIR LANGUAGE ARTS TEACHER! If it happens again? The school board says I can fire you." He jabbed his finger at Mrs. Dunaway. But he happened to be holding the question book in his hand. Which flopped onto the floor and lay there in the open doorway. I watched the pages flutter in the hallway breeze, from first to last in less than a second. "If I were you?" the principal muttered. "I'd be more worried about drilling grammar into my kids' skulls than asking Arthur about that stinking lawn mower."

"Aaron," said Mrs. Dunaway. "Wheelbarrow."

"Whatever," scoffed Principal DuPlessy. "Shape up."

"Brianna Bishop," said Mrs. Dunaway, stepping back into the room. "I cannot *wait* to hear the poem you've prepared for us."

"'Anecdote of the Jar,'" said Brianna. "By Wallace Stevens. 'I placed a jar in Tennessee,'" she began, "'And round it was, upon a hill.'"

"A jar," muttered Principal DuPlessy in disgust as he snatched the test booklet from the linoleum and stomped away. "In Tennessee. For the love of Pete."

But I had everything I needed to help Mrs. Dunaway. And I was *going* to help Mrs. Dunaway. Because when a teacher makes you recite insanely hard poems and thinks up special questions just for you, even if you don't understand what they mean, then her heart is in the right place and you need to make sure she keeps her job.

* * *

When that test booklet came fluttering past the classroom doorway and lay on the floor flapping in the breeze, my brain took a snapshot of every single page. After I got home, I looked at the snapshots again, and I picked out three questions I knew everybody in the class would get wrong, because they were hard, and because never in a million years would Mrs. Dunaway spend time teaching us stuff like this when she could be grilling us about poems.

I only needed three because Mrs. Dunaway wasn't that far from making the grade. According to the numbers on the floor, if everybody got approximately 2.1 more answers right, then she'd get to keep her job.

On Monday, as soon as the bell rang, I knocked all of Jimmy Stell's orange pencils onto the floor and stumbled around helping him pick them up. When I was sure I had the whole class's attention, I said, "Oh. By the way. Mrs. Dunaway?"

"Yes, Aaron?" she replied.

"Is a good example of a transition word A, prestidigitation; B, Glimmerglass; C, moreover; or D, thoroughly? I'm pretty sure it's C, moreover. Aren't you pretty sure it's C, moreover?"

Mrs. Dunaway was busy rummaging in her drawer for her roll book and didn't bother looking up. "It's moreover,

Aaron," she answered, "as I feel certain you already know."

"Did you hear that, Hardy?" I said. "Hey—Nate and Alexander. Listen up, Andrea! A good example of a transition word is C, moreover! Amazing. Wow. Cool. What do you know! Moreover! Who would have figured? Wow!" I figured if I repeated it enough times, it would sink in where it was needed most, even if not everybody was totally paying attention. It would work like hypnotism. Or osmosis.

On Tuesday, I did the same thing, only with Stephanie's lunch and a question about passive voice constructions. The answer to that one was D, none of the above.

On Wednesday, I spilled Hardy's gym bag, and while everybody watched me stuff his socks back in, I made sure they knew that the narrative point of view of "The Tell-Tale Heart" by Edgar Allan Poe was B, first person unreliable.

Since I had a long history of blurting out odd facts, I don't think Mrs. Dunaway thought twice about any of this. At least not at the time.

On Thursday, we took the test.

In the front of the class, Mrs. Dunaway read a novel while we worked. *David Copperfield*. She glanced up at me and smiled. She didn't have any idea that what I'd been doing for the past three days was giving away answers.

Well, I told myself. *I'd already known the answers before*

I ever saw the questions, so, technically, they were mine. Right? How could it be cheating for me to give away three answers that I already knew? Plus, in a way, Mrs. Dunaway had taught everyone the answers. I mean, she was the one who'd said they were correct. Am I right about this? Somebody tell me I'm right.

The classroom clock ticked.

The pencils of the class scritched inside the ovals.

The clock ticked.

The pencils scritched.

I couldn't take it. I was *not* right. About any of what I'd told myself. My insides collapsed. I began to visualize everything that was going to happen. I thought through all the angles I hadn't thought through before. As soon as we turned in our tests, Mrs. Dunaway was going to take them to the office, where they were going to scan the results and send them to a central computer in Ames, Iowa, which would spot strangely improved scores on questions 77, 93, and 99. Investigators would immediately buy airplane tickets and, by the next morning, converge on Dolley Madison Middle School and begin pulling students out of Mrs. Dunaway's room one at a time, extracting their statements, comparing notes. Soon they'd figure out the method I'd used to give away three of the hardest language arts answers, and finally they'd call me in and ask me questions that would make me incriminate myself, not to mention Mrs. Dunaway, Hardy Gillooly, and everybody else who'd paid attention while I was busy leaking information. Mrs. Dunaway was over eighteen. About fifty years over eighteen. She'd probably go to jail!

My palms got sticky. I shivered. I stood it as long as I could. Then I jumped out of my seat. "I did it!" I cried.

I ran out of the classroom, down the hallway, and around the corner, and I burst into Principal DuPlessy's office. There sat a policeman whose name tag read OFFICER HANRAHAN. Beside him sat a colossal German shepherd.

Wow, I thought. *These Central Standards guys don't waste any time.*

"I admit it!" I cried. "I admit the whole thing! I tried to fix the Central Standards Exam!"

"The what?" said Officer Hanrahan as the dog peered at me with his ears at attention.

"The exam," I began. "I . . . uh—"

"Wahoo and I are just here for the SSFT assembly," said Officer Hanrahan. He pointed out the office window at the hallway, where shrimpy sixth graders filed by on their way to the libracafegymnatorium. "What's all this about a Central Standards Exam?"

"What's all this about SSFT?" I asked.

"Summer Safety Fun Tips!" explained Officer Hanrahan.

As he said it, he fished a miniature tube of sunscreen

out of his pocket and tossed it in the air. Leaping like a trained seal, Wahoo snatched it in his teeth. "First, no matter what sort of fun you enjoy, always wear sunscreen!" said Officer Hanrahan. Wahoo dropped the slobbery sunscreen in my lap, wagging his tail.

"In that case," I said, wiping it off, "never mind." Wahoo was so well trained he'd only left three faint toothmarks. I stuck the sunscreen in my pocket.

"No problem," said Officer Hanrahan as he and Wahoo headed for the assembly.

I stood up to follow. But Principal DuPlessy said, "Could you please stay here, Aaron? I have a few questions for you."

"So," the principal began, "what exactly do you mean by 'fix'?"

"Fix, to make firm or stable," I replied. "To give permanent form. To preserve for microscopic study. To make a photograph permanent."

"I think you meant something different," ventured the principal.

"To attach," I continued. "To hold steady. 'He fixes his eyes on the horizon.' To repair or mend. 'He fixed the broken lock.'"

"No, I don't think that's what you meant either," mused Principal DuPlessy.

"To get even with. To influence an outcome by improper or illegal means," I continued. *Whoops.* A prime example of something I should've previewed before I said it out loud.

"That sounds closer," mused the principal, rubbing his shiny head. It still wasn't clear if his hair was going to grow back.

Mrs. Dunaway knocked on the door. The principal must've called her before he started in on me.

An ice age dawned inside my rib cage, and a glacier began to coat my spine.

"Are you shaking?" asked the principal.

"Yes," I said.

"Good," said the principal. "Have a seat, Mrs. Dunaway. I'm just finishing up your termination letter." He jotted his initials on a sheet of paper and handed it to her.

Everything inside me started to sink. "But I did it!" I cried.

"But I can't fire you," said the principal. "So I'm firing your teacher. I've been looking for an excuse. I need somebody new and fresh who can improve my statistics."

"But it was *me*," I repeated miserably. "I saw the questions when you dropped that quiz book on the floor, and

I revealed the answers to the class! Mrs. Dunaway, I was only trying to help."

"I have to hand it to you," said Mrs. Dunaway. "You failed spectacularly."

"I'm really, really sorry," I said.

"Don't be," said Mrs. Dunaway, tearing up the letter Principal DuPlessy had just handed her. "As I said, it was spectacular."

"What do you think you're doing?" asked the principal.

"Going back to class," said Mrs. Dunaway, standing up and motioning to me.

"But you're fired!" cried the principal. "As for Aaron, he's suspended."

"I don't think so," said Mrs. Dunaway, giving the principal a stare.

"But he just admitted leaking answers to the Central Standards Exam!" bellowed the principal. "That's cheating! The Central Standards Committee will not be happy!"

"I agree," said Mrs. Dunaway. "They certainly won't. When they hear how Aaron got those answers. How the principal of Dolley Madison Middle School stood right in front of him and broke the seal on the test SIX DAYS EARLY and dropped a question book ON THE FLOOR FOR HIM TO SEE!"

I could almost hear the air leak out of Principal

DuPlessy. He turned white. He slumped in his chair.

"You've certainly got some explaining to do for the benefit of the Central Standards Committee," observed Mrs. Dunaway. "Good luck."

"I . . . you . . . ah . . . ," stammered the principal.

"Bye," said Mrs. Dunaway.

As Mrs. Dunaway and I walked back to class, she said, "You're a smart kid, Aaron. Smarter than you realize."

"But everything I touch turns into a disaster!" I said. "I think I'm actually some kind of *idiot*. How can I *possibly* be smarter than I realize?"

"That's the kind of question you have to figure out on your own," she said.

"The same way I have to figure out how much depends on a red wheelbarrow?" I wondered.

"A lot like that, yes," replied Mrs. Dunaway. "But it sounds like you're already on the right track."

"This could take a while," I said.

"It might," agreed Mrs. Dunaway. "And now, one last thing: I'm afraid a parent-teacher conference is called for."

Evidently, the principal made some kind of excuse and filled out a waiver and signed a form and convinced the Central Standards Committee to let Mrs. Dunaway's homeroom retake the test the following week, since we never got to finish taking it the first time, due to unspecified "technical difficulties" (in other words, me).

And believe it or not, Mrs. Dunaway's score went up four whole points! Mrs. Dunaway said it was because of all the adrenaline rushing through everybody's bloodstream because of the excitement I'd caused. I think she was joking, but she also told the whole class thanks for saving her job, and when she said that, she sounded serious.

After the parent-teacher conference, during which Mrs. Dunaway revealed pretty much the whole story, except the part about blackmailing the principal to avoid punishment, my mom and dad and I went home to discuss everything. We sat at our kitchen table and my mom told me the same thing Mrs. Dunaway had told me: "You're a smart kid."

My dad snapped, "You think you know everything." He was a little mad at me because of all the trouble I'd caused. Actually, so was I.

"I *don't* think I know everything," I said. "I think I *remember* everything. But I don't *know* anything."

"Oh, son," my dad said much more softly. Suddenly, he was over being mad. He put his arm around me. "I realize it's hard."

"Mrs. Dunaway is the greatest teacher I've ever had," I explained. "She was trying to teach me something important. She gave me a nutty poem. She asked me questions with no answers. She's awesome. And the principal was going to fire her. Because of that test. I just wanted to help her!"

"We know your heart is in the right place," said my dad. "But things have to change. You could've gotten yourself expelled."

"Maybe we've let you down," reflected my mom. "Maybe when you memorized all fifty-seven countries in Africa just by walking past the globe at the pediatrician's office when you were three—"

"Sixty-one," I corrected. "Including independent territories."

"Maybe then we should have consulted an expert. But we thought you'd outgrow it."

"I probably would've ended up this way no matter who you consulted," I reassured them.

"Your mom and I talked it over earlier," said my dad, "and we did some research and conferred with the school counselor, and we think maybe you could use a change of scene, a brand-new start, a blank page for the summer."

"What kind of place?" I asked.

"A place where you have to *think*, instead of just *remember*," said my mom. "Like you said."

"There's a place like that?" I asked.

"We believe so," said my dad.

"Where is it?" I asked.

"We said a *blank* page," my dad reminded me.

"What are you talking about?" I asked.

"We're not telling you where you're going, honey," sighed my mom. "Because what good will it do if you memorize every known fact about it before you get there?"

CHAPTER FIVE

Audrey Alcott

El Viaje a la Confianza Trailhead

Pumpjack, Texas

THE VIAJE A LA CONFIANZA brochure hadn't been lying about the "stunningly beautiful" landscape. Even from the window of the airport shuttle that took me to the camp, I drank in the spice colors of the earth and noticed the way the clear sunlight made everything sharper than at home. When I got off the van at the trailhead in a tiny town called Pumpjack, beside a low, plain stucco ranger station with a red tile roof, I just stood there for a moment, blinking and greedily breathing in what felt like an entirely new kind of air.

But I'd hardly gotten my bearings when a voice boomed across the parking lot, "I'm Jare Eastbrook, your mentor and guide along el Viaje a la Confianza. Parents, see you in six weeks!'"

A few tearful good-byes continued while Jare made this

announcement, but I grabbed my backpack and jogged over to a patch of silvery-green grass to join what I guessed must be my fellow campers, a group of pretty dazed-looking kids. Jare's wasn't the kind of voice you disobey.

"No. Really. I'm serious," shouted Jare as he seemed to loom over the parking lot. "See you, parents. Skedaddle. Vamoose. Let me start earning all that money you just paid me."

My shuttle was long gone, but the few moms and dads who'd driven their kids all the way to the trailhead shot him doubtful looks.

"I know what I'm doing," Jare assured them. "Bye."

Less than a minute later, all the parents were gone, and he turned to us. "We're gonna hike from this ranger station to el Presidio de la Norte. Two hundred and ten miles of scenic Texas desert in six weeks. Which means we have to cover approximately five miles a day of mountains, gullies, badlands, and worse lands. Smile. That's a joke."

A minivan idled on the highway in front of the ranger station. Somebody's mom peered anxiously out the passenger window. *"HASTA LA VISTA!"* cried Jare. The minivan sped away.

"To find our way, we'll use maps, compasses, trail markers, the sun, the moon, the stars, and our wits, at least those of us who have any. We will supply our needs from stores of water and food I have cached along the trail. Six times during el Viaje, we'll take a break from walking and undertake wilderness challenges of my devising, which will reveal what you're made of. In the meantime, there will be plenty of sun, fresh air, and pure open country. And here is some advice: don't *ever* let me catch you wasting water in the desert!"

"I've got a question," said one of the campers, a small, dark-haired girl.

"The answer is no," said Jare. "Now. Dump your packs. On the ground. Everything out. Here's what you can keep: headlamps, tweezers, water treatment pills, clothes, sleeping bag, and tent. Here's what goes in the Dumpster, the dead weight: teddy bears, photo albums, and favorite blankets."

I made sure not to let him see the picture of my parents and me that I'd slid inside a luggage tag and clipped to my pack.

"One last thing," said Jare as the "dead weight" thudded into the trash. "Your priorities in the desert: PHWSS. Pack a Hat, Water, Sunscreen, and Socks. Whatever you do, always PHWSS, and your chances of catastrophe are minimal. Let's go. Three hours to camp."

"PHWSS" was pronounced with a sound like running over a broken bottle on your mountain bike.

"Wait," said a blond boy. "You mean we're leaving? Now?"

Jare didn't answer, just lowered his head and stared at him.

The kid's face turned red. "Um. Sorry. I just thought, since we just got here, since we were at, you know, our *houses* this morning, maybe we weren't, you know, ready."

I knew what the kid meant. It had all happened really fast. But somehow, unexpectedly, I found that I *was* ready. Yes, I was nervous, but right at that moment, with that odd, beautiful place stretching out on every side of me, the world felt bigger than it ever had, and I wanted to see it.

After an hour of hiking, I started thinking about gravity, which got me thinking about how, back in my regular life, I never thought about gravity, unless you counted in science class, and even then, I never thought about it as part of my everyday life. I never considered that gravity tugs on me just as much as it ever tugged on Sir Isaac Newton's apple. I don't know what I thought was keeping me from flying off the face of the Earth back then. My school schedule? Homework? My friends (back when I had them)? But when you've been hiking for an hour in the hot sun with a hippopotamus-sized pack on your back, you suddenly understand how, every time you lift your foot off the rocky, sandy ground in order to take a step, gravity is trying with all its might to keep it glued to the spot.

Weird, maybe, to tromp through the desert thinking about gravity, but what was even weirder was that I found myself liking it, all of it. Yes, it was hard, achy, sweaty work, but even though, literally, I'd never been so weighted down in my life, I also felt light. No schedules, no school, no family, no friends, no lies, just me and gravity and my heavy, heavy feet and, underneath them, the ground, which was so pale and crumbling and stony that it might have been the moon (except for the gravity, of course).

There were over a dozen other people hiking around me, but for that first couple of hours, I hardly noticed them. For one thing, I tried not to notice them, and for another, we were all too hot and busy—and possibly also shy—to talk. Even when we took our first real break, I kept my distance from the others, tossing down my pack at the very edge of the group and, after a few desperate gulps of water, settling in to look at the land around me.

The place was oddly beautiful, like almost everything soft had been peeled away to reveal the Earth's bone structure, which was as stark as truth. The mountains in the distance were faceted like crystals. There were clusters of cacti shaped like Ping-Pong paddles and spatulas, minus the handles; agave plants bursting out of the ground like artichokes gone haywire; gray-green grass that looked like fur but wasn't soft; and a sky so vast, I felt my brain and rib cage expanding to make room for it.

I leaned back on my pack, and stared at the completely cloudless sky, and thought, lazily, *How did the sky get that blue?* At least, I thought I only thought it, but it turns out that I must have said it out loud, because right after I said it, the boy closest to me piped up with, "The blue of the sky is due to Rayleigh scattering. As sunlight passes through the Earth's atmosphere, longer wavelengths such as red, orange, and yellow travel with very little impediment. But shorter wavelenths such as blue are captured by air molecules and scattered in all directions, making it appear that blue light is emanating from every part of the sky."

Reluctantly, I turned to look at him. A skinny, brown-haired kid, he was red-faced and sprawled out on the ground like he'd been spilled there, just like the rest of us, but unlike the rest of us—now that I actually looked around at the other campers—he wasn't bleary-eyed with fatigue. In fact, his face was wide-awake and peppy, and he talked like a person who was just getting started, who might go on talking for hours.

"That's interesting," I said. "Thanks." I hoped my tone conveyed a combination of politeness and dismissiveness, but just in case he didn't get the dismissiveness part, I turned away from him, lay back against my pack again, and closed my eyes. After what had happened with Janie, I was more resolved than ever to keep people at a distance, to leave camp with exactly as many friends as I came with: zero. But the boy didn't seem to notice I was giving him the cold shoulder.

"Rayleigh scattering also causes sunsets to appear red," he continued cheerfully, "because as the sun drops near the horizon, light must travel farther through the atmosphere to reach your eyes. Therefore, more of it gets scattered. Short-wavelength blues and greens become so scattered they're virtually lost, while the longer wavelengths of red are all that's left to be seen."

I hauled open one eyelid a fraction of a centimeter and darted my eyeball sideways to sneak a peek at the kid, just to see if he was talking to me or to the group as a whole. I couldn't quite make out his face, but right before I closed my eye again, I saw a rock the size of a grape come winging in from the boy's left to hit him on the shoulder, not lightly. The boy's mouth twitched a little in a way that was maybe nervous, but he just swatted vaguely at his arm like a fly had landed on it and kept talking about the red waves.

"There's gonna be some red waves coming out of your skull if you don't shut up," growled a voice.

Someone—a girl—laughed like this was the cleverest

thing she'd ever heard. It was a mean laugh.

"Great," mumbled someone else, a boy, worriedly. "Threats."

Just ignore them, I told myself. *If you keep your eyes closed, maybe they'll all disappear.* But I could feel myself getting interested in the conversation—if you could call it that—in spite of myself. I squeezed my eyes shut, and was trying to think of a way to put my fingers in my ears without anyone noticing, when a whistle cut through the clear air like a razor.

"Break over!" Jare, the big, meaty camp director, barked. "Up and at 'em, people. We've got ground to cover."

Everyone started groaning, but I was relieved. Now we could go back to the silent walking, where I could pretend it was just me and gravity.

But it was like the tall skinny boy with his Rayleigh whoever and his scattered whatever had poked a hole in the silence that wouldn't close back up. The farther we hiked, the bigger the hole got. Not everyone talked. Mostly the skinny kid would unroll these long encyclopedia-sounding streamers of information; the rock-throwing kid, who was red haired, freckled, and muscly in that weight-lifter, no-neck, short-guy way, would call him stupid and tell him to shut up; and the mean-laugh girl, who had hair the color of ketchup, fingernails the color of dried blood, and boots like anvils, would laugh, meanly. But I could tell that even the nontalkers were part of it. They were listening, clumping together in twos and threes so they could exchange glances or roll their eyes at each other over what the three talkers were saying.

Every now and then, Jare would stop to hurl a piece of education at us: "That's a prickly pear. Edible, from the fruit to the pads to the seeds. Store that information away. You'll need it!"

Or, pointing to an innocent-looking bush with a smattering of white flowers: "Beebrush! Deadly poison to horses. Don't even think about eating it!"

"Who would think about that?" I mumbled.

"Nobody," a tiny, black-haired girl with big sad eyes mumbled back. "Ever."

"Bumblebees!" bellowed Jare, pointing at some fat, fuzzy, striped bees. "Fat! Fuzzy! Striped! Harmless. But there are other bees in the area. Honeybees! Not indigenous! Some are harmless. Others are Africanized, aka *killer* bees!"

The boy to the left of me, who was almost as large as Jare and walked like he was stepping across hot coals, gulped and said, "Killer?"

"If they chase you," yelled Jare, "run! Zigzag pattern!"

"Zigzag?" croaked the large boy.

Pointing to an agave plant, Jare shouted, "Agave! Also called century plant because they bloom once every hundred years!"

"*Agave havardiana*, a monocarpic succulent, lives up to fifty years and blooms once, just before it dies," said Skinny Kid, "sending up a seed stalk that can be twenty feet tall."

We all swiveled our heads to stare at him, but I swiveled mine back fast and braced myself, waiting for Jare to start shouting.

"I'm sorry," barked Jare. "Did you say something?"

Skinny Kid nodded, smiling like someone who hadn't just been yelled at by a man the size of a grizzly bear.

"What do you do?" asked Jare, whipping off his sunglasses to squint at the boy. "Memorize encyclopedias?"

"Sometimes," said the boy, shrugging. "But not on purpose. I mean, mostly not."

Glaring at him, Jare shoved his glasses back onto his face and said, "Let's pick up the pace, people!" and took off hiking at about sixty miles an hour. "One last thing. Watch out for rattlenakes!"

"Nice work," said the no-neck boy, giving Skinny Kid a shove from behind. Then he added, "Memory Boy!" with a sneering tone and a snicker that suggested that "Memory Boy" was the most creative insult ever invented. He looked at the ketchup-haired girl for validation, but she just shrugged and hiked past him. After a disappointed beat, he scurried after her.

I had to hand it to Ketchup Hair: she might look like something out of a bad vampire TV series, but, in her own furious, stomping-something-to-death way, the girl could hike through the rocks and cactus in those Frankenstein boots like a pro.

"Memory Boy," murmured Sad-Eyed Girl in her flat voice. "Good one."

I smiled at this. I couldn't help myself. After I did it, I let out a groan, and this time, it wasn't because of the heat or the hike. I saw that it was starting: We'd all keep talking and arguing and shoving and smiling at each other and *interacting*, and soon these people would stop being Ketchup Hair and Sad-Eyed Girl and Skinny Kid. Soon they would have names; soon they'd be full-fledged people, like Lyza, like Janie, and I knew that's when the real trouble would start.

By the time we got to our campground, it was almost evening. We'd gone uphill for the last thirty minutes or so, and while we weren't exactly in the mountains, we were in an in-between area where the shrubs ("Mesquite! Long taproot! Edible beans!" "Creosote bush! Distinctive smell!"

"Ocotillo! Medicinal! Makes good walking sticks!") were starting to mix with some good-sized trees ("Piñon pine! Edible nuts! Good bird food!" "Juniper! Berries used to make gin! Don't try it—or else, ha ha ha!").

Even though the desert floor was interesting, I was glad we would be sleeping with trees nearby. Somehow, trees made me feel safer. I wasn't sure yet what I needed to be safe from, but I figured that before long, Jare would probably tell us, in a tone of sinister glee. He sure had a lot of fun hinting at how we'd sooner or later all be wandering through the desert, alone, starving, foraging for food, and getting attacked by bees.

I have to say that, even though I'd been grumpy about how many times my parents had made me practice setting up my tent in our backyard before I left, I was proud of how well I did it, Tinkertoying the skinny rods together and sliding them into the fabric channels like I'd been doing it for years. Except for Jare and Ketchup Hair, I was the first one done. The big kid who'd worried out loud about the killer bees took twice as long as any of us, but while the rest of us had narrow, one-person tents, his looked big enough for three or four people. The only tent bigger was Jare's, but I figured that Jare had to stow a lot of stuff inside. Big Kid was definitely large, but a tent this huge seemed like unnecessary weight to me. I wondered what was up with Big Kid.

Dinner was a bland beef stew and hard chunks of cornbread like dull, yellow stones, but after the hard day, it all tasted good. I thought about Henry David Thoreau, hoeing his bean fields in the hot sun and then eating the beans for supper. I bet they tasted good too. Maybe that's the way this camp was going to work: we'd suffer so much all day that even the stuff that was just okay or even kind of crummy would seem great in comparison.

After dinner, Jare gave a speech. When he'd met us that morning at the park's visitor's center, he'd barely introduced himself before he'd started barking out orders. I'd taken it as a good sign, since, as I've mentioned, I wasn't in the market for a big, chatty, get-to-know-each-other excursion. I had liked his impersonal, businesslike approach.

But now, as we all sat around the campfire in a semicircle, Jare stood up, cleared his throat, and turned into a different person. He pointed his finger a lot; he clapped his hands together *a lot*. It was like he was part inspirational speaker, part football coach, which made sense, since he was a former football player. A Darn Good One! High School All-American! College Player of the Year in his rookie season!

"Yeah, right," mumbled No-Neck. "I bet he rode the bench."

But I could tell Jare was telling the truth. He really had

been good—not that anyone seemed to care, because why would we?

"But I wasn't one of those guys who wanted to devote my entire life to tossing an oblate spheroid around an Astroturf field," Jare went on. "I wanted more."

For the first time, I saw his truthfulness falter. Before I could think much about why this might be, Skinny Kid interrupted him.

"A football is actually a prolate spheroid with the profile of a vesica piscus." He said this cheerfully, as though he was honestly trying to be helpful.

Even in the fading light, I could see Jare's face turn red. Maybe that had been the problem with what he'd said about the oblate spheroid. Pretending to know what you're talking about can look an awful lot like lying. I felt a little sorry for Jare; he'd probably used the term so we'd all think he was smart, not just a dumb football jock, and here he was, looking sort of dumb after all. After giving Skinny Kid the evil eye for a full ten seconds, Jare clapped his hands together and continued.

"My point is, I know how to fight. How to work hard. How to win. And I know how to do it out here, in a wilderness like you've never seen in your lives. A place where all the rules are different."

"Please," said Ketchup Hair in disgust. "This is, like, my fourth wilderness camp. They're all alike."

Jare's jaw tightened, but he didn't even glance at Ketchup Hair. I could tell he was gearing up for the grand finale part of his speech. He bent over a little, narrowed his eyes, and leveled a piercing gaze at us, stabbing his finger at random campers as he talked.

"Whatever you were back home—a delinquent, a smart mouth, a spoiled brat behind the wheel of a BMW . . ." The camp was for kids ages thirteen to fourteen, which meant none of us was old enough to drive.

". . . captain of the math league . . ." Jare sneered, like there was nothing stupider in the world than captain of the math league.

". . . a punk-rock skateboarder punk . . ." Ketchup Hair guffawed acidly at this.

". . . valedictorian, class clown, class president, Annie in the school musical, first chair trombone, et cetera! Whatever you were, you're not that here. You're nobody."

"Fine with me," murmured Sad-Eyed Girl.

"You can look at this as a fresh start or as the worst thing that's ever happened to you," said Jare, his voice getting louder, "but what you can't do is escape. This land doesn't play. It bites. It stabs. It stings."

Big Kid (with the big tent) flinched three times, like each of those verbs was actually happening to him as Jare spoke them.

"Rise to it, ladies and gents," boomed Jare. "Show yourselves worthy of it and all its challenges—or end up bleached bones in the desert sun!"

Silence settled over us. Thinking about yourself as a skeleton will do that, I guess. For a long moment, we all just listened to the fire crackling and contemplated our own deaths, and then Jare smacked his hammy palms together one more time and said cheerily, "Okay, let's get down to business, people! First thing to work on: mind-set! Sometimes, the difference between victory and defeat is less this"—he flexed his arm muscles—"and more this." He tapped his forefinger to his temple. "Although plenty of *this* sure doesn't hurt." He flexed his muscles again. "Ha ha ha!"

"Who laughs like that?" I whispered to myself. "'Ha ha ha'?"

Someone to the right of me chuckled after I said this. It sounded like Big Kid, but he was sitting at least twenty feet away from me. If he'd heard what I'd said, the guy had hearing like a bat's.

"Question: what is the thing that will be the difference—for you, personally—between throwing in the towel and surviving el Viaje? What thought will keep you hanging in there when the vultures are circling, when the wilderness has you in its clutches, ready to crush you?" asked Jare. "Let's go around the circle, introduce ourselves, and share with the group the one and only thought that will have any hope of keeping you alive."

Great, I thought, bleakly, *a getting-to-know-you game.* I'd hoped Jare was too tough for that touchy-feely camp stuff, but even though his touchy-feely game had vultures circling around it with their hideous shriveled red heads, it was touchy-feely all the same.

Jare started walking around the circle, pointing to each camper in turn. People said things like parents, dog, baby brother, and even in the dark, I could tell most of them were telling the truth.

No-Neck turned out to be Randolph. He said, "My gang back home." Lie.

Ketchup Hair was Daphne. She said, "My dad and getting revenge on my mom and all the other losers who have crossed me." Truth.

Big Kid was Louis. He said, "Being in my house with my books and my computer and my food and my sheets on my bed." Truth.

Sad-Eyed Girl was Kate. She said, her voice flatter than ever, "What's the point of holding on to stuff when it all just goes away in the end anyway? I don't have anything. Unless you count the same reason I get out of bed every morning: why not? Like, I know what it's like to be alive, and I don't know what it's like to be dead, so why not just go with what I know?" Truth. She wasn't just being dramatic. She was really as sad as her eyes.

Skinny Kid was Aaron. He said, "Well, first of all, the world's a pretty interesting place, but mostly what I think is that I haven't had the chance to give anything back to it. Like I've had this basically decent life, but because I'm a kid, I mostly just take what gets handed to me. The last time I tried to help someone was kind of a disaster. But it would stink to die without, you know, making a contribution." Randolph and Daphne mimed vomiting, and yes, Aaron sounded eerily like a Miss America contestant, except that all of them are always lying, and Aaron was—oddly, amazingly—telling the truth.

I said, "My parents. They're pretty great people, and I'm their only kid. They'd be crushed if they never saw me again. And, you know, vice versa."

Daphne shot me a venomous glare, which was weird because, even though my answer was true, I also thought it was pretty generic.

While we were all still squirming with discomfort but were also feeling relieved that it was over, Jare broke us into four groups of four. Mine was me, Aaron, Kate, and Louis. Uneasily, we got up and sidled toward each other, with weary "heys" and nods, except for Aaron, who shook hands with each of us in turn and said, "Aaron Archer, nice to meet you." When he held out his hand to Louis, Louis looked at it like it might electrocute him, and after one quick shake, he dropped it like maybe it had.

"This is your team!" Jare told us. "Team! Starting tomorrow, you will go out into the desert alone with your team! You will face unimaginable challenges together, challenges of my own devising! If you expect to rise to those challenges, you will need to rely on each other in ways you've never relied on anyone else! At some point in this journey, every member will be the difference between triumph and defeat! Don't mess up, people! Don't let your team down!"

He gave us another question to discuss. "What do you bring to the table? What special talent will you contribute to the team's survival?"

Louis, Aaron, Kate, and I eyed each other shyly for a moment. Then I said, "I can't believe he didn't say 'There's no I in team.' He's definitely a no-I-in-team kind of person."

"Yeah, but of course," said Aaron, "in the Spanish word for team, there actually *is* an I."

For a second no one said anything, and then Louis, in a perfect imitation of Jare, laughed, "Ha ha ha!" and we all cracked up. When we were finished laughing, Kate said, "I guess we should sit down?"

So we all plopped down, except for Louis, who lowered himself slowly and gingerly, like the ground was as prickly as a cactus. I noticed that his curly hair was so long and shaggy it could almost have gone into a ponytail, except that he didn't seem like the ponytail type.

"Um, okay," I said. "So what special talent will you contribute to the group's survival? Anyone want to go first?"

"Sure," said Aaron brightly. "I guess my talent would be—"

I held up my hand. "Let me guess," I said. "You have a photographic memory."

"That's not really it," said Aaron, "because it's not just what I see, but what I hear too. It all just stays in my brain."

"Do you use mnemonic devices?" asked Louis. "You know, like Every Good Boy Deserves Fudge? Always Add Acid? King Henry Died Unexpectedly Drinking Chocolate Milk?"

"Nope," said Aaron. He looked almost embarrassed. "I never really talked to anybody about how it works before. Everything I see and hear just kind of . . . sticks."

"Like Post-its," said Kate.

"If you had about three tons of them, and a thousand regrigerator doors to stick them on," said Aaron. "Although what happens to me is not as overwhelming as hyperthymesia, where people recall nearly every event of their entire lives through uncontrollable and unexpected associations."

"Still. Doesn't it get cluttered?" I asked. "How do you think straight with all that stuff stuck to the inside of your brain?"

"It's not like it's all there all the time. Well, it is there, but I might not even know, because it's kind of put away. I can usually get it out if I need to, though."

"Like clicking open a folder on your computer desktop?" asked Louis.

"Exactly!" Aaron said excitedly. Then his thoughts seemed to shift. "The first modern analog computer was a tide-predicting machine, invented by Sir William Thomson in 1872."

"What's analog mean?" I asked.

Aaron squinted up at the sky. "I don't know," he finally said.

"I thought you knew pretty much everything," I said.

"I only know what I've seen, or heard, or looked up, and there's only so much time in the day," Aaron replied. "So there are definite gaps. I mean, sometimes I just have to put down the books and go eat dinner."

"Well, anyway," I said, "your talent could definitely come in handy."

"Thanks," said Aaron, and then added sheepishly, "except I don't know if I have much information about the desert southwest. A few things here and there maybe, along with whatever Jare's already told us."

"I'm surprised you didn't read up on it before you came," said Kate.

"I would have, but my parents wouldn't tell me where I was going until I got on the plane."

"Really?" said Louis. "Didn't they want you to store information that would help you conquer the wilderness?"

"I think the idea was for me *not* to have the information. I think they want me to use my other strengths to figure things out." He looked embarrassed. "Except I don't *have* any other strengths."

"I'm sure you do," I said, but I sounded uncertain, even to myself.

"Thanks. Uh, so, what about you?" Aaron asked me. "What's your special talent?"

I'd never told anyone about the lie-detecting thing, except for my parents, who had already figured it out on their own. There was no way I was telling these strangers. So I just said, "I spend a lot of time outside. And, uh, I'm good at setting up a tent."

"Great!" said Aaron. "How about you, Kate?"

Kate sighed. "I don't know. My parents used to tell me I was good at walking around in other people's shoes."

Aaron looked puzzled. "Really? That's an interesting, um, skill."

"I think she means she's good at imagining what it would be like to be someone else," said Louis.

Aaron laughed, embarrassed. "Right!"

"But I haven't felt like doing that lately." She paused gloomily. "Haven't talked to my parents much lately, either."

Then she added, with more fire than she'd shown so far, "Also, I stick by people I care about. I don't just ditch them when things get rough." Then, just as suddenly, the dullness came back. "Of course, I don't really care about anyone anymore, so I guess that doesn't matter."

Kate looked down at her hands in her lap. I noticed that she had beautiful hands, with the kind of oval fingernails I'd always wanted. We all sat for a second, not saying anything.

Finally I said, "Okay, Louis. What special talent will you contribute to the group's survival?"

"Can we just maybe not say survival?" asked Louis. "I've been here less than a day, and I've already pictured like ten ways I'm probably going to die, which, even for me, is a record. Can we say . . . success?"

"Sure," I said. "Louis, what special talent will you contribute to the group's success?"

"Nothing," said Louis. "I am useless. A total liability."

"Aw, that can't be true," I said encouragingly.

Maybe it was and maybe it wasn't, but Louis definitely believed it was.

"No, trust me, it is," said Louis. "I have this weird sensory disorder, which basically means all my senses are like ridiculously heightened."

"That sounds sort of cool," said Kate, shrugging. It was almost funny how even when she was saying something was cool, she sounded sad, dull, and like not one thing on the planet had ever been or ever could be cool.

"Jewel beetles have infrared detectors under their legs that enable them to sense forest fires fifty miles away," said Aaron. "The greater wax moth is capable of sensing sound frequencies of up to three hundred kilohertz, which means its range of hearing is almost twice as great as that of the bottlenose dolphin. Grizzly bears' sense of smell can have an eighteen-mile radius."

I saw what he was doing, trying to put a positive spin on Louis's sensory issues, but Louis stared blankly at Aaron for a few seconds and then said, "I can't wear pants with regular waistbands." He snapped the elastic waist of his pants, just to demonstrate, and then winced like he'd been shot.

"Oh," said Aaron.

"I can't go to the movies without throwing up because it's so loud."

"It *is* really loud," said Kate, shrugging, "especially the previews."

"I've never gotten *past* the previews," said Louis.

"Wow," I said.

"I can't stand things coming at me unexpectedly. I've gotten better in that I don't scream anymore, I mean not usually." His face took on a haunted look. "I hope there won't be dodgeball here. Dodgeball is hell."

"We unpacked our bags and repacked them back at the visitors' center, remember?" I said. "Not a red rubber ball in sight."

Louis looked relieved, then smiled wryly. "A good idea, right? Sending a kid who is terrified of a playground game and can't wear clothes with tags in them to the wilderness."

"Were your parents maybe thinking along the same lines as Aaron's?" I asked.

"I guess the idea is that if I face my challenges head-on, I'll develop ways to cope with them," said Louis. He rolled his eyes. "Yeah, right. Like the wilderness could suddenly make me like dodgeball."

"Or make me happy," said Kate.

"Or make me into someone besides . . . Memory Boy," Aaron said quickly.

"Or make me trust my fellow human beings," I said. It just slipped out.

They all looked at me, waiting for more. Just then, a rock-hard lump of cornbread flew out of nowhere, hit Aaron in the side of the head, and fell at our feet.

Randolph's mocking voice came out of the darkness. "Tomorrow, you're vulture bait, Memory Boy!"

We all stared down at the cornbread. Aaron rubbed the side of his head.

"Trust your fellow human beings?" said Kate dryly. "Good luck with that."

CHAPTER SIX

Aaron Archer

El Viaje a la Confianza

I JOLTED AWAKE. IN A sleeping bag. In a tent. Lying on the rocky ground, next to the rusting tracks of an abandoned railroad. Before we'd bedded down the night before, Jare had made sure to tell us the story of the poor people who'd tried to build the railroad long ago, only to be defeated by the sun, sand, and heat of the desert. He gave us the impression it was mostly because they'd failed to PHWSS.

I heard an enormous creature crashing away through the bushes, and then everything fell silent, like in a museum or a church. At first I thought I was the only camper awake, but across the clearing, I saw Louis sitting bolt upright in the door of his tent, wrapped in his sleeping bag, staring glassily at the stars like he hadn't slept a wink.

Suddenly, loud screams rang out. Everybody woke up in a panic and tried to thrash out of their tents before they'd even unzipped their bags.

Except me. Because I knew the screams weren't screams. I recognized the sound of Helm Brütson of Garroted Artery shredding the guitar solo from "Beast Wagon." Two feet from my left ear. In the dimness of the dawn, I spied a beatbox hidden in a tumbleweed next to my tent flap.

"Guys! Guys!" I hollered, fumbling with the switch to kill the music. "It's okay! Stop! Everything is fine!" Slowly everybody calmed down. "It's just Jare's idea of an alarm clock."

"I hate Splutterkick," grumbled Randolph.

"It's worse than Splutterkick." Louis shivered, his hands still covering his ears. "It's Garroted Artery!"

"Shut up, freak," snarled Randolph, and shoved Louis into a bush, which made him whimper. "It's Splutterkick." He stomped off toward the campfire, dragging his pack behind him.

"Actually, you're right," I whispered to Louis, who was rubbing his ribs where Randolph had shoved him as he extracted himself from the bush. "Randolph made a mistake." I figured it'd cheer Louis up to know he'd been correct. "What most people don't realize is that Helm Brütson of Hang Time and Vhing Sharapova of Splutterkick were members of the same middle school marching band in Galveston, Texas, and during a hiatus in their rock-and-roll careers, they joined forces to form the supergroup Garroted—"

I noticed Louis's eyes grow wide at the sight of something behind me. I turned around in time to see Randolph, who must've come back for something he had forgotten, looking really annoyed and drawing back his—

BLAM.

Everything went white, and static crackled in my ears.

I found myself lying in the dirt watching birds fly through the purple dawn while my fellow campers stared down at me with wide eyes and silent mouths shaped like Os. All except for Randolph, who carefully placed his bootheel on my forehead and said, "Listen up, Memory Boy. If I say it's Splutterkick, it's Splutterkick, even when it's Garroted Artery. Got it?"

I thought maybe I did.

Because of my encounter with Randolph, I got to breakfast a little late.

The other campers were just finishing up PHWSS, which was how we were going to begin every day in the desert, I realized: Pack a Hat, Water, Sunscreen, and Socks. The breakfast bowls were cleaned and packed, and there was nothing left to eat but half a box of raisins that somebody had dropped in the sand and picked back up, so when I chewed them, they made a lot of noise inside my head.

Jare was concluding a speech about the purpose of our upcoming el Viaje challenge, whatever it was. I'd missed that part while I was stretched out on the ground near my tent, contemplating all the stars in the daytime sky. "You're going to work as *teams*," he said. "You're going to *trust* each other! Remember, you might not get back here until tomorrow! So take your sleeping gear and plenty of water! This heat has been killing everything from mastodons to mountain lions for the past ten million years! Now go beat the other guys! Win that air mattress!"

"What air mattress?" I asked.

Audrey turned to me with an exasperated look, but when she saw me standing there covered in dirt, my eye swelling up, her expression softened. A little. "It's our first team challenge. Kind of a scavenger hunt. We're supposed to follow Caesar's Nose," she explained.

"Right," I said. "Follow it where?"

"Somebody else want to explain while I fill our water bottles?" asked Audrey, holding a canteen under the spigot of an orange cooler Jare had cached in a tree before we arrived.

"Don't spill a drop!" hollered Jare as he lumbered past.

"Not one! It's a crime to waste water in the desert!"

His bellowing made Audrey jump, but she managed not to spill any water, which almost seemed to disappoint Jare, who stalked off to torment somebody else.

"Caesar's Nose is one of the clues Jare put on the sheet he passed out at breakfast," volunteered Louis.

"Jare's clues," continued Kate, "are supposed to lead us to a flag hidden somewhere in the desert. Have a look." She handed me the clues to the challenge, which came in the form of riddles to solve at turning points along the way.

The first step is easy—follow Caesar's Nose.

Benedict Arnold the river's ghost.

Do not go gentle into that good night, caballero.

Delve back into time.

By turning, turning, we come out right.

"This makes everything clear," I joked, but nobody was in much of a mood to laugh.

Audrey told me Jare had said to pack tents and sleeping bags, as if the search might last overnight, but he had also promised it would be worth the trouble, no matter how long it took, because at the end waited a prize. The team that found the flag and brought it back got an air mattress to sleep on.

Which didn't sound like much, especially since, even if your team won, you only got it one night out of every four. But I noticed that Louis seemed excited for the first time since I'd met him. And I remembered the look I'd seen in his eyes that morning, after he'd stayed awake tossing and turning on the desert gravel for nine whole hours. An air mattress would mean a lot to him. I wouldn't have minded one either, and I could tell by the gleam in Audrey's and Kate's eyes they felt the same way. Of course, so did everybody else on el Viaje a la Confianza. But our team had to win. For Louis.

"Hey. Look at that," said Louis, after I'd gotten my sunscreen smeared on (the tube still had Wahoo's toothmarks in it) and my extra socks stowed. He stared at something above my head. I looked. The peak of the mountain we were camped beside was actually a colossal rock outcropping, shaped like the head of an ancient nobleman with a regal nose. Simultaneously, all four members of our team glanced in the direction the nose pointed, where an almost invisible path led behind the tents and disappeared into the desert.

"Awesome, Louis," whispered Kate.

"Good eye," murmured Audrey. "Let's go."

As silently as we could, while the other teams rushed around slopping water into canteens and slathering on sunscreen and arguing about how much gear to carry, we shouldered our packs and slipped out of camp.

On the trail, Audrey led the way. Then came Kate. Then came Louis. I picked up the rear. About thirty minutes out, we stumbled upon a bush swarming with hundreds, probably thousands of bees, and Louis panicked. He ran off the trail, straight into nowhere. Kate managed to catch him after a few hundred yards. She was tiny, but she moved fast. By the time Audrey and I got there, she had slowed Louis to a stop by putting her hand on his arm, and she was talking to him in the quiet voice a jockey uses to calm his horse after it bolts. After that, she walked beside Louis to keep an eye on him.

We hiked for an hour. We hiked for two. On our left, the mountain still loomed, the nose still pointed. On our right, the desert rolled in waves to the horizon, like an ocean of stone, frozen in place. And dry as dust. I could see for twenty miles. I could see a million acres. Maybe this was what it felt like to be Louis.

I breathed in the air. It was clean. And clear. And smelled of something sharp and exciting, like a city on a spring day when you ride the school bus to visit the science museum. Creosote. A sizzling wind blew up the trail, chasing away the cool air of morning. The sun turned into a fist and began pounding the back of my neck.

I saw a tiny cactus beside the trail that had figured out how to grow on bare rock. Its spines were so fine that they looked like mist hovering around it.

I heard birds cheeping, and when I looked for them, I saw a pair—flitting along the ground from shadow to shadow. I realized they were staying hidden, from anything that might eat them, and from the sun. As I watched, one lit on a prickly pear. It knew where to perch without getting stabbed. Quickly it took a drink from one of the yellow blossoms.

We walked and we walked some more. The sound of our footsteps crunching together on the path, the equipment clinking in our packs, and our breathing made a rhythm. Almost a song. Caesar's Nose loomed above, showing us the way.

Then Louis hissed, "Somebody's following us."

We stopped.

"I don't hear anything," said Kate.

"I thought we had a huge head start," said Audrey.

"People are back there," said Louis, apprehensively cocking his ear. "Maybe half a mile. I definitely hear them."

"We better hike faster, then," said Audrey.

So we did. And soon I realized something. We were hiking in step. We were a team. We were almost a single person. Right there, in that second, I felt like I was about to make friends with Audrey, Kate, and Louis. If only I could remember the right thing to say, the way I'd remembered Heisman winners on the day I'd dropped all those passes and made friends with Hardy Gillooly . . .

I thought about satellite images and geological reports. I thought about weather patterns and American history and the Spanish-English dictionary I'd thumbed through when I was in fourth grade. I wished my parents had told me I was coming here while I still had internet. I felt totally unprepared. But the more I thought, the more I realized I *did* know things about the desert . . . a few, anyway.

"Certain factors remain constant in all high-temperature exertion," I called to the rest of the group. "Ideally, sustained heart rate should not exceed fifty percent of maximum capacity, and personal water consumption should remain high enough to produce a clear, steady stream of—"

"It's okay, Aaron," said Audrey, so softly I almost couldn't hear her. "It's okay if things are quiet."

But I really wanted them to like me.

"The band America," I tried in a softer voice, "had a smash hit in 1972 that contained the lyrics 'I've been through the desert on a horse with no name—'"

"Really," said Kate, "it's fine not to talk."

Louis nodded. "I think the point of the desert is . . . sometimes there's no noise," he added.

I felt the lightness inside me replaced by a weight. I felt Audrey, Kate, and Louis slipping away, even though we were all right there hiking together.

The heat beat down. We moved more and more slowly. Finally we came to a gully in the foot of the mountain. It cut so deep into the desert that its sides cast shade on the bottom. Our trail led down one side, back up the other, and headed into the distance. Audrey scrambled in and out to follow.

"Wait," I said. I thought maybe I saw Audrey roll her eyes as she stopped and turned around. "Sorry," I apologized. "But this might be important. Look at the next clue." She dug the clue sheet out of her pocket. "Benedict Arnold the river's ghost?" she read. "Yeah. I don't really understand what—"

"The river's ghost," murmured Kate, pointing at the arroyo. "There was a stream here. But it died."

"I get it," said Louis. "This is the next place we have to make a decision."

"Benedict Arnold?" said Audrey uncertainly. "What does Jare know about Benedict Arnold? What do *we* know about Benedict Arnold?"

"Benedict Arnold," I said, "was an American Revolutionary War general who originally served in the Continental Army but later defected to the British side."

"So he was a double-crosser," said Kate.

"Which means we cross back to the other side," whispered Louis, aiming his ears down the trail we'd just hiked. "They're still back there."

"All right," said Audrey quietly, gazing at the trail we'd almost taken, which would've led us off into the wide-open desert. She gave me a fist bump and then Louis. "Hurry. Let's turn around and see if we can ditch our tail before they see us," she whispered. "I bet none of them know who Benedict Arnold was."

We located the fork in our trail leading back over the gulch. We followed it, trying not to leave footprints in the gravel. Soon the path began to climb, like it wanted to lead us over the mountain. The empty streambed ran beside us.

Before we'd gone half a mile, Louis held up his hand. "Hear that?" he asked.

"Somebody's still following us?" asked Kate.

"No," said Louis. "This is different. He cocked his head toward the arroyo. "This way," he said, sliding gingerly down the side and following it uphill as it cut farther into the mountain, until it got so deep it became a tiny canyon, a slot between two walls, shady, dark, and cool at the bottom.

I still didn't hear anything. But then I did. Crying?

A tall blond kid who'd told us his name was Kevin

Larkspur hovered with two of his teammates over the last member of their team, a guy named Enod Marx, who lay on the ground, moaning. Kevin had said he'd go to the ends of the earth for his pet beagle. Enod for his little brother, who had autism.

"What happened?" Audrey asked Kevin. "How'd you get here before us?"

"We wanted to beat everybody. We really didn't understand the clues, so we just took the first trail we saw. It cut over the side of the mountain. I guess we were in the sun more than we thought," he said.

"I went too fast putting on my sunscreen," moaned Enod.

"What do you mean?" asked Audrey.

"Look," said Enod.

Grunting, he rolled over and pointed at the backs of his knees.

Louis turned white and sat down with his arms over his head. Tears sprang to Kate's eyes.

Enod had put sunscreen almost everywhere, but he hadn't reached the soft skin behind his knees. They were as red as fire, and blistered.

"Second-degree sunburn," I said. I'd seen pictures in a first-aid manual.

"I can't bend my legs," said Enod. "I can't walk."

"What do we do?" asked Larkspur.

"Fire your Jare flare," I said, because I knew Enod needed first aid fast. Audrey had told me that Jare had given each team a flare to fire in an emergency, so he could come get us. He'd made it clear that if you had to fire yours, you were a stinking loser on a team full of losers. Larkspur reluctantly pulled the flare out of his pack, sighted down the tube, and yanked the cord. The flare scorched a white streak through the blue sky.

"You guys keep going," moaned Enod. "Maybe you'll be able to capture the flag. And keep those jerks Daphne and Randolph from getting the air mattress!"

"No," I said. "Look at the sun. It's almost straight above. We should all just stay here in the shade. There's no point in trying to hike until things cool off. For every hour we hike during the heat of midday, we'll go two miles at most, and use a quart of water each. It's not worth it."

Kate took a T-shirt out of her pack, poured a cup of her precious water on it to cool it, and laid it across the backs of Enod's knees. "How does that feel?" she asked.

"Better," said Enod, even though he muttered it through his teeth, so I could tell he was still in pain.

"Daphne's group isn't far behind," Kevin told us. "We saw them below you on the trail when we were lost on the mountain."

"We're still waiting until Jare gets here," I said, even though I could tell by the shadows on the arroyo floor that the sun had already dropped a little. "In the meantime, everybody, check your water." It turned out, even though we'd started with eight gallons, we were already down to four.

Suddenly Jare vaulted over the edge of the gully and landed in our midst, raising a cloud of dust. A handful of maps tumbled out of his vest pocket and fanned out on the dry bed of the ghost creek. As I picked one up, he snapped, "Give me that!" and snatched it.

"How'd you get here so fast?" Kevin asked.

"I have ways," muttered Jare. He took a look at Enod's knees and said, "Happens every year. Usually not on the second day, though. Son, I think you just set the el Viaje record for quickest calamity. Stick a fork in you. You're done."

"What do you mean—done?" moaned Enod.

"You ain't gonna die, but the next few days around camp ain't gonna be fun," said Jare. "Other guys in his group. Larkspur, and whatever, and whoever?" Enod's other team members, a tall skinny girl named Sara and a chubby guy named James, stood up out of the gloom. "You're gonna carry him. And be careful. You break those blisters on the backs of his knees, then he's in real trouble."

"Carry him?" asked James. "All the way to camp?"

"No way," said Enod. "I'm heavy."

"Shoulda thought of that before you blew it with your sunscreen," said Jare. "You're their teammate. You screw up, they pay the price. Everybody get cracking. Hup, two, three, four. What are you staring at?" He glared at our team.

"We just . . . stopped to help," replied Audrey.

"What do you expect now?" shot back Jare. "A medal?"

"No . . . we . . . ," stammered Kate.

Jare snorted derisively and stomped up a trail we hadn't noticed before. Kevin and the rest scrambled to follow.

"Good luck, guys," Enod called as they headed over the shoulder of the mountain.

After that, we hiked as fast as we could. We knew Daphne was right behind us, and nobody wanted to spend the next six weeks listening to her and Randolph gloat about all the sleep they were getting. My feet hurt, and I could feel thirst creeping up the back of my throat. At least my pack was feeling lighter. But so was everybody's. Because our water was nearly gone.

Louis panicked at the sight of a stick in the bushes and had to stop three times to take twigs out of his boot, and once an ocotillo stuck to his pack like the tentacle of an alien, scaring him stiff. Every time we halted, we asked him about Daphne's team. And when he got calm enough, he almost always heard their footsteps behind us. One of the team, he said after a while, was limping.

"Wait until I tell Hardy Gillooly about you," I told Louis.

"Who's Hardy Gillooly?" he asked.

"A friend of mine. From back home. He's interested in superpowers," I said.

"What I have is anything but a superpower." Louis sighed.

We crested a rise, and Caesar's Nose was gone. The double-cross trail was fading beneath our feet. All I saw were white rocks, stained red by the setting sun, scattered across the peak. We'd hiked onto a new mountain without realizing it. I checked, but I didn't have a map or a satellite photo or even a travel brochure in my head to tell me where we were.

I saw Audrey stumble, and I realized that as soon as we'd hiked over the pinnacle, the sun had disappeared. "Hold on," I said. "Maybe we should look at the clue sheet again."

Audrey reached into her pocket. Then she reached into another pocket. Then she squirmed out of her pack straps and unzipped the flap. "It's gone!" she said. "What happened to our clues?" Frantically, she dug through her pack.

"Does anyone have it?" she cried. Louis and Kate shook their heads.

"Maybe we dropped it when we stopped to help Enod," surmised Louis.

"Aaron? Do you have the sheet?" asked Audrey.

"'The first step is easy—follow Caesar's Nose,'" I recited, because of course I had the clue sheet. Right there in my brain, beside everything else.

Benedict Arnold the river's ghost.

Do not go gentle into that good night, caballero.

Delve back into time.

By turning, turning, we come out right.

"Are you sure that's right?" Audrey asked.

"Oh, yeah," I said.

"But what does it mean?" asked Kate, shivering. The nighttime chill was setting in fast now that the sun had begun to fade. "'Do not go gentle into that good night, caballero'? Jare wrote these?"

"Maybe his girlfriend wrote them for him," said Audrey.

"Or his English teacher," I said. Everybody stared at me. "What?" I asked. "Some people are friends with their English teachers."

"No," giggled Kate. "They're not."

"'Do Not Go Gentle into That Good Night' is a poem written in the form of a villanelle by the Welsh poet Dylan Thomas in 1951. It's addressed to his dying father."

"Maybe," said Audrey, before I had a chance to go any further, "it just means what it says. Don't go into the night."

"Maybe," agreed Louis. "But why not?"

I heard the narrator of an educational show start to speak inside my head. He sounded like Morgan Freeman. He was talking about the exact place we were standing: "Los Cañones de los Muertos y Sus Caballos . . ."

"Hold on," I told the team. "Let me listen to something." Because even though I'd been doing my sixth-grade math homework at the kitchen table when it came on, I could hear the documentary my dad was watching on PBS in another room. I repeated what Morgan Freeman was saying so the rest of the team could hear: ". . . is an isolated stretch of desert, where, in 1553, the Piñones expedition, in their quest to find a mythical town of gold, foolishly rode into complete darkness. Their leader plunged down an unseen ravine. Twenty riders followed. Every horse and every horseman died. Hence the name: the canyons of the dead men and their horses."

"And that was—" said Audrey.

"A PBS documentary," I said.

"Then it's definitely trustworthy," declared Kate.

"Sounds like this clue is telling us to learn from their mistakes," said Louis. "And to stop for now, since once it's fully dark, even I can't see."

"It's sort of flat here," I observed, "since we're at the top of the mountain. It'll be cold, but we have tents and sleeping bags. There aren't too many rocks—"

"—THE HECK YOU LOOKING AT?" I heard somebody shout.

"Randolph?" whispered Kate.

Randolph had just limped over the peak. Daphne and her other two teammates, two kids who hadn't said much yet besides their names, Cyrus Ramsey (the guys on his soccer team) and Edith Mendez (her guinea pig) followed. Louis stared blankly at Randolph. "What?" bellowed Randolph.

"Nothing," said Louis, looking away quickly.

"What're you doing in our campsite?" demanded Randolph.

"This is *our* campsite," said Kate.

Randolph glanced at Daphne. One corner of her mouth twitched upward. Just a little. I almost didn't see it. But Randolph sure did. And was highly encouraged. "Get off!" he shouted. Randolph grabbed Kate's backpack, took a running start, and heaved it over the side of the mountain. I could hear it tumbling into the darkness.

Nobody said anything. Nobody moved. Randolph grinned in pride. I could see his yellow teeth in the fading light as he looked hopefully at Daphne.

"Are you waiting for a Scooby snack, Randolph?" asked Audrey.

"Huh?" said Randolph. Some of the shine faded from his grin.

"Come on, guys." Audrey sighed. "Let's go."

"But—" I said.

Randolph glared at me and balled up his fists.

"We should go find Kate's pack," Audrey said calmly, "and finish this conversation another time." When she turned away, I saw how hard she clenched her teeth, and I realized how mad she was. Almost as mad as I was. But Audrey seemed to know how things like this worked, and I didn't, so I followed her. Kate and Louis fell in behind.

"That's right, losers," scoffed Randolph. "Run. Edie, hand me my water." Edith dropped her pack with a colossal thud and rummaged around in it for Randolph's water, which he'd evidently made her carry up the mountain. "And fix my blisters," he added, yanking off his boot.

We found Kate's backpack at the bottom of the mountain, lying in a gulley. It wasn't in great shape. Her last water bottle had cracked and soaked everything. Louis gave her a swig of his water.

"Look at all these lines in the rock," murmured Louis as he studied the sides of the gully in the last of the light.

"Strata of sedimentary stone provide a useful historical record," I said, "because the layers were deposited sequentially as sheets of mud at the bottom of a prehistoric sea, hardening into rock after aeons of heat and pressure. The top layers represent the most recent eras, while the deepest represent the most ancient."

"Wait," said Audrey, gazing at the gully cutting deeper and deeper into the layered rock as it led across the plain into the darkness. "This is where we use the next clue—what was it—about going back in history?"

" 'Delve back into time,' " I said.

"The deeper we go, the father back we go," said Kate thoughtfully.

"But we don't start until tomorrow, right?" asked Louis, shuddering as he gazed into the depths of the gulley. "Why don't we leave at first light? That way, we can see where we're going *and* lose Daphne's team."

"What do you mean?" said Audrey. "They're at the top of the mountain."

"No, they're not," said Louis. "They're just over that

ridge. They trailed us down the slope and stopped right behind us to camp. I can smell their fire."

The rest of us sniffed the air.

"Believe me," said Louis. "They're there."

"Why did they follow us?" I asked.

"Maybe," said Audrey, "because we can figure out the clues and they can't?"

"Or maybe they're just up there planning to break more of our stuff," said Kate darkly, staring up the trail.

"We need to go find out," said Audrey, leaping to her feet.

"We're just going to ask?" Louis said. "I don't think that will go well."

"We're going to eavesdrop," said Audrey. "It's not cheating to spy on cheaters, is it?"

"No way!" was our unanimous verdict.

We heard something giant crash through the creosote bushes. "Probably a javelina," I guessed. Louis looked alarmed. "Just a midsized wild pig," I added. "They're not hostile, but they have terrible eyesight, so sometimes they get confused and run over people by mistake. Who's coming to spy on Daphne's team?"

"Not me." Louis shivered.

"You'd be super at eavesdropping," I said.

"Sorry," sighed Louis, grinning. "Stick a fork in me. I'm done."

"I'll stay here with Louis," offered Kate.

"Let's go, Aaron," Audrey said.

CHAPTER SEVEN

Audrey Alcott

El Viaje a la Confianza

EVEN THOUGH AARON AND I were on a mission, we hadn't walked twenty yards before we got to a clearing in the bushes, stopped dead in our tracks, tipped our heads back, and stared upward. We did it at exactly the same time, like we'd planned it, although of course we hadn't. The sky was just this irresistible force, as gargantuan and shiny as a limousine; you could practically hear it shouting, "Look!" There seemed to be twenty times as many stars as usual. In all those dots and islands and swarms of light, the few normal constellations I could usually recognize, like Orion, got lost. It was like we were on a planet in another galaxy.

"They look like somebody spread them on with a knife," I whispered. "Like peanut butter, except stars."

"Famed African-American botanist George Washington Carver is often credited with inventing peanut butter," whispered Aaron, "but the Canadian chemist Marcellus Gilmore Edson actually secured the first patent, back in 1884."

I had always thought George Washington Carver invented it, but I didn't say this because who did or did not invent peanut butter was so completely beside the point. Who wouldn't know that? Aaron, that's who. As smart as he was, I was starting to realize that a lot of times, he needed the point pointed out to him.

"Okay, but I was talking about the stars and how they look," I whispered, never taking my eyes off the sky. "They're amazing."

"Oh. Right," whispered Aaron, embarrassed.

We kept staring.

"You're right. They are. They're amazing," whispered Aaron, and he didn't sound embarrassed anymore. He sounded so dazzled that I had to smile.

We kept walking.

"It's funny how good Kate is with Louis, isn't it?" I said. I kept whispering because, even though I was pretty sure we were too far away for Louis to hear us, I wasn't positive.

"Funny? I . . . guess?" said Aaron. After a little while,

he said tentatively, "Maybe it's funny because she's so small, and he's so big?"

"Yes! She's like one of those tiny companion ponies, the ones that go around tethered to racehorses to calm them down."

"Seabiscuit had one named Pumpkin, but he also had a companion monkey."

"Named Jo-Jo," I said.

Aaron stared at me, shocked. I laughed. "Hey, you're not the only one who reads books."

Aaron smiled sheepishly. "Sorry. I guess I sometimes forget that other people know things."

"That's okay."

After a minute or so, Aaron said, "I smell the campfire now."

"So do I. We must be close. Also, I think the wind shifted."

Just then, as if it had heard me, the wind shot cold air straight at us. I shivered and tried to zip my jacket, but the zipper stuck. Before I knew it, Aaron had pulled a tiny flashlight from his pocket and was handing it to me.

"Here, you hold this," he said.

I switched on the flashlight. As small as it was, its beam sliced through the dark like a laser. I lifted the flashlight and slid the beam through the bushes and across the sky.

"You could play connect the dots with the stars with this thing," I said, and then I found the dipper part of the Big Dipper and did just that: one, two, three, four.

"You could also shine it on your zipper," said Aaron. "Sometimes it's easier to fix a zipper when you're not the person wearing the jacket."

"Oh. Thanks."

As he worked on the zipper, he said, "Whitcomb L. Judson invented the zipper, but Gideon Sundback perfected and marketed it. The word for how the teeth interlock is interdigitate, which is what happens when two people hold hands, with their fingers interlocking."

For a second, Aaron's hands on the zipper froze, and I could tell he was embarrassed again.

"Not that I've ever, uh, you know, uh, done that," he said. Usually he spoke with casual confidence, but now he was stammering. I realized that as much as Aaron talked, he hardly ever said anything about himself.

"Yeah, me neither," I said. "That's cool about the word, though. I'll probably think about that every time I zip something from now on."

He gave one final tug and said, "There. Try it."

I zipped my jacket shut. "Great, thanks. But can I ask a question?"

"Sure!" Aaron's face took on a focused, soccer-goalie

expression, like he was gearing up for whatever question I might shoot at him.

"You have to read something to have it imprint on your memory, right?" I asked.

"Read or hear or see, but a lot of times it happens with reading."

"So why were you reading about zippers? Was it a zipper book? The history of clothing closures or something?"

As soon as I said it, his shoulders tensed up, and I wondered if there might be Lyza Turnbills at his school too, "cool" kids who smiled and acted interested, even though they were laughing at him behind his back the whole time. I hoped not. Because I was really and truly interested, I quickly said, "I mean, I read a lot of quirky stuff too, like *Walden* by Henry David Thoreau, for example, which is why I was wondering."

He relaxed. "Oh, well, yeah, I read the weird letter sections of the dictionary sometimes. You know. Q, Z. Or relatively rare letter combinations, like Ps . . ."

"Cool. But why?" I said, and I really wanted to add, *By the way, if your school does have a version of Lyza Turnbill, never, ever tell her that you read the dictionary.*

"I guess I find words interesting." He shrugged and smiled a half smile. "But also sometimes I just need stuff to talk about with people. So anyway, I found the word zipper, which got me wondering about zippers, so I checked a book out of the library."

We'd gotten to some taller, thickset shrubs and brush. Aaron went first, occasionally holding branches so they wouldn't spring back and hit me. I thought this was really nice of him, but when I whispered, "Thanks," he looked puzzled, like he had no idea what I'd be thanking him for. We'd only gone a little way into the woods when Aaron stopped, turned around, and put a finger to his lips to tell me *Quiet*. Through the trees, I could see the tangerine glow of Daphne's team's campfire.

Slowly Aaron and I made our way closer, staying low and trying not to step on anything noisy, until we were right on the edge of the clearing where the team was camped. Daphne and Randolph sat near the dying fire. They were facing us, but I was pretty sure we were lost in shadow. I really, really hoped so. Their other two teammates, Cyrus and Edie, must have been sleeping or just lying in their tents, and I would have bet that they'd been there since setting up camp. If I were on Daphne's and Randolph's team, I knew, I would take off and zip myself into my tent before it even got dark.

"We've got to figure this out," said Daphne. "No way am I letting that pack of misfit, preppified, math-club dorks get their dweeby hands on the air mattress."

Aaron and I exchanged a look that said, *Those misfit, preppified, math-club, dweeby-handed dorks would be us.*

"Hey, maybe it means we should set our watches back!" said Randolph excitedly. "But how *far* back? That's the question."

Daphne snorted. "That might the stupidest idea I've ever heard. You're kidding, right?"

Randolph forced a laugh. "Yeah. Duh. Totally kidding."

A lie. Obviously. He ended it with a squeak, a classic Helium Liar.

He stared up at the sky, squeezing his hands into fists and pounding them gently against his thighs. After I watched him for a few seconds, I realized this was Randolph's version of thinking, as if even just using his brain required hitting something. He stopped pounding.

"Okay, how's this? Maybe we should hike *backward*? Like *face* one way and *walk* the other way?"

Aaron touched my shoulder and mouthed the word "Clue."

To delve back in time. They hadn't figured it out yet! And obviously, if it were up to Randolph, they never would.

"Why would we have to do that?" scoffed Daphne. "What would that lead to, besides you walking off the edge of a cliff?"

Randolph laughed uneasily again. "Well, what do *you* think it means?"

"I think it means we should walk back the way we came."

"Really? But that would be, like, backtracking, right?"

Daphne gave him a withering stare and then sighed. "Look, everyone will assume the flag is up ahead because they haven't seen it yet, but I'll bet Jare is out there in the dark, sticking it someplace back along the trail right this minute. *That's* why he didn't want us searching at night."

Randolph narrowed his eyes and nodded, slowly. "Whoa. I bet you're right."

Viciously, Daphne stabbed at the fire with a stick. "This whole thing is so stupid. I'd run away except the only place stupider than here is home with my so-called mom."

"Is she not really your mom, you know, biologically?" asked Randolph.

Daphne gave him a shove. "Don't be an idiot. Yeah, she's my mom, biologically! What do you think, I'm adopted? Or some pathetic foster-care kid?"

Randolph's face drooped. "No way," he said, a little halfheartedly. "Foster care? Seriously? I don't even know what that is."

Lie. Randolph knew what foster care was. Who didn't?

But something about his tone made me worry that Randolph hadn't just heard about it or seen it on TV, that his knowledge was more of the firsthand variety. I hoped not.

"I *meant* that she acts more like a prison guard. All she does is make insane rules just so she can punish me when I break them. She says she wants me to be responsible, but if that means turning out like her, I'd rather drop dead. All she does is work at her stupid office job. She's like a rat in a cage on one of those rat wheels."

"Rat wheels," said Randolph sagely. "I know what you mean."

"It's why she keeps sending me to these camps. She thinks if I spend enough time roughing it, I'll finally get how great our life is and appreciate all she does for me. Like that'll ever happen. No wonder my dad left when I was a baby. He is so awesome, it's not even funny. Totally fearless. He helicopter skis. He surfs ridiculous waves. He scuba dives the Great Barrier Reef, like, annually."

Daphne wasn't lying. Her dad's awesomeness might have been debatable (helicopter skiing sounded plain stupid to me), but Daphne didn't doubt it at all.

"Cool!" said Randolph. "Why don't you go live with him?"

"Brilliant idea," said Daphne. "Gee, why didn't I think of that?"

"Oh, yeah. I guess you probably did think of it."

"Uh, once or twice, moron. My witch mom hired some fancy lawyer who tricked my dad into giving up custody of me. But as soon as he can work it out, he's totally taking me back. We'll go live in this amazing town in Montana where he grew up. It's so far north that it's practically Canada. Which means I'll never see my mom again, thank god. She hates the cold *and* the wilderness, anyplace she can't wear her hideous blue suits."

"Oh, yeah, my mom wears those suits too. And she's super strict. Last July, on my *birthday*, she made me do yard work all day because I talked back to her. I got blisters all over my hands and got stung by a hornet on my freaking birthday. *And* sunburn!"

Lies. The suit, the yard work, the hornet, all of it. Possibly even the mom was a lie. It almost annoyed me, feeling sorry for Randolph, but no matter how big a jerk the guy was, I really hoped he had a mom.

"Hey, I was born in July, too. The sixth. When's your birthday?" asked Daphne.

"July seventeenth. And we live in this town on the Georgia coast, which is a million degrees in July."

"You're a Cancer, like me," said Daphne. "Cancers are the best!"

Randolph's eyes glittered, as though being a fellow

Cancer of Daphne's was the best thing that had ever happened to him. She raised her hand, and he high-fived her, then stared down at his palm, awestruck. Daphne kicked sand on the fire.

"Let's get some sleep," she said. "We need to get out of here as soon as it's light if we want to beat Little Miss Perfect Ponytail and her band of freaks."

"Yeah! What a bunch of losers!"

"She and I left from the same airport. Her parents walked her all the way to the security line and then hugged her like she was going off to war or something. Her *dad* actually got teary eyed. It was sickening."

It took me a second to realize that Little Miss Perfect Ponytail was probably me. I felt a jolt of anger and wanted to slap Daphne for having the nerve to even talk about my parents. But right then, Aaron turned and nodded at me, and we carefully, silently backed deep into the thicket of creosote bushes.

When we were a safe distance away, I said, "Did you see Randolph's face when she high-fived him? I bet he won't wash that hand for a week."

"Like he was going to wash his hand anyway," said Aaron.

Surprised, I laughed.

"What?" said Aaron.

"That was funny."

"It was?"

"Yeah, and I think it was also the first mean thing I've heard you say."

"Oh," said Aaron, a little guiltily. "Well, I guess maybe I don't like Randolph that much. He's not exactly nice to me, right?"

"Well, there was that brutally-smacking-you-to-the-ground incident."

Aaron smiled. "Yeah, there was that."

"He was lying, you know, about his mom making him do yard work on his birthday."

"I know. Last July seventeenth, Hurricane Ernesto hit coastal Georgia. It started at noon and hovered over the region all day. There were hundred-mile-per-hour winds. No one was doing yard work that day." Then he gave me a puzzled look. "But how did you know?"

I made an offended face. "What? You're just assuming I don't know the weather conditions in Georgia on July seventeenth of last year?"

"No!" Then he scratched his head. A Poison Ivy liar, unless he only scratched his head, which would make him a Lice Liar. I tried to remember what he'd done before, but then I realized this was the only time I'd ever heard him lie. And he took the lie back about three seconds later.

"Well, yeah, I was. Sorry. Like I said, sometimes I forget that other people know things."

"I was *kidding*," I said, elbowing him. "I had no idea what the weather was."

"Oh, well, how did you know he was lying, then?"

"I knew because—" I had never told anyone about my special ability, my unsuper superpower, but I decided, right there on the spot, to tell Aaron. I don't know why. Maybe because he was so open about his own weird gift. Maybe because he just seemed like someone you could trust. Maybe because I knew I'd never see the guy after camp ended, so it didn't matter what I said to him. But really I think it had more to do with the night sky, how immense and starry it was. I know it doesn't make sense, but there was something about being under that sky with Aaron that made me want to tell him the whole truth. I took a breath. "Because my brain can do this strange thing."

And then I told him. After I finished, he didn't say anything at first, but I could tell from his expression that he was mulling it over. I braced myself, waiting for him to spurt out some fact about the prefrontal cortex of the brain or about a world-famous pathological liar, or maybe he was even going to lie to me to see if I could detect it, but when he finally spoke, he said, "Do you ever wish people wouldn't talk about it all the time?"

"About what?"

"Your lie-detecting ability." He smiled. "Your superpower."

"I don't really call it that. Sometimes, to myself, I call it an unsuperpower."

"I don't call it that either," said Aaron, "except as a joke. But whatever you want to call it, both our brains can do strange things. I just wondered if you ever get tired of people talking about *your* strange thing."

"Do people talk about yours a lot?"

Aaron nodded. "Sure. All the time. They're not being mean or anything; at least, most people aren't. They think it's cool. They think *I'm* cool because of it, and when they talk about it, they're, like, cheering me on. But now, for some reason, I wish they wouldn't talk about it so much."

I thought for a second. "Well, yeah, it probably gets old being known for just that. You wouldn't want it to become your entire identity."

Aaron's eyes clouded with confusion. "I'm not sure what you're saying."

"You know, your amazing memory is, well, amazing. But you probably wish people saw the other interesting things about you."

Aaron looked even more confused, as if it hadn't occurred to him before that there might be other interesting things about him. I didn't see how that could be true, though. He was probably just tired.

"Well, *I'll* try not to talk about it a lot," I said, nudging him with my shoulder. "And I'll definitely never call you Memory Boy."

Aaron smiled. "Thanks."

"Although it is a really clever nickname. Sounds like something a first grader would make up," I said, "which isn't that surprising, since it was Randolph."

"Right." But Aaron didn't jump in and start talking about what an idiot Randolph was, which is what most people would have done. I figured that with the hand-washing insult, maybe he'd used up his meanness quota for the day.

"I don't get tired of people talking about my lie-detecting ability because no one knows about it," I said.

Aaron looked at me, startled. "Seriously? Why not?"

"I guess since it's something I hate about myself, I don't feel like going around broadcasting it to everyone. Only my parents know."

"Hold on. You *hate* it?"

"Anyone would hate it."

"I don't know about that. I mean, I can see how it would be a problem sometimes, but it's part of who you are."

"So?"

"So hating it seems . . . counterproductive."

I stopped walking and put my hands on my hips, annoyed. "My so-called gift messes up my life on a daily basis. So what am I supposed to do? Just start—*poof!*—liking it? Does that sound easy to you?"

"I guess not," said Aaron. "Sorry."

He sounded so downcast and regretful that I felt bad about snapping at him. *Why should you feel bad?* I chided myself. *He's not your friend, remember? You don't have any friends.*

Even so, I flashed back to him patiently fixing my zipper when I hadn't even asked him to.

"That's okay," I said.

When we got back to our campsite, Kate and Louis were waiting up for us. Kate pointed and said, "Here they are!" and I noticed that she seemed less sad than usual. I thought about how maybe those companion ponies (or monkeys) weren't only helping the racehorses. Maybe taking care of the racehorses helped them too.

We filled them in on what we'd overheard.

"Do you think they're right?" asked Louis. "About heading back down the trail?"

He sounded hopeful, and I thought he was probably thinking that he might not have to hike through that dark, narrow crevice in the rock after all. But Aaron was shaking his head.

"'Delve' comes from the Old English word *delfan*, which means 'to dig.' It's an odd choice of words, so I think Jare must have done it on purpose. We're not just supposed to go back; we're also supposed to go *down*, into the ground."

"Not to be negative or anything, but do you think Jare *knows* Old English?" asked Kate.

"Maybe his girlfriend or his mom or his English teacher does. Whoever wrote the clues also knows about Benedict Arnold and Dylan Thomas's poetry. He—or she—could easily know about the word 'delve.'"

Louis shuddered but then sat up straighter. "Okay. So we'll get up tomorrow morning and go."

"It'll be fine, Louis," said Kate. She reached out as if to pat his arm but, as if remembering that he didn't like to be touched, stopped a few inches from it and patted the air instead. Louis gave a shaky smile, but he didn't look one bit convinced.

"Actually," I said, "I think we should leave before morning."

Louis's eyes widened. "You mean go in the dark?"

"Well, it would only be dark at first, before we get to the gully, and we'll use headlamps," I said. "Look, I don't love the idea of hiking in the dark either, but Daphne's team is planning to start first thing in the morning. I bet it won't take her that long to figure out they made a mistake. So I think we should get a head start."

"'We need to get out of here as soon as it's light if we want to beat Little Miss Perfect Ponytail and her band of freaks,'" quoted Aaron.

Louis and Kate stared at him. He shrugged.

"Sorry. That's just what she said," he explained.

"Yeah, thanks for repeating it word for word," I told him, but I wasn't really mad. Aaron was somehow a hard person to be mad at.

"Your ponytail *is* nice," said Aaron helpfully.

Maybe we were giddy from exhaustion, but this struck us all as hilarious. When we stopped laughing, we agreed that Aaron would set his watch so that we'd be up a half hour before sunrise.

"I wear earplugs when I try to sleep, so you might need to talk extra loud to wake me up," said Louis, climbing into his big tent. "If I sleep at all. Anyway, good night, guys."

"Yeah, good night, everyone," said Kate sadly. She sighed as she unzipped her tent, and I thought that nights must be especially hard for her, lying there alone with whatever it was that made her so miserable.

"Night," I said.

"Good night," said Aaron. Then, when the other two were in their tents, he added, quietly, just to me, "I was thinking. Maybe you don't have to actually *like* it, your unsuperpower."

"What do you mean?"

"Well, maybe you don't have to go all the way to liking it. But remember what you said about my memory? That it doesn't have to be my whole identity? Maybe if you thought about your lie-detecting ability as just another part of who you are, like your brown hair or whatever, it wouldn't seem like such a big pain," said Aaron.

I know I should have been irritated that this kid I wasn't even friends with was giving me advice I hadn't even asked for, but somehow all I could feel was touched. All this time, just because he wanted to, Aaron had been thinking about how to help me with my unsuperpower problem. But I realized that showing him I was touched would be a mistake—it would make him think we were friends or something. So I just shrugged.

"Who knows?" I said breezily. "Maybe."

But that night, I stayed awake inside my tent for a long time, thinking about what Aaron had said.

I'd expected that Aaron would have to come wake us all up when his watch alarm went off, but even though I was two tents away and sound asleep, I heard it, a bright, hard, mechanical pinging, bouncing like a tiny hammer against the soft, wide quiet of the desert night. I knew it was actually early morning, but most of my brain and my entire body thought it was still night. It was only by sheer force of will—and picturing Daphne instead of Louis sleeping on that air mattress—that I was able to drag myself up and out of my tent. But when I stood, stretched, and breathed in, the air smelled fresh and crisp and lush and alive.

I figured I was the first one to emerge, but after a moment I noticed that Louis's tent was already down, and then I saw his large, bunched silhouette against the backdrop of trees. Either he'd decided not to wear his earplugs after all or he'd been too nervous about hiking in the dark to sleep. He was sitting on his pack, and his hands were around his face. His shoulders were slowly rising and falling. I thought he might be crying.

"Louis?" I whispered his name so softly that it was more like a breath, because I knew he hated things coming at him out of nowhere, and I wasn't sure if this included his name. But he didn't jump at the sound, just turned his head in my direction and nodded. I walked over and saw that he had one hand clamped over his mouth. The forefinger of his other hand was pressed against the side of his nose, squeezing shut his right nostril.

"Oh. Do you feel like you're going to throw up?" I asked him.

He shook his head, moved his hands away, and exhaled, long and slowly, like he was blowing out birthday candles.

"I do that too, sometimes," he said. "Throw up. I guess I still could. It's early." He gave a shaky laugh. "But no, I was reducing my oxygen levels and increasing my carbon dioxide."

"Because . . . ?"

"I was overbreathing," he said. "Also called hyperventilating. But just the word 'hyperventilate' makes me anxious, which is basically the last thing you want when you're panicking. I find the word 'overbreathing' more calming."

I considered this. "I can see why you would. Are you feeling . . . better?"

He squeezed his eyes shut and lifted one finger to tell me to wait, and I wondered if he was trying to look inside his own head to see if it was all finished panicking. Finally he opened his eyes and nodded.

"I think so."

"It'll be okay, you know. It really will."

He gave a decisive nod. "Definitely."

And it was okay, mostly. Kate had the brilliant idea of tying two bandannas together to make a scarf about two feet long, then tying one end to her pack and giving Louis the other end to hold.

"I'll walk ahead of you," she said. "If you get nervous in the dark, it might help to know you're connected to someone."

Louis eked out a smile. "It'll help. I'm sure it will."

When he said this, I met Aaron's eyes, and he smiled. I knew we were both thinking about Seabiscuit and Pumpkin; I also knew that once you started having inside jokes with people, it was really, really hard not to become friends with them. But I couldn't help it. I smiled back.

We retraced our steps from yesterday, heading back toward the gully. Because the path through the creosote bushes was narrow, Aaron went first, then Kate, then Louis, then me.

A couple of times, I heard Louis's breathing get faster, but each time he used the birthday-candle blowing to calm himself down. It didn't take us long to get to the deep cleft in the rock that we'd found the day before, and by then, the eastern sky had gone from black to smoke gray to rose. Just as we stopped hiking and stood staring uneasily into the gully, the sun popped up behind us and turned the rocks the color of pumpkin pie.

Aaron said, "Okay, how about if I go first? Then I'll yell back to let you know how long it took, and also if there's anything specific to watch out for."

"Are you sure? I can go first," I said, but he was already

going. The space was narrow enough so that if he opened out his arms, both hands could brush the sides of the crevice, and after about twenty feet, it curved down and away to the right. Something like two minutes went by before we heard him call out, "Through! It gets a little bit narrower for about ten steps, but then it opens up. It's brighter in there than you'd think. Don't worry, Louis. It'll be fine!"

"It'll be fine, it'll be fine," said Louis, in a squeaky whisper, to himself.

"You got this, Louis," I said.

Kate gave him a quick look over her shoulder. "Ready?"

"Ready," said Louis.

The three of us stayed close together, shuffling more than hiking, Louis clutching the bandanna rope with both hands. I could hear his breathing growing shallower and shallower. Soon he was trembling so much that his pack was quaking.

"The walls won't actually close in on us, right?" he asked.

"No way," I said. "Never. This crack in the rock has been here for a million years."

When we got to the narrowest part, he stopped and leaned against the rock wall. His face was pale and beaded with sweat. "I can't. I can't, I can't, I can't."

"We know you can do it, Louis," I said. "Right, Kate?"

Kate nodded, and then she did something I'll never forget. In a soft, steady voice, she began to sing.

"'My bonnie lies over the ocean. My bonnie lies over the sea. My bonnie lies over the ocean. Oh, bring back my bonnie to me.'"

I joined in. "'Bring back, bring back, oh, bring back my bonnie to me, to me. Bring back, bring back, oh, bring back my bonnie to me.'"

It was all we knew of the song, but it didn't matter. At the beginning of the third round of it, in a small, quivering voice, Louis started to sing too. By the chorus, he had picked up the bandanna rope again, and we were walking, singing in time with our steps. Kate was amazing. I would never have thought of singing, but it was exactly the right thing. Her parents knew what they were talking about when they told her she was good at walking around in other people's shoes. But about five paces into the narrowest section, I heard Kate's voice falter, and she stopped walking.

"Hey," she said quietly, without turning around. "Louis, why don't you close your eyes for this part."

"Oh," he said. He seemed to be about to ask why, but then he didn't. "Okay."

When I got to the place Kate had stopped, I saw why she'd done it, and my heart took off like a racehorse. On the rocks, about two feet above my head—which would have made it about one foot above Louis's—was a tarantula as big as my hand and looking exactly as hairy and terrifying and magnificent as tarantulas always look in pictures. I had to swallow a screech at the sight, but Louis's singing hadn't missed a beat. With his eyes closed, he'd walked right by the tarantula like it wasn't even there.

With a loud, collective sigh of relief, the three of us spilled out the end of the slot where Aaron was waiting. We all just stood there for a while, feeling the huge space around us and the sun on our faces. Louis was still pale, but he seemed to be breathing normally. When we'd caught our breaths, Aaron said, "Hey, follow me. I need to show you something!"

He led us over a small round hill like a swell in the ocean of desert and pointed.

"What?" I asked.

And then I saw it: a cardinal-red flicker against the sky. The flag!

"What's that?" asked Louis nervously.

"It's the flag!" said Aaron. "We've won! Or almost."

"No," said Louis, cupping his ears with his hands and scanning the sky. "I mean, what's that noise?"

It took the rest of us a few more seconds, but then we heard it too. It sounded like a faraway waterfall: a high, fragile singing and a splashing, splashing, splashing. Even though I couldn't see anything yet, I knew what I was hearing: hundreds of voices, echolocating; hundreds of wings, flapping. Then a black boiling cloud poured over the hill in front of us.

"A flock," I said through clenched teeth.

"A colony," said Aaron, correcting me.

"Oh, no!" cried Louis.

Kate just stared with her big, bottomless eyes.

Bats. And they were headed straight for us.

CHAPTER EIGHT

Aaron Archer

El Viaje a la Confianza

WE FROZE. THE TORRENT OF bats narrowed like the tail of a twister as they swarmed into their cave in the base of the cliff. They flocked from every direction, so there was no escape. In half a second, Louis went—I hate to say it—bats. He screamed. He clawed at the air. He ran in place so fast I couldn't see his feet, but he got nowhere. "Get them off me, get them off me, get them off me, get them off me, help me, help me, help me, get them off me . . . ," he wailed.

"Louis!" called Kate, like he was half a mile away. But he couldn't hear. Because in a way, I guess he *was* half a mile away. At least.

"Get them away, get them off, help me, help me, help me . . ."

"Bats," I yelled into his ear, "are equipped with onboard

sonar capable of locating objects in complete darkness, enabling them to avoid collisions. Their brains construct detailed three-D acoustical images of nearby hazards or prey—"

"You mean they know what we look like?" shrieked Audrey, grabbing wildly at one of Louis's windmilling arms. "Gaaaah."

"Bats almost never collide with stationary items," I shouted.

"If you're telling Louis to stand still, it's not gonna happen," cried Kate, lunging for the other arm.

"Aaaah, baghabaaaa, horrrghggggfffff," gasped Louis weakly.

"The average brown bat poses far less danger to a human being than a mosquito," I added.

"Aaron!" shouted Audrey. "Do you really think this is the time for a science lesson?"

"I just mean," I said, "if a bat can locate a gnat in the dark, don't you think it can tell where we are?"

Louis's flailing hands whacked a bat, which veered off course and smacked into his forehead. It fell to the ground and staggered away like a leather crab on its little claws before wobbling back into the air.

"Get behind this boulder!" Kate shouted to Louis. "The swarm is splitting apart to fly around it." She managed to catch one of his hands so she could drag him behind a big rock. Audrey and I followed. Bat wings fluttered so close to my face, it felt like they were vacuuming my breath out.

Louis's too. He gasped for air like he was suffocating. Then he collapsed.

"Louis! Louis!" screamed Kate. "Louis!"

Audrey hollered something about increasing carbon dioxide levels. And reducing oxygen. If I remembered anything about this, I didn't remember that I remembered. My brain went staticky.

"Please, please, please," sobbed Kate. Audrey held her hands over Louis's face and clamped his nose shut. "Louis! Wake up!"

But Louis didn't look asleep. He didn't look like he'd fainted. He didn't even look knocked out. In fourth grade, Hardy Gillooly had cold-cocked himself on the edge of Mrs. Mattson's door in the school hallway, but even lying on the tile floor, he'd seemed alive. His face still had "Hardy" written on it, and I could tell by looking that any second he'd roll over and stand up. But Louis looked—dead. While I watched, his hands and feet twitched, and then his body went slack.

Time stopped.

All at once, I realized how many things could go

wrong out here, and I realized that if we really needed help, we didn't have a prayer.

"Louis! Louis!" screamed Kate.

"He'll be okay," said Audrey. But she didn't sound convinced. She kept her hands covering his mouth and nose.

"Let him breathe," cried Kate.

"Breathing is the *problem*," said Audrey.

"What?" sobbed Kate. "What does that mean?"

The bats had all flown into their cave and latched onto the ceiling like a squirming, breathing, squeaking, furry drape. A roadrunner streaked across the trail ahead of us. The woody arms of an ocotillo clattered together in the wind.

Kate collapsed into tears.

"Hyperventilation," I finally remembered. "He doesn't have enough carbon dioxide in his blood. And he has too much oxygen. The blood vessels in his brain are constricting."

"Wake up, Louis," whispered Kate. "Please just wake up."

"Ohhhh," groaned Louis, his eyes blinking open. "Did I overbreathe?"

"If that's what you call it," gasped Kate.

"That's what I call it," said Louis, struggling to sit up.

"Then that's what you did," said Kate, laughing through her tears.

Gravel skittered down the rock face and spattered in the dust around us. We glanced up to see where it'd come from, and I caught a flash of orange hair disappearing along the cliff above us.

"Randolph!" said Kate.

"And Daphne and the rest," added Audrey. "They really did go the wrong way! They're stuck at the top of the cliff!"

"Did they see us?" I asked.

With a massive effort, Louis tried to pull himself together. "I'm pretty sure Randolph did," he said, squinting upward.

"So now they know where we are," said Kate, who had wiped her eyes and shouldered her pack.

"But they still have to double back to the beginning of the canyon and hike down it to get here," Audrey said.

"How much of a head start do we have?" wondered Louis.

"Maybe an hour?" I said. "Maybe a little less."

"And the flag is right there," said Louis, pointing up the next hill.

"Come on," said Audrey. "Let's go!"

We heaved on our packs.

But Louis took one step, and his feet walked off in two different directions. He sat down hard. His arms dangled by his sides. His head lolled like Pinocchio's before the magic spell, when he's still a marionette and nobody is holding his strings.

"You guys go on," Louis mumbled, staring at the ground. "I'll be okay."

"We can't leave you by yourself!" Audrey protested.

"I'll stay," said Kate.

"No. You guys go. Hurry," said Louis. "I'll be fine. Get the flag. And you can come back for me once you've got it."

"Don't be ridiculous," said Audrey. "We're not leaving you here. You're still shaking."

"No, I'm not," Louis replied. He shivered. "Okay. I am. But you still have to go. It's our only shot."

"Actually," I said, "studies have shown that in situations like this, teamwork is key. Statistically, our chances are better if we stay together."

Audrey looked at me quizzically.

"It's true!" I said. "Overall! According to many experts!"

Audrey shrugged and turned back to Louis.

Ten minutes later, we had him on his feet. He tottered like an eighty-year-old man, but he was walking, and the good news was, there was no sign of Daphne, Randolph, Edie, or Cyrus. The sun was still less than a quarter of the way up the sky, and what was left of the morning breeze cooled our faces. I stayed in front, but now Louis came second and Kate walked behind him, because she wanted to keep an eye on him. Audrey took up the rear.

We walked for an hour, but the flag refused to get any nearer, although the day sure got hotter. Louis kept getting wobblier, and Kate started to drag her feet like they were too heavy for her to lift. But we could see the flag, and nobody felt like giving up or slowing down. I tried to think of something to tell everybody about. Something that would help us get to the flag sooner. I wondered if there *was* anything like that to tell everybody about. The Robert Scott expedition to the South Pole? No. Not quite right. They'd gotten there second, and then all died. Sir Edmund Hillary and Tenzing Norgay climbing Mount Everest? Didn't seem to fit.

"Aaron," said Louis while I was still thinking, "should get the air mattress the first night. Because without him, we'd never have figured out all those clues."

"No way," Kate replied. "You should get it. You need it most."

"Sure, Louis," I pitched in. "You get it first."

"That's the whole point," said Audrey. "So you can get a good night's sleep."

"But I don't *want* it first," said Louis as we dropped into a crease in the desert floor and the flag disappeared from sight. "I want it last, so I can dream about it longer. If I know I'll get to sleep on the air mattress soon, just looking forward to it will make me feel so good, I might get some sleep."

"Louis," said Kate, "you always get *some* sleep. I mean, you don't stay awake all night."

Louis didn't say anything.

"Do you?" asked Audrey.

I thought about how he'd looked the first morning.

"Do you?" I chimed in. Louis just kept walking. Slowly. It was about all any of us could manage. "All night long? Without any sleep?" I remembered the two times in my life I hadn't been able to sleep. Just for a few hours. Until one a.m. In my own bed, at home. I remembered how the darkness swirled and formed itself into a tunnel, and how the tunnel led through hours and hours that seemed endless, deserted, pitch black, and sinister. I remembered feeling like the only person in the world, and feeling afraid I would always feel this way. I remembered wishing that dawn would hurry, and knowing that it wouldn't, and couldn't, and didn't want to, because it was huge and slow and, like night, didn't care about me.

"When it's daylight," said Louis quietly, "I'd rather not talk about the dark."

So then I did what Kate did when she listened to Louis talk about his life, and I thought about what night must be like for him, on the ground, rocks grinding into his bones no matter which way he turned, with the hours stretching into the darkness. And I realized that if he'd been to sleep since we'd begun el Viaje a la Confianza, it hadn't been for very long.

"But," said Louis brightly, "things are about to change."

I glanced up at the hillside. For some reason, that flag didn't seem to be getting any closer. It must've been farther away than we'd thought.

"You can have my night," I said. "That's two out of every four."

"You can have my night," said Audrey. "Three out of four."

"You can definitely have my night!" said Kate. "And sleep every night!"

"Not fair," said Louis. "No way I'm taking your awesome air mattress nights."

"If you don't take mine," said Kate, "I'm filling your bag with fire ants while you sleep."

"I don't sleep," pointed out Louis.

"Then I'll do it while you're awake!" said Kate. "Take the air mattress!"

"Okay," said Louis. "Sheesh. Bullies. Now what will I worry about? Warthogs?"

"They're javelinas, not warthogs," I pointed out.

"Then I guess I have to scratch them off the list too,"

joked Louis, shaking his head. "How about . . . foot-long millipedes!"

"Those you can worry about." Audrey shuddered.

Kate giggled.

Louis laughed. He'd stopped chewing on his fingernails. He wasn't cringing like he thought a safe was about to fall on him from the sky. In fact, he was grinning. Louis was actually a funny guy when he wasn't freaking out.

The desert quiet fell over us again. A rhythm set in. Our footsteps. Our breathing. Our rattling cookware. It was nice. Soothing. Like a lullaby. One you enjoy while walking under a burning sun wearing a fifty-pound pack while the temperature rises ten degrees every hour.

But I didn't mind the heat, because I felt strong. We all did. I could tell just by the sound of everybody's boots on the trail. I saw why it was taking so long to get to the flag. Our trail had taken a wide swing to go around a boulder field as big as a small town. But we didn't care. We dropped into a dry creek bed, which was a long, smooth, undulating sheet of rock slithering between two cliffs made of laminated red-stone outcroppings. We came to a bowl as big as a hot tub. The creek, when it ran, had scoured out the bowl with sand and gravel, and its side curved and bulged and swelled and heaved like billows of cloud set in stone. Layers of color swirled through it all, red, yellow, blue, green, and black. At the bottom lay three feet of crystal-clear water.

We scrambled around, because this water was for wild animals, not for boots, although I did jot down its location on my mental map in case we needed it later, when we had the flag and weren't in such a hurry.

And now we were so close, we could hear the flag flapping on the other side of the streambank. The trail led up and over.

The climb was steep, and hard, and a lot longer than I'd have thought. Carrying a fifty-pound pack didn't help. But after I took a few sharp steps upward, my heart stopped pounding and settled into a steady beat, and I filled my lungs with clean air, and my thigh muscles quit burning, and it felt great! We made it nearly to the top of the bank and paused in its shadow to gaze back down at the green pool sparkling like an emerald amid the red rocks.

Louis was the first to talk. "That's the prettiest thing I've ever seen," he said. His words echoed faintly, the last bits bouncing off everything like the final chime of a tiny handbell.

—een —een —een

He stood up straight. Louis was nearly six feet tall.

"Louis," I said, looking around us, "maybe this is your red wheelbarrow. Maybe it's your white chickens."

“Chickens?” repeated Louis.

“I mean,” I said, “you know, how so much depends upon a red wheelbarrow, glazed with rainwater, beside the white chickens?”

“I, um,” said Louis. “What?”

“I mean—I mean—” I stammered. And for a second, in the quiet, while the colored rocks from millions of years ago shimmered in the rising heat, I thought I knew what William Carlos Williams wanted to say, and I thought I knew what I wanted to say, and I thought maybe I could tell Louis and Audrey and Kate before they concluded I was a complete lunatic. “I just think . . . ,” I said, motioning toward all the beauty and peace. But I had to stop. Because I didn’t know what I thought.

Everybody stared at me. They were trying. Really trying. Trying to understand me. But *I* didn’t even understand me. Time ground to a halt and silence fell and the whole thing turned into a disaster.

Finally a redwing blackbird whistled a song. “Listen,” whispered Kate. It was beautiful.

“Wait. What’s that?” asked Louis when the song was done. He cocked his head curiously and turned to look behind us. And then he was lying on his back in the trail.

Randolph had smashed into him from the rear and was

sprinting up the trail, Daphne hot on his heels. They'd sneaked up on us while I was yammering about wheelbarrows. Daphne shoved Audrey down as she and Randolph disappeared up over the edge of the creek bank. For someone who tromped around in boots as big as Frankenstein's, she could move fast.

"Come on!" cried Kate. "We have to catch them!" The sun beat down. All the strength I'd felt half an hour before was gone. My thigh muscles twisted into knots.

By the time we got to the flag, Randolph had yanked it out of the ground and was waving it in both hands. Audrey tried to tear it away, and Daphne struggled to pry her off Randolph. I did my best to peel Daphne loose from Audrey, but Edie and Cyrus panted up the hillside at that moment, carrying their packs *and* Daphne's and Randolph's, and they dropped the packs and each of them grabbed one of my arms. Just as Kate and Louis laid hold of them, Randolph gave a huge heave and tore the flag out of Audrey's hands. Holding it above his head, he sang, "We are the champions, my friend!"

Atrociously.

Louis covered his ears.

Daphne rolled her eyes.

"What?" Randolph asked her. "We got the flag!"

"It's not fair!" cried Kate. "We were in the lead all the

way. We figured out all the clues. We did all the work. We won it!"

"Nevertheless," said Daphne, "we have it."

"But *we* have to have it," I said. "I mean, we really really *have* to have it."

"Shut up, Memory Boy," snarled Randolph.

"No. Wait a minute. Hold on, Randolph," Daphne said. She looked at me with interest. "Memory Boy has something to say. I think we should listen."

Randolph's eyes just about popped out of their sockets. He ground his teeth so hard, I thought they would shoot sparks.

I glanced at Louis. He sat in a dusty patch where nothing grew. He looked at me, shrugged, and pulled his hat brim over his eyes. "We need it for Louis," I blurted.

"Aaron, don't—" said Audrey, glaring at Daphne.

"Daphne really wants to hear this, Audrey," I said.

"I really want to hear this, Audrey," Daphne said sincerely.

So I told her. I told her how hard it was for Louis out here, how he didn't sleep. Kate jumped in to tell her how we'd volunteered to give Louis the air mattress on our nights, so he'd have it all the time. Audrey didn't say anything during this. She just stared at Daphne, and once in a while, she shook her head.

"Amazing," marveled Daphne.

"Thanks," Kate and I said. Wow. We'd had Daphne all wrong.

"Just plain astonishing," Daphne said. "What are the chances, Randolph?"

"What are what chances?" he said sulkily.

"That of all the stupid survival camps in all the lame deserts in the entire world, the four biggest losers on the planet end up right here, on the same team, losing to me?"

"Yaaaaahaaahaaa!" brayed Randolph like a delighted donkey when he realized what Daphne had been up to. "I don't know, Daphne. I don't know!"

"Had you going, didn't I, Memory Boy?" Daphne smirked. "You've sure given me a lot to think about while I relax on my air mattress."

"What?" I said. "I mean—I thought you were—"

"It's not enough to win." Daphne snarled. "The other guy has to lose. And you, my friend, are the other guy. And so is she and so is he and so is she," she added, glancing at Kate, Louis, and Audrey.

"Hah!" crowed Randolph.

Daphne's group shouldered their packs and started back the way they'd come.

"Daphne, you forgot the last clue," piped up Cyrus timidly.

"What?" barked Daphne.

" 'By turning, turning we come out right,' " he said.

At the word "turn," I saw Audrey glance over my shoulder. A look of disbelief appeared in her eyes.

I looked too, and right behind me jutted—Caesar's Nose? I peeked at the trail under our feet, and I realized that the shadows were falling in the same direction as when we'd started the day before.

"No way," I whispered.

"Did he really do that?" murmured Kate.

It looked like Jare had hiked us around in a great big circle with all those peculiar clues of his. Sure enough, through the scrubby trees on the hillside below, I could see the sun glimmer off pots and pans beside the campfire, and the orange water cooler glinting in the tree.

"Shhh," I hissed quietly, because Daphne hadn't figured it out yet.

"Shouldn't we use the last clue, Daphne?" persisted Cyrus.

"No, Ant Brain," snapped Daphne. "We already have the flag, don't we?" And she took off in the wrong direction.

As he shouldered past Louis, Randolph fished something out of his pocket, wound up, and pitched it at Louis's face. Louis flinched, but just before it hit him, the bat unfurled its leathery wings and flew away.

Louis yelped and collapsed in a heap, and Randolph laughed.

"I'm going to kill you," muttered Kate, lunging for Randolph. Audrey and I managed to grab her. She thrashed like crazy, but she was tired, so we managed to keep our grip.

"I'm a licensed cage fighter," chortled Randolph. "I'd like to see you try."

"What you are is a liar," said Audrey.

"I'm not a liar!" cried Randolph.

"You're not a licensed cage fighter, and you don't hate your mom, and your mom didn't make you work on your birthday," said Audrey slowly. "You just said all that to impress Daphne."

"What—I—how do you—you were spying?" stammered Randolph. "Cheaters!" He turned to Daphne. "Daphne," he whined, "they're cheaters! They were spying on us!"

Daphne didn't seem too upset at this news. In fact, she looked like spying was the only thing we'd done since she'd met us that she actually admired.

"And let me be the first to inform you, Randolph," Audrey went on, "Daphne is not impressed by your wild stories."

It was true. Daphne didn't look impressed with Randolph. She looked disgusted.

Randolph charged at Audrey. Kate managed to yank one arm free in time to grab my water bottle and squirt it in his face.

"Well now, what have we here?" said Jare, who'd hiked up the hill just in time to catch her. "You weren't wasting water in the desert, were you?"

It only took about three minutes to walk to camp, because Jare *had* hiked us around in a giant circle, which meant that even though we'd trekked ten miles, we'd never been more than three miles from where we started. This was his way of keeping track of us. "Hey, Little Miss Sunshine," he said to Kate as soon as we got back. He picked up a ten-pound railroad spike from beside the abandoned tracks. "Come over here and turn around." Kate did. Jare unzipped her pack and dumped in the spike. Now Kate's pack probably *did* weigh as much as she did. Audrey had to catch her as she stumbled backward, and help her stand up straight.

"What's that for?" cried Kate.

"To carry," said Jare.

"Carry where?" asked Kate.

"Everywhere," said Jare.

"Why?" asked Kate.

“’Cause you need to learn a lesson,” said Jare.

“What lesson?” asked Kate.

“Don’t waste water in the desert,” said Jare.

“How long do I have to carry it?” moaned Kate.

“Till your lesson is learned,” said Jare.

The only bright spot in the whole episode was that even though we didn’t win the air mattress, Daphne’s team didn’t either. Jare wasn’t too happy with the way Randolph had treated that poor bat. So he kept the mattress for himself.

That night, when the fire was nothing but embers far dimmer than the stars, and the other groups had wandered off to sleep, and Daphne crouched in the brush staring daggers into the dark for reasons she didn’t bother to explain, and Randolph hid in the shadows watching her, I told Louis I was sorry we hadn’t done a better job. Audrey and Kate said they were too. But Louis said *he* was the one who was sorry. He said next time we found ourselves chasing a flag, and he started wigging out, just leave him behind and go capture it. Maybe even choose the fastest one of us to go alone, for instance Kate. But definitely ditch him.

I said, “Experts agree that individuals in survival situations may be prone to loneliness, face greater individual responsibilities and workload, and may not be able to establish full perimeter security, while members of large groups will enjoy the benefit of a full support system, more numerous solutions to problems, a divided work effort, and the ability to sleep in shifts, not to mention companionship and the ability to establish full-perimeter security. So, um, like I said earlier, it's better to keep groups together."

"Okay," Louis answered. It didn't quite seem like he believed me. But it seemed like he wanted to believe me. "If you say so!" He almost sounded cheerful. "By the way," he asked, "what's full-perimeter security?"

"That part I'm not totally clear on," I admitted.

"I guess I'm going to sack out," yawned Louis. I could hear the fear returning to his voice. Nighttime. The long black tunnel.

"How about," said Kate, "if the rest of us stay awake with you two hours at a time? That way you won't feel so lonely. Maybe you'll get some sleep?"

"No," said Louis. "You're all tired. I couldn't ask you to do that."

"You don't have to ask," said Audrey.

"Because we're doing it," I added.

Louis unrolled his bag, and Kate sat in the doorway of his tent.

"You made that up," Audrey whispered to me after they were gone.

"What?" I asked as innocently as I could.

"That it's better to stay together. I mean, the main facts were probably right," she said. This seemed important to her. "But you made up the last part."

I didn't quite know what to say. Because I *had* made it up. The jury is still out on the question of splitting up in survival situations. Nobody knows if sticking together is better. So I admitted it. But I also told Audrey that since there's no way we could ever leave Louis behind, it was clear sticking together was better for *us*.

"Maybe *you're* Louis's white chickens," Audrey said.

"What *are* white chickens?" I wondered.

"You're the one who brought them up," Audrey said. "I thought you knew."

"Just because I bring something up doesn't mean I know what it is," I reminded her.

"Maybe it's time to turn in," said Audrey, as if this conversation had gone on long enough. But I swear I could see her smiling in the last of the firelight.

CHAPTER NINE

Audrey Alcott

El Viaje a la Confianza

I WON'T GO SO FAR as to say that the camp started to feel like home after the failed flag contest. For one thing, the whole point of the camp, at least for me, was that it *wasn't* home. No school, no Lyza, no best friend who turned out to be a liar and a thief and—worse than either of those—not my friend at all. For another thing, I wouldn't feel at home with the likes of Daphne and Randolph if we were the last three people on Earth. And then there was Jare. In moments, I suspected that Jare might be a total psycho, even though Aaron said it would be more accurate to call him an individual with antisocial personality disorder. Either way, the guy didn't exactly give off homey vibes.

But I will say that the days started to take shape, arrange themselves into a pattern. I'm not really talking about the camp's routine, although that had its own pattern: we'd wake up; make, eat, and clean up after breakfast; PHWSS; hike, either as a group or in teams, breaking once for lunch; have wilderness survival training—orienteering, fire building, wildlife identification—make, eat, and clean up after dinner; have campfire time; go to bed. That was the daily, predictable stuff.

I'm talking about the pattern that the daily, *un*predictable stuff took on. Or maybe the pattern I imposed on it. When I mentioned this to Aaron, he went on for some time about a guy named Klaus Conrad, a German psychiatrist who studied apophenia, which, I think, is the tendency to see patterns in completely random and meaningless data. After about thirty seconds of scientific jargon, I got confused and told Aaron to stop, which caused him to shift gears and start talking about a related phenomenon called pareidolia. I had to admit that this was more interesting, especially when Aaron got to the part about people seeing faces in inanimate objects: the man in the moon, a face on Mars, the Virgin Mary in a tree stump, the Virgin Mary in a grilled cheese, Jesus in a grilled cheese, Jesus in a pierogi, Mother Teresa in a cinnamon bun (as if religious figures had nothing better to do than show up in pieces of food). Anyway, whatever the reason, after a while, our days seemed to fall into a kind of rhythm.

Maybe because we were in the desert, which is an

extreme place—extremely hot, extremely dry, extremely beautiful, extremely scary—the rhythm wasn't a relaxed one. It was full of highs and lows. In my tent at night, when I took inventory of my day, I took to calling them "hells" and "heavens." Every day had a hell. Every day had a heaven. I guess it was a way to organize it all in my head. Also, I think it was a way to not forget what was happening at the camp, because the longer I stayed, the more I understood that, for better or worse, it was an experience I'd want to hang on to.

Day Four

Hell

I grabbed a cactus. I wasn't even falling or anything, at least not at first. I just leaned over to look at what I thought was a rattlesnake's rattle—minus the rattlesnake—on the ground and used the cactus for balance. It burned so much—sent flames of pain shooting up my arm—that at first my discombobulated brain thought I'd grabbed a hot coal. *Then* I fell. Fell and rolled around awhile, not just shrieking but actually yelling "Ow, ow, ow," just like a comic-book character in a seriously unfunny comic book.

Kate ran for Jare, and when he came, he said, "And here I thought you were the one member of your group who might have some common sense," thus neatly insulting four people with a single sentence and making me feel even more like an idiot than I already felt. With a sneer but with no explanation whatsoever, he tossed a bottle of craft glue and a plastic bottle of witch hazel in my general direction.

"What are we supposed to do with this stuff?" asked Louis, but Jare had already lumbered off.

"In addition to using witch hazel bark and leaves for medicinal purposes, Native Americans also used its Y-shaped branches for dowsing," said Aaron.

"What's dowsing?" asked Kate.

"Finding underground water sources," said Aaron. "Well, mostly. People also dowsed to find precious stones, oil, even gravesites, although I'm not sure if they used witch hazel for all those purposes. Dowsing is also called divining and doodlebugging."

"Doodlebugging? I thought doodlebugs were roly-polies," said Louis. "You know, those little gray bugs that look like armadillos."

"The Latin name for the roly-poly or pill bug or wood louse is *Armadillidium vulgare,*" said Aaron.

Just as I was starting to wonder if that was because both armadillos and roly-polies curled up in balls, I remembered that I was in horrible, excruciating pain.

"Who cares about wood lice?" I yelped. "Hand. On. Fire!"

About thirty seconds later, Kate was pouring craft glue all over my palm. About a minute later, Kate and Aaron were debating about whether to pull it off fast, like a Band-Aid ("No!" cried Louis) or peel it off slowly, like when you apply a fake tattoo ("No!" cried Louis), and I reached over with my good hand and ripped the darn thing off, so fast that the white-hot flash of pain almost didn't register. Almost. We all leaned over to examine my palm at exactly the same time so that we blocked the light and no one could see a thing, and then we all leaned out again. I closed my eyes and stuck out my hand in Kate's direction.

"Kate, you look."

After a few seconds, she said, "It's swollen and red and kind of terrible looking, but I don't see a single spine."

I opened my eyes and stared down at my poor, throbbing palm. Gingerly, I ran a finger over it. Smooth. I squeezed my eyes shut and thrust out my hand again.

"Witch hazel," I said. "Please."

I heard Kate struggle with the lid to the bottle, and then someone must have gotten it off because suddenly the inside of my nose was prickling with a medicinal smell. It wasn't bad, really. I mean, you wouldn't want to use witch hazel for perfume, but at least it smelled powerful, and I was hoping for a powerful cure. But I heard a gagging noise and opened my eyes. Louis, looking, as my mom would say, a bit green around the gills.

"I'm okay," he said, following it up quickly with "I'm not okay."

"Go," I said.

"Sorry."

He bolted for the brush at the edge of the trail. Later, when we were hiking again, my hand better, if a tad smelly, Louis caught up with me to say, "I'm sorry I'm hanging back, but that smell—it's like a cross between cleaning fluid and pink erasers and the inside of airplanes."

"No problem, Louis," I told him.

And it wasn't a problem, but just the three of us hiking together—Aaron, then Kate, then me—felt incomplete, off-kilter. Kate's narrow back, her swinging, shining bob of black hair, was a new view, not a bad one, but unfamiliar and also oddly faraway, like I was looking at her from a distance. That's when I realized it: without meaning to, I was leaving a Louis-sized gap, saving his place.

Heaven

After dinner that evening, Kate, Aaron, and I climbed a hill and sat on its stony, nearly bald top to watch the sun drop down into the scooped-out place between two faraway mountains. A glowing strawberry pink filled the scooped-out space, while thin, flat, opalescent clouds floated above like ice islands in a punch bowl. We didn't speak, but if we had, it would have been under our breaths, in the most reverent of whispers. Just as the colors hit their supersaturated peak, I heard someone scrambling up the hill behind us, and there was Louis.

Kate started to move over to make a space between her and Aaron, but Louis walked over and sat down right next to me. I could smell the witch hazel glazing my palm—I'd just smeared on a fresh coating after dinner—so I knew Louis could. But he sat, steady as the red rocks surrounding us, and he watched the sunset.

We stayed until the pink faded and the dusk lay down in layers of shimmering gray, violet, and a smoke blue so lonely and perfect, you felt it at the base of your throat and the pit of your stomach and all the way down your spine. It was the perfect moment, and even though I was keeping to my no-friends vow, I was happy we were all there to see it. When the first stars came out, I said, "I'm glad you came up, Louis," and Louis said, "Me too."

Day Five
Hell

During a break in a hot, long desert-floor hike, after I resisted the urge to frantically gulp water from my bottle and instead drank it down in long, careful swallows the way Jare had told us to, I flipped over my pack to take a quick glance at the photo of me with my parents. It was something I did when the going got especially tough. I'm not sure why. Maybe because seeing us smiling through the clear plastic of the luggage tag reminded me that the going wasn't always going to be this tough. Maybe to remind myself that if I died of exhaustion and vultures picked my bones clean, at least two people out there would definitely miss me. Either way, looking at the photo made me feel stronger, if a little bit homesick, every single time.

Except this time.

Someone had scratched out my parents' faces. Not just their faces, but their whole heads were obliterated with white scratch marks, some so deep that they'd ripped through the photo paper. Whoever had done it had probably used a rock, but the paper looked clawed. For about ten seconds, I felt slammed by fear and grief, as if my real mom and dad actually had been attacked by some vicious animal and were gone, clawed right out of the world. I eased the photo out of the luggage tag and held it in my two hands, my eyes burning with tears. Then I looked up and saw Daphne, perched on her pack and staring at me with her beady eyes like the bird of prey she was. Slowly her mouth twisted into a mean smirk, and I felt a fiery rush of rage. I wanted to body-slam her, rip out her ketchup-colored hair by the fistful, and I had just jumped to my feet to go do it, when a voice right behind me said, quietly, "Don't give her the satisfaction."

It was Aaron. I handed him the photograph.

"I know," he said. "I saw it just now."

"Why?" I demanded furiously. "Why would she do this?"

Aaron's dark eyes got that narrow, thinking look, and I prepared myself for a jargon-laced paragraph about the latest scientific research on photo-destroying psychopaths. Or something. But slowly, tentatively, Aaron said, "Remember what she said about seeing your parents at the airport? I think maybe, even though she would never admit it, she wishes her family were more like yours. That"—he pointed at the photograph—"is her way of trying to take your parents away from you. Which is stupid. Because that's just a picture, a piece of paper. It's not them."

I stared at Aaron, blinking, so surprised that I forgot my plan to yank out Daphne's hair.

"What?" he said.

"That's it? No facts?"

"Oh! Sorry. Hold on."

I shook my head. "No, no, I think you might be—"

"What?" he said nervously.

"Right."

Aaron looked shocked. "Seriously?"

"Seriously. Thanks."

Aaron smiled. "Anytime."

I looked down at the picture that was nothing but a picture, and I folded it up and slid it into my pocket.

Heaven

It was at the tail end of the most grueling hike we'd done so far. Twelve miles on the desert floor, although "floor" conjures up an image of a flat, smooth surface, and what we discovered is that it's not flat or smooth or anything close to easy. The land was pitted and scarred and scattered around with these little hills, so you had to watch your step—every step—and the terrain was so up and down, up and down, that my thighs practically cried out in pain. And it was hot. Oven hot. Kiln hot. We were like clay pots in a kiln, except that clay pots don't have to hike, endlessly, and we did. The only breezes were dragon's-breath gusts that did not deserve to be called anything so breezy as "breezes."

And did I mention that we were on mile *twelve*. We had just taken what Jare announced (with evil satisfaction) would be our last break before we got to our next campsite, and along with everyone else, I groaned, and stood up on my aching legs, and slung my monstrously heavy pack over my aching shoulders, and started to hike, and I'd gone maybe ten steps when I realized that even though it was hard, it wasn't *that* hard, and I also realized that just a few days ago, it would have been *impossible*. My heart gave an exultant leap. I was getting stronger, sturdier, learning to work hard and get along with the bare essentials. Henry David Thoreau would have been proud.

Day Six

Hell

In the middle of the night, or I guess it was very early morning, I woke up to the sound of someone crying. It was muffled, as if the person doing it was trying to keep anyone from hearing, and somehow that lonely, dreary, low-key weeping was more heartbreaking to hear than loud sobbing would have been. I sat up and listened more carefully, and I could tell that the crying was coming from the tent next to mine. Kate's tent. I started to get up to go talk to her, but her crying just sounded so turned inward, so private, that I changed my mind. I lay in the dark, listening, for a long time before she finally stopped.

Heaven

After an hour of the dry, stony, uphill hike Jare had sent us on, Aaron, Kate, Louis, and I came upon a little grove of madrone trees. It's what the desert does: you think you know where you are and what's around you, and then, suddenly, there's something unexpected to knock the breath out of you, cactus flowers the color of lemon drops; two brilliant blue birds on a branch; a peregrine falcon, wings folded, plummeting like a soundless missile; or, like with the madrones, a flash of emerald when you least expect it. The trees had skin-smooth, tawny bark on their curving, twisting limbs, and they seemed to spring out of a kind of cup in the side of the hill, which I guessed trapped enough water for them to thrive. The madrones were a gathering of rarity and grace, like a family of gazelles. We stood, hushed, and drank in the sight of them.

And if that had been all, it would have been so much more than enough, but then, afterward, as we kept walking, it was like my eyes had changed, like the madrones had woken them really and truly up. I noticed everything, every sharp edge, every curve, how all the trees and rocks broke the sky into shapes, every variation in color or texture. The colors were so vivid they seemed to shout, and as I looked around at the world, I wondered if this was how Louis saw all the time. When we got to a cliff face, I noticed that the rock wasn't plain red or plain anything but seamed with a thousand shades of color—honey, rust, coffee brown, cat's-eye gold—some seams as thin as pencil lines, some hundreds of feet wide. And I felt this huge presence that I understood was *time*, because those ribbons of rock weren't just sandstone and shale but years. Centuries. Millennia.

"If the four and a half billion years the Earth has existed were compressed into a single twenty-four-hour day," said Aaron, very, very quietly, "humans would have appeared one minute and seventeen seconds before midnight."

All that time, without us.

A shiver went from my heels to the top of my head.

Who cares if people lie? I thought. *This—right here—is why the word "awesome" was made.*

Day Seven

Hell

Randolph put a millipede down Louis's shirt. I saw it happen, but I was too far away to stop it. We had just gotten to the campsite, and we were all setting up our tents, all of us except Randolph, who was putting a millipede down the back of Louis's shirt. And it wasn't one of those threadlike ones you find under rocks in the woods, either. It was fat and orange and at least six inches long, way more animal than bug (and, yes, I knew that millipedes weren't really bugs, but arthropods in the class Diplopoda, a word that means "two feet" because they have two pairs of legs for each body segment; or, at least, I knew after Aaron told me).

The screams. The shrieks. The rolling around on the ground. The slapping of his back with his own hands. The spasms of trembling that came and went for hours afterward. Sheer terror. Poor, poor, poor, poor Louis.

Heaven

As Randolph stood red-faced and bent over with laughter, Kate dropped the pieces of her tent, screeched "You!" and came charging at him like a wild animal. Kate can't weigh more than seventy pounds, but it turns out that seventy pounds of pure fury packs quite a punch. Randolph hit the ground like a sack of flour, and Kate sat on his back whacking away at his shoulders, the back of his head, occasionally his round cheek, with her tiny, almost golf-ball-sized fists, shouting, "You think you're funny? Do you? Do you?"

No one jumped in for what felt like a long time. We were all too shocked. Well, almost all of us. Daphne stood a few feet away, one hand on her hip, amusement all over her face, watching. Jare was where he usually was when there was trouble between the campers—nowhere to be found. He'd told us on one of the first days that this was the wilderness, where survival of the fittest wasn't a theory but part of the daily routine—and it was his job to let it "play out" even among us humans. As soon as I could unfreeze myself, I started to run over, but my shoelace caught on a prickly pear and I almost fell. By the time I'd untangled it, Aaron was there, behind Kate, catching hold of her flying arms and saying, "It's okay, Kate! It's okay!"

And, sure, I know it's not nice to celebrate physical violence, but after Aaron gently tugged Kate off Randolph, and Randolph had gotten to his feet and was rubbing the back of his head, before he could get himself together enough to act tough, the look he gave Kate—this amazing combination of scared and stunned and even sort of awestruck—made me want to hoist that girl onto my shoulders and carry her through an imaginary town square. I didn't, for obvious reasons, but if I had, I guarantee that everyone, all the people lining the streets and hanging out of their car windows and sitting on their porches, would have cheered themselves hoarse.

Day Eight
Hell

It started out as an ordinary meal. Jare got the ingredients for dinner out of the metal, bear-proof storage box where he'd stowed them sometime before our camp started. Cans of beans, chili spices, Worcestershire sauce, wheat tortillas, dehydrated tomatoes and broccoli, all the makings of a bland-if-filling-and-fairly-nutritious dinner for sixteen. Aaron and Louis helped cook, because it was their turn. Kate and I served, because it was our turn. Jare went off to eat by himself, the way he sometimes did (Louis suspected that he had better food stashed someplace else just for him). And we all started eating.

Then Edie, the other girl in Daphne's group, started to cough. Actually, a number of us were coughing, because the chili spices were pretty hot. But then Edie started to cough *differently*, and soon after that, she started to scratch her head and her arms.

"What's wrong?" I asked her.

She put her hand to her throat and croaked, "I'm having an allergic reaction. I need my shot."

My heart started beating fast at this. When I was in first grade, a kid at my school named Rocco had gotten stung by a bee on a field trip to a petting zoo. Since no one had known that he had the allergy until then, no one had medicine ready for him, and his symptoms came on fast. I can still see him lying on the grass in the goat pen, his eyes rolling into the back of his head. The teacher had to scoop him up and carry him, running at full tilt, toward the petting zoo office, where, luckily, they had some epinephrine, and, luckily, it worked. I can remember reaching for Janie's hand, and how we all stood in the pen, looking at each other, while the forgotten goats butted against us, asking for the food that we were still holding in our hands. A few kids started to cry, and nobody made a single joke, because even though we were really little and had seen almost nothing in our lives, we all knew we'd just seen someone almost die.

Randolph, who happened to be sitting next to Edie, jumped up so fast he spilled his chili. Once he was up, he slowly backed away.

"Allergies aren't contagious, Randolph," said Kate in her flat voice.

"Like you know," retorted Randolph.

"Where is your shot?" I asked Edie.

"Jare has it!" Her eyes filled with tears, and she made some fluttery motions in front of her mouth that I hoped weren't sign language for "I am going into anaphylactic shock."

"I'll go!" said Aaron, jumping up and running toward Jare's tent, which we couldn't even see from where we were. Jare always set up his tent at the very edge of the camp, as far away from the rest of us as possible.

"What are you allergic to, anyway?" asked Daphne, turning to Edie with a sneer. She had this amazing talent for making everything she said sound like an insult.

"Fish," said Edie in a harsh whisper.

"Fish?" Daphne raised an eyebrow. "Uh, last time I checked, three-bean chili didn't have any fish in it, E-death."

E-death was Daphne's nickname for Edie, whose real name was Edith. I thought that calling her that at this particular moment, while her throat was closing up, was crossing the line, even for Daphne.

"Well, obviously this chili does," I snapped.

Daphne turned to Randolph. "E-death's probably faking. Just trying to get attention."

"Definitely!" said Randolph.

Edie was lying on the ground now. Her eyes and lips were swelling up, and her breathing made a high-pitched whistling noise. Only a lunatic could think she was faking.

"Don't worry," I told her. "Everything will be okay."

Aaron came running up, looking worried.

"Where's Jare?" I asked.

"He's coming. I think."

"You *think*?" I stood up. "Did you tell him we have an emergency here?"

Aaron nodded, fast. "I did! But he, uh, didn't believe me at first."

"He thought you were lying?"

"I don't know. More like he thought Edie was? Or something?"

I grabbed Aaron's sleeve. "Aaron! What did he say?"

"He said that he knew all about Edie's allergy. He said he'd put together the menu for the entire camp, personally, with Edie's allergy in mind. So she couldn't be having a reaction."

"Told you!" said Daphne.

I tugged Aaron's sleeve so hard he almost lost his balance. I knew he was doing his best, but frankly I was getting frantic. *"But she is having one!"* I shouted.

"I know! That's what I told him. So he said he'd come."

We all looked in the direction of Jare's tent, and sure enough, there he was, coming. But he wasn't exactly in a rush. He wasn't even walking his usual fast-Sasquatch walk. He was *strolling*, one hand in his pocket, like he'd just decided to take a nice turn around the campsite on this lovely evening. If he'd broken into casual whistling, it would not have surprised me.

"Hurry!" I yelled. "She needs her shot!"

Jare shook his head and waved his hand dismissively. "She's fine." But I could tell he was faking his nonchalance now, maybe because he'd heard the fear in my voice. He picked up the pace, but only slightly, a shift from strolling to sauntering.

My face got hot. My hands balled into fists.

"Now!" I yelled. "She needs it *right now*! *Run!*"

And, amazingly, he ran.

After it was all over and Edie was asleep in her tent, breathing normally, Aaron asked, "Hey, does anyone know what she's allergic to?"

"Fish," said Kate.

A light dawned on Aaron's face. "Worcestershire sauce is made with anchovies."

"You should tell that to Jare," said Louis.

Aaron glanced nervously at the path to Jare's tent. After Jare had given Edie her shot, with one sudden jab that made all of us flinch except for Edie, he'd been in a black mood, yelling at us and barking out commands before he'd stomped away, seething.

"Uh, I will," said Aaron with a sheepish grin. "But maybe I'll wait until tomorrow."

"Told you he was a psycho," I said.

"According to the *Diagnostic and Statistical Manual of Mental Disorders,* commonly known as the DSM, an individual with narcissistic personality disorder—"

"Aaron! Edie could have died. What kind of person is

so full of himself that he'd risk someone's life because he didn't want to admit that he'd made a mistake?"

"Well, according to the—"

I narrowed my eyes at him menacingly. "What kind of person, Aaron?"

Aaron's eyes met mine, and his face broke into a smile. He shrugged. "A psycho. What else?"

Heaven

That night, after we were all in our tents, I heard Kate crying again, the same doleful, lost, continuous, undramatic crying as before, as if sorrow didn't take hold of her as much as it simply leaked out of her. It wasn't the middle of the night this time, though, so none of us was asleep yet. I wanted to go to her, try to comfort her, but I knew that this was exactly the kind of act that binds people together, turns them into friends, so I stopped myself. But finally I couldn't stand it anymore. She was just so sad.

As quietly as I could, I unzipped my tent and got out, and as I did, I saw two other people emerge from the darkness, their faces pale ovals in the moonlight. Aaron and Louis. We all walked to the door of Kate's tent and just stood there, looking helplessly at each other, unsure of what to do, and listening to the awful sound of Kate's crying. After a while, it started to slow down and get hiccupy, and then it stopped abruptly, and there was Kate's familiar, dry little voice, saying, "Well, are you going to stand out there all night or come in?" Which made us all smile with relief.

"In?" said Louis doubtfully, eyeing Kate's one-person tent.

"Right," said Kate. "Go sit in Louis's tent. I'll be there in a second."

We obeyed. Louis's tent wasn't so big, really, not for people who were used to rooms. But for us, sitting there, it felt as spacious and high ceilinged as a cathedral.

"Wow," said Aaron, looking around. "This is great."

"I have this thing about walls closing in on me," said Louis, shuddering, and I flashed back to his hiking through the narrow gully in the rock, singing "My Bonnie Lies over the Ocean" as if his life depended on it, which maybe it had, or almost. He smiled a lopsided smile. "I guess I have a lot of 'things.'"

The tent flap opened, and Kate came inside. In the light of the flashlight we'd set on the ground between us, she looked tired and puffy eyed, but not the least bit embarrassed, which I admired. Whenever I cried in public, I wanted the ground to swallow me.

"I wanted to explain," she said, "because—" She

paused, thinking, her beautiful hands lying perfectly still on her crossed knees. "Well, I don't really know why."

We sat in silence, being patient. With the four of us sitting there, so close together, time somehow didn't matter; if we had to wait all night, we would. Even Aaron seemed okay with the quiet. Then Kate looked up at us. I could see her black eyes shining in the dark.

"I guess I don't want you guys to think I'm this depressed person."

It was on the tip of my tongue to say "You aren't?" when Louis said it for me.

"You aren't? I mean, you seem happy sometimes, and you're, like, really nice and all, but I thought maybe you were . . . depressed."

Kate sighed. "That's what my parents think too. Well, what they say is that I'm 'in a funk' or 'in the doldrums' or 'moping' or 'brooding.' "

"Oh, I wouldn't say any of those things," said Louis quickly. "I don't even know what some of them mean."

I watched Aaron open his mouth, no doubt to fill us in on the dictionary definitions of all those words, with maybe some history about how they came to be (I myself recognized the Doldrums from *The Phantom Tollbooth*, which I spent fifth grade being obsessed with), but then he closed it again. He caught my eyes and smiled. It occurred to me that he was getting better at knowing when to keep his total recall to himself. It also occurred to me that he had a nice smile.

"Basically, they all mean the same thing: I'm going around sad for no good reason," said Kate. "They also mean I'm starting to get on everyone's nerves."

"Well, what do you think you are?" I asked.

Kate lifted her chin. "Sad. My grandmother lived with us for a year and a half, and then she died." Her chin started trembling, but she didn't start crying.

"Oh, no," I said. "Right before you came here?"

Kate shook her head. "That's the problem. It was five months ago, and according to my parents, that's like four and a half months too long."

"Aren't they sad too?" asked Aaron.

"No!" said Kate bitterly. "Not even my mom, and Granny was her mother!"

But I heard the lie, and right afterward, Kate scratched her elbow. A Poison Ivy Liar.

"Okay," she said, shrugging. "My mom was sad, a little, at first. The thing is that my grandmother was kind of . . . difficult."

Truth. And a hard one for Kate to tell.

"She'd had a rough life. I never knew my grandfather

because he left when my mom was a baby, so my grandmother raised her on her own. She worked in a chair factory and then, when the factory closed, she cleaned houses. And she never got to go to college, even though she was really smart, and I guess in a lot of ways, she wasn't a very nice mom. She wasn't abusive or anything, but she was tough and didn't talk much and had a bad temper. My mom said she was a cold fish. She said she was like a person who'd had all the love wrung out of her when she was a young woman, so she didn't have any left for her daughter."

"What do you think?" I asked gently.

Kate faltered. "I think she was probably not the nicest mom." Tears filled her eyes. "She felt bad about it, though, later. She told me that."

"Did she tell your mom?" asked Louis.

"I don't think so. She had trouble saying stuff like that to most people." She pressed her fingers to her eyes, then moved them away. "But she said it to me. She loved *me*! And I loved her. I took care of her. I always tried to put myself in her place, think about what she'd like best. I read her books out loud and sat and watched TV with her, even though she loved really, really, really bad reality shows, and when she got super sick at the end, I helped her eat and massaged her hands and feet to distract her from the pain. She said I did a better job than the home health lady. *I loved her!*"

Truth, truth, truth, raw and painful, almost too much truth to bear. I scooted closer to Kate and put my arm around her small shoulders.

"I'm sorry, Kate," said Aaron.

"Same here," said Louis.

"But the worst thing is that no one ever talks about her," said Kate. "After she'd been gone for a while, I would try to tell some of the stories she'd told me or just say how much I missed her and how it hurt to see her empty room, and my parents and my sisters just acted exasperated. They'd say I needed to get over it, but how am I supposed to get over being sad if no one lets me *be* sad?"

"Is that why they sent you here?" asked Louis. "To get over it?"

"Yes, but those, those . . . layers!" wailed Kate.

Layers? Louis and I looked at each other questioningly, but Aaron had the answer, as usual. The thing is, it wasn't his usual kind of answer at all.

"In the rock face, you mean," he said.

"Yes!" said Kate.

"The way it makes human life feel infinitesimally small," said Aaron.

I stared at him.

"Exactly," said Kate, tears falling down her cheeks. "My

grandmother isn't even a hair-sized line. She's too tiny to leave any kind of mark on those rocks. And no one wants to even talk about her. She's been dead five months, and all anyone wants to do is forget her. Soon it will be like she was never here at all."

A hush fell over us, and I wondered if Louis and Aaron were doing what I was doing: trying to think of a way to comfort Kate, to tell her she was wrong about her grandmother and time and the rocks, without lying to her.

"But Kate," ventured Aaron at last, shyly, "does knowing about those rocks make you not, um, love her?"

"No! Of course not. I'd never not love her."

"Right," said Aaron, getting more and more embarrassed. "You came here and saw the rocks and realized how small your grandmother is compared to, you know, the history of the Earth or whatever, and you love her *anyway*. Which is maybe the whole point."

We all just looked at Aaron, who looked down at his lap. I puzzled over what he'd just said: "the whole point." The whole point of what?

"Oh!" I said. "I get it. You mean the anyway."

Without looking up, Aaron nodded.

"The anyway is the whole point," I said, and Aaron nodded again.

"I'm confused," said Louis.

"The anyway is the whole point of—" I broke off, as embarrassed as Aaron.

"Love," said Kate, amazed. "Even if no one cares, even if no one else remembers her, even if she could be not so nice, even if time lasts forever and those rocks tower over everything, and my grandmother isn't even a speck, I love her anyway."

"And that's the whole point," said Aaron. Then he groaned and fell backward, hitting the ground with a bump. "Sheesh. Thinking is a lot harder than knowing. Why didn't anyone warn me?"

We all laughed, especially Kate. Louis, the person who didn't touch people, lifted his hand and hesitated only a second before he slapped Aaron on the shoulder.

"Good job, man," he said.

Lying in my tent at night, dividing my days into hells and heavens, I could see how nothing was tidy, how the hells had some pretty sweet parts, how the heavens were a mixed bag too, which is maybe how it goes in the desert. Or maybe it's how it goes anywhere, although back home, good and bad sure seemed a lot easier to tell apart.

I also saw that I was coming dangerously close to forgetting my resolution to not have friends. Some outside observer might even have said that when it came to sticking to that resolution, I was failing dismally. But I didn't panic. I knew it was all temporary. We would go home and never see each other again. If these people ended up lying and betraying me like Janie had, well, I wouldn't know them for long, anyway.

And come on, those rocks? Those trees? That sunset? The Milky Way trailing down the sky every night like spilled glitter? It was all so beautiful, but it also felt unreal, otherworldly. And if this wasn't the real world, nothing that happened in it was real, was it? No matter how real it felt.

CHAPTER TEN

Aaron Archer

El Viaje a la Confianza

ONE MORNING WHILE ENOD'S TEAM was scraping the last of the oatmeal off the breakfast dishes with handfuls of dried creosote leaves, which got the dishes clean but made all our food taste like railroad crossties, Jare took a seat on a rock in the shade of an abandoned ranch house beside the trail, got a funny look on his face, felt around on top of his head, and pointed to three columns of stone looming like watchmen in the faraway desert. He said, "Your second el Viaje character-building challenge is to bring me my hat. I left it on one of those hoodoos." Then he ducked into his tent. "Let's hope you do better than you did capturing that flag."

"What are hoodoos?" asked Kevin Larkspur.

"Those," said Jare, ducking back out to point at the stones, "are hoodoos." He disappeared into his tent again, and we could hear him throwing his things around.

"Those stupid rock fingers that stick up in the desert," said Daphne, rolling her eyes.

"Thanks, that clears things up," said Audrey.

"Actually, a hoodoo, tent rock, or fairy chimney is a spire of stone that protrudes from the bottom of an arid basin. Ranging from the height of a human being to the height of a skyscraper, hoodoos consist of soft rock capped by harder, less easily eroded stone that protects each column from the elements," I supplied. After all, I'd spent a whole afternoon studying geology to get ready for Quiz Masters season.

Jare stuck his head through the tent flap again. "Could you just," he asked from between gritted teeth, "go?"

"I don't want to," Daphne announced.

"Yes," said Jare, climbing impatiently back out. "You do."

"No," said Daphne, "I don't."

"Yes," hissed Jare, "you do!" He raised one eyebrow.

Daphne thought his assertion over for a second, and then, to our surprise, she shrugged and said, "Okay. You win, Jare. I *do* want to. By the way, does this field trip have a catchy name, like the other one?"

"I've got more important things to think about right now, Daphne," muttered Jare, jabbing his thumb toward his tent. "And it's a challenge, not a field trip."

"Are there clues to help us get there?" asked Edie.

"Good question, E-death," said Daphne, clapping silently. "Very good question." She turned to Jare. "Jare, are there clues?"

"Yeah. Here's your clue. Look over there. See the hoodoos? That's where the hoodoos are. Now get going."

"This one seems kind of thrown together, Jare," observed Daphne. He glared at her.

"Um," said Louis, "before we go, could you tell us the purpose of this challenge? I mean, what is it supposed to teach us?" He must've figured if he knew what Jare was trying to do to us, he might be able to guess what shocks to expect. "Are we team building?"

"Or problem solving?" tossed in Enod.

"Or improving our cross-country navigational skills?" asked Kevin.

"Yes!" said Jare, glancing impatiently at the rising sun. "You are doing all of that! Now get going!"

"How much do we need to pack?" asked Kate.

"Everything!" cried Jare. "Plus . . . an extra gallon of water. Be prepared! And you better not forget your railroad spike, Little Miss Sunshine! Now vamoose!"

"What's the prize?" asked Kate.

"Prize? Prize?" burst out Jare, coming back from wherever his thoughts had taken him. "I don't know. What do you clowns *want* for a prize?"

"The air mattress," said Kate.

"Are you still fixated on that stupid air mattress? Fine. The prize is a nice, comfy, brand-new air mattress, 'cause nobody managed to win it the first time. Now get lost!"

Which didn't seem like such a great way for Jare to put it, given how much time he'd spent rounding up lost and injured people during the capture-the-flag challenge, but even I knew better than to point this out.

We grabbed our packs and started toward the hoodoos. There wasn't really a trail, so after we'd wound through the agave, lechuguilla, candelilla, cholla, and ocotillo for five minutes, the groups had scattered far and wide.

"We have to hurry," said Kate. "Or Daphne and Randolph will beat us again."

"Hold on," I said. "First, let's hike up to a high spot to have a look around. I know Jare must have some kind of surprise waiting between here and the hoodoos."

But when we got to the top of the nearest hill, the surprise was—there was no surprise. The desert floor stretched out plain and flat all the way to the hoodoos. And all the other groups were way ahead of us.

"What the heck!" cried Kate. "He tricked us. Because he didn't trick us!"

"Just when you think you've got Jare figured out,"

muttered Audrey, skittering down the hillside, "you don't have Jare figured out. Come on. Let's go!"

"What's he doing?" murmured Louis, pausing to stare back at camp.

"Who?" I asked.

"Jare," said Louis.

I looked, and thought, possibly, with my regular old eyes, I could make out Jare wandering among our tents. "I can't tell," I said. "What *is* he doing?"

"Leaving camp in the other direction," said Louis. "With his pack."

"Hey!" Audrey called to us. "Get moving up there!"

"We've got a contest to win!" added Kate.

So Louis and I slid down the hill after them.

We hiked as hard as we could. I could tell we were in better shape than ever, because even though we were nearly running among the cacti, we still had enough breath to talk. As Kate and Louis walked side by side in the lead, we dropped into a gully and the hoodoos disappeared from sight. Louis glanced up and said, "Where the heck's that doggone hoodoo?"

Kate said, "*You* know just as well as I do."

Louis said, "Who do?"

Kate said, "You do."

"I do?"

"You do."

"Hoodoo?"

"You do, I do, we do, they do."

They fell down laughing. But I noticed that they checked for cactus first. We were getting the hang of this place.

And then, as soon as Kate and Louis had yanked each other back to their feet and we started hiking again, we topped a small ridgeline and realized that actually, the desert *did* have a surprise in store for us. The hoodoos stood right there, along with all the other campers. It had hardly taken an hour to get to them. Their distance from camp had been an optical illusion, because they weren't nearly as big as we'd thought. The tallest one, which was wearing Jare's hat, turned out to be twelve feet high. From far away, I guess we'd thought it was a hundred. Still, even with only a twelve-foot hoodoo, there was no way to get the hat down. The other teams had all dropped their packs and were dragging out their belongings, looking for something that might help scale the hoodoo.

Cyrus and Edie tried to tie their group's sleeping bags together to form a rope, but from what I could tell, that's the kind of plan that works mainly in the movies.

Enod had a pair of underwear in one hand and was collecting sticks with the other. "Stretchy," he said, tugging on the waistband. "Should make a good slingshot."

"Why not?" I replied.

"Looks like Jare just walked over here and tossed his hat on top," observed Kevin Larkspur, pointing up at the hoodoo.

"The whole thing feels really impromptu," added Enod.

"Impromptu," snickered Randolph, as if he thought it was a naughty word. Which he probably did. Randolph had his pack scattered all over, looking for something to throw at the hoodoo, I guessed, but instead, he'd found a bunch of pistachios at the bottom and gotten distracted by cracking them in his teeth.

Kate rummaged around inside her pack and came up with her railroad spike.

"What are you gonna do with that?" sneered Randolph. "Comb your hair?"

"Just shut up, Randolph, okay?" requested Daphne.

And then Randolph wasn't on a roll anymore. He dropped to the ground and sullenly began destroying the burrow of a field mouse with a stick.

Kate circled the hoodoo a couple of times, examining its sides. She seemed to spot something, because she stopped, motioned to Louis, and said, "Louis? Can you give me a leg up?"

Louis lumbered over, took a breath, dropped to his knees, and made a stirrup from his hands for Kate to step into. As soon as she did, he stood up. And lifted her feet all the way to his chest. From there, in one quick motion, Kate stepped onto his shoulders. She slipped her railroad spike out of her pocket, stuck it into a crack about eight feet off the ground, and used it like the rung of a ladder. With a sweep of her hand, she swiped the hat off the hoodoo, stepped back onto Louis's shoulders, pulled her railroad spike out of the crack, and dropped to the ground.

"Impressive," said Enod.

Kevin began to clap, and everybody but Daphne and Randolph joined in. Kate took a bow.

Daphne didn't waste a second. She marched up and put her face in Kate's. "And now, Little Miss Sunshine," she said, grabbing Kate by the elbow, "give me the hat."

Kate laughed scornfully and yanked her elbow away.

"Or," said Daphne, "if you want, I can just take it."

"Go ahead," said Kate, glaring at her eyeball to eyeball, which meant basically staring straight up.

"Randolph?" said Daphne. "I think we have a problem."

"Leave her alone, Daphne," I pleaded. "We won fair and square."

"Yeah. Lay off, Daphne," chimed in Enod.

"Shut up, spud," warned Randolph.

Sheepishly, Enod fell silent and stared at the ground.

"Seriously, Daphne," I said. "Enough."

Daphne turned to me. "I'm starting to wonder," she said, "if Memory Boy is really the right name for you. Because it seems like you *forgot* what happened the last time you messed with Randolph. I heard you ended up on your butt, counting stars." She turned back to Kate. "You should go ahead and give us the hat. I want to get back to camp to have a nap. On my new air mattress."

"If you want the hat," whispered Kate, "then come and get it."

"Fine." Daphne smiled. She turned to Randolph. "Randolph?"

Randolph snickered softly.

"Don't just stand there giggling," said Daphne impatiently. "Take the hat!"

"Uh," said Randolph. He studied the ground, where he spotted a little blue rock he suddenly needed to kick into the bushes.

"Randolph?" said Daphne.

"Well," said Randolph, waving a hand in Kate's direction. "I mean, she . . . I . . . you—"

Everybody had gathered to watch.

"Get the hat, Randolph," ordered Daphne. "I want it!"

"I had to deal with her last time," Randolph whined. "It's *your* turn."

"Oh, for the love of—" began Daphne.

Kate dangled the hat in front of Daphne. “Do you want it or not?” she asked.

Daphne thought this over. But it was pretty clear that she didn’t want the hat badly enough to tangle with Kate. “Oh, who cares about Jare’s stupid dandruffy hat!” Daphne burst out. “Just keep it. Loser.”

“All right, I will,” said Kate agreeably, unzipping her pack. First she dropped in the railroad spike. Then the hat. “Come on, guys. Let’s go claim our prize.”

“Hold on a second,” I said. “I’ve got to put everything back in my pack.” I’d dug all my stuff out too, just like everybody else.

While we all repacked, a breeze picked up and wafted among the hoodoos. They loomed silently over us. I began to think they knew something we didn’t, and I wondered what it was. Something made me want to tell everybody how I felt, and whatever that something was, it was so strong I couldn’t stop myself. “Hoodoos form from sedimentary rock and volcanic stone in desert landscapes across the globe,” I said. “They often exhibit a variable thickness, which contributes to the totem-pole shape of their bodies. Minerals deposited within different rock types cause varied colors throughout their height—”

This didn’t feel like what I wanted to say.

Above us, the sun moved just enough to cast downward

shadows over the tallest hoodoo's head, and as I watched, I saw his eyes, nose, and chin emerge. I heard myself tell everybody, "Look at his face."

"Who?" scoffed Randolph. By now he'd gotten distracted by half a PowerBar he'd found in the bottom of his pack and was gnawing on it.

"Him," I said, because the hoodoo that had been wearing Jare's hat, in this light, looked like an old man, a nice old man, a nice old man who was frowning a little because he was deep in thought.

"What's he looking at?" Louis asked, seeing the old man too.

I scanned the hills, mountain, rocks, arroyos, river bottoms, cliffs, valleys, trails, roads, caves, abandoned farms, frozen windmills, rusting rails, reds, yellows, oranges, and blues stretched out in front of us. "All of it," I said.

"Who *is* he?" wondered Audrey, gazing at his expression.

And all the facts I knew about hoodoos started rearranging themselves. I said, "First, he was seashells and the spines of ocean creatures collecting at the bottom of a prehistoric sea. It took him millions of years, but after a while, he got stronger and harder and turned into stone. And then the sea dried up. And then a volcano erupted and made his bones. And the desert formed above him. And the rain and the wind began to carve him out of the stone. He got taller and taller. And he watched everything. He's been watching since before the dinosaurs were born. He's seen everything. I'm going to come back to visit him."

When I stopped, I realized everybody was staring at me. Quickly Louis and Kate and Enod shot their gazes up at the hoodoo and stood silently contemplating it. And Audrey scanned the desert. Then they all stared at me again. But the words had stopped, like a flood that'd washed itself away. I didn't have anything else to say. But maybe, I thought, I didn't need to say anything else.

In the silence, Daphne gazed at the base of the hoodoo. Slowly she picked up a giant rock, so huge she could hardly lift it, and as we watched, she started to run. Not very fast. Her rock was as big as a bathroom sink. Nobody quite understood what she was up to. Faster and faster Daphne staggered with her stone, and finally, after it was too late, I realized what she wanted to do. With a shout like an Olympic hammer thrower, she spun around once and let her stone go. It crashed into the delicate, fragile base of the old man hoodoo, knocked a rock chip loose, and slowly, very slowly, the hoodoo began to topple.

For a second, I must've thought I could hold it up, because I ran toward the falling stone. Audrey did the same thing. But we were too late. The hoodoo had been doomed the second Daphne picked up that rock. Audrey and I had to leap back to keep from being crushed. As he fell, the worried old man began disintegrating, and when he hit the ground, he shattered into so many pieces, it was like he'd never existed. He was nothing but dust in the dust.

"What does he see now, Memory Boy?" sneered Daphne, and she shouldered her pack and marched away toward camp.

I felt like I was the one she'd just toppled with a rock.

Nobody said anything. We just gazed at the fragments that used to be the old man hoodoo, and then we began wandering back to camp in ones and twos, completely silent.

All except for Randolph, who hurried to catch up to Daphne. Maybe he wanted to give her a high five.

After a while, our group managed to collect itself as we hiked through the brush and the ocotillo, and once we'd walked silently for half a mile, Kate said, "What's Jare going to do when she gets back? I mean, he'll see the missing hoodoo, and who else would have knocked it down but Daphne?"

"He'll call her names. Take her tent away," said Audrey.

"Make her carry a railroad spike," I suggested.

"Fifteen railroad spikes," said Kate. "And a crosstie."

"For about a hundred miles," I added.

"Scream," said Louis, grimacing at the thought. "Definitely scream."

"It's not going to be pretty," said Kate. "In fact, it'll probably be horrible."

"As horrible as what *she* did to the hoodoo?" I asked.

"Not that horrible," said Kate.

But as we all straggled back into camp, Jare didn't do any of the things we'd predicted, at least not right away. In a very quiet voice, he asked a few questions. "Would you knock over a gravestone, Daphne? Would you dump garbage in a church? Would you spray paint the *Mona Lisa*'s face? Would you set the Declaration of Independence on fire?"

Out of the corner of my eye, as I watched her smiling stonily at the ground, I glimpsed an expression on Daphne's face that made me think yes, she might actually find one or two of those activities enjoyable, now that he'd mentioned them.

And then a tear leaked out of Jare's eye. He wiped it away with his sleeve. This was unnerving. Another one formed and ran down Jare's cheek. I shuddered. Watching Jare cry was a thousand times worse than listening to him scream.

Audrey, Kate, Louis, Enod, Kevin, and I looked at each other. Who knew he cared so much about this place?

Jare finally got hold of himself and smeared away his tears with his fists, leaving muddy streaks on his face. He took a deep breath, and after that, he got mad.

"You," he barked at Daphne, "don't know when to quit!"

"And you," she said sweetly, smiling at him like he was three and had just said something incredibly silly, "don't know *anything*."

"This is public land," hollered Jare. He pointed to the gap on the horizon where the old man used to stand. "That hoodoo belonged to everybody. You didn't have the right!"

"It would've fallen down sooner or later," yawned Daphne.

"It took the forces of nature millions of years to create that hoodoo!" cried Jare. "It took you a second to destroy it!"

"Daphne one," Daphne laughed, doing a victory dance in the dirt, "nature zero!"

"Just keep laughing," Jare snarled. "What if you'd knocked it down on somebody, and broken a leg or fractured a skull, or worse?"

Daphne pretended to think this over. Then she shrugged. "I give up," she said. "What?"

Jare seemed to have run out of ideas for getting through

to her. He stared at her silently, seething. Then he said, "For one thing, this place would be crawling with sheriffs and rangers, and our timeline would be off by a day, or more—" Then Jare stopped talking again.

"That's right, Jare," said Daphne patronizingly. "It's probably time to stick a cork in it."

"This is why," whispered Jare, staring furiously at her.

"This is why what, Jare?" asked Daphne brightly.

"This is why," said Jare, "your dad didn't want you."

"What?" gasped Daphne, all her cockiness gone.

"I said—this is why your dad left!" Jare shouted.

Daphne's hand moved so fast I hardly saw it, but I sure did hear the sound of the slap.

"Charming," Jare muttered at her back as she disappeared into her tent. And without another word, he slipped into his own tent, tossed the air mattress out over his shoulder, and zipped the flap. We didn't see him anymore that night, so all we had for dinner was a squashed box of saltines Edie had hoarded in her pack.

"Jare went a little too far tonight," commented Kevin.

"Got that right!" bellowed Randolph, and stomped away to sit by Daphne's tent.

We split the crackers fourteen ways, since Daphne never came back out and Randolph crouched by her door, panting in the heat like he was her faithful Irish setter, until we all got in our tents and fell asleep.

Even Louis fell asleep that night, *especially* Louis, because despite everything that had happened, when darkness fell, he floated atop a cushion of air.

CHAPTER ELEVEN

Audrey Alcott

El Viaje a la Confianza

THE NEXT MORNING, WHEN JARE blasted his usual pleasant, person-screaming-bloody-murder-over-the-sound-of-tearing-sheet-metal wake-up music, Daphne did not come out of her tent. I noticed she was missing right away. I'm sure everyone noticed. Daphne's absence was so conspicuous—no stomping, glaring, growling—that it was almost a *presence*, a nice one, like the smell of baking bread or an unexpected snowfall during a heat wave. But I guess because we were all so busy enjoying the presence of her absence, no one pointed it out for at least twenty minutes. Even Randolph didn't mention it, just darted wary but questioning glances at her tent. And like the rest of us, he stayed as far away from that tent as possible. When any of us had to walk by it, we left a margin of at least ten feet, as if there were an invisible fence around it that might shock us if we got too close.

Despite the fact that Randolph was a gargantuan jerk, once again I felt a little sorry for him. Daphne was his best friend at camp (at least, I'm sure *he* thought so), and even he was uneasy around her. In fact, without her there, he seemed uneasy, period. Sure, he did some blustering, but you could tell his heart wasn't in it, and it was obvious that Randolph was a born henchman, lost without someone bigger and meaner to attach himself to. Randolph was the remora; Daphne was the shark.

Finally, when Daphne's tent was the only one still standing, Randolph said, "Someone's gotta wake up Daphne. Jare'll be here any minute, and she'll get in trouble if she's not packed up."

We all looked at Randolph expectantly. Since he was the only one who cared whether or not Daphne got in trouble, obviously he was the one to wake her up.

"Go for it," I said, and I swear he blushed.

"But . . . shouldn't a girl do it? I mean, what if, uh, you know, she's in the middle of, uh, you know, dressing?" he said.

"He's turning the color of a *Pyrocephalus rubinus*," said Aaron under his breath.

"Yeah, Aaron, just what I was about to say," I whispered back sarcastically.

He grinned. "Vermilion flycatcher."

I gave him a look.

"Those red birds we see all the time," he said.

"Ah," I said. "Yep. He sure is."

Kate walked up to Randolph until she was standing a couple of feet away from him. *Within smacking distance,* I thought with satisfaction, as Randolph leaned away from her.

"What?" he said.

"You wouldn't have to unzip her tent," said Kate.

"Yes, I would," said Randolph belligerently.

"No. You could just go to the flap and yell her name."

Randolph rolled his eyes and said, "Yeah, like that'll work."

"Actually, it probably would. Your voice tends to . . . carry," said Cyrus, using the tone of a person who got yelled at by Randolph at least five times a day.

Randolph stared at the tent, swallowed hard, and started walking toward it like he was sneaking up on a sleeping rhino, but just before he got there, a voice boomed out, "What pathetic, hopeless, godforsaken loser has yet to break down and pack up her tent?" so loudly that Randolph nearly jumped out of his skin. We all turned and stared at

Jare. He loomed huge, a wall of rage. His nostrils flared like a crazed bull's.

Because asking a question you already know the answer to is its own kind of lie, even before it totally registered that Jare had just said "*her* tent," I knew he'd already figured out whose tent it was. The guy just couldn't resist putting on a big, scary, name-calling show, a *loud*, big, scary, name-calling show. When I noticed Louis, standing in the back of the group, looking completely miserable, his shoulders bunched up, his hands cupped around his ears to muffle Jare's stupid bellow, I wanted to tell Jare that people who shouted when everyone was listening anyway were pathetic, hopeless, godforsaken losers too. But of course, I didn't.

"Name!" he barked. "I need a name, people!"

No one said anything. Nothing happened at all, which struck me as odd because this was the perfect time for Daphne to unzip her tent, climb out, yawn, and stretch, all the while smirking (because if anyone could yawn and smirk at the same time, it was Daphne), and gaze coolly into Jare's bugged-out-with-rage eyeballs, as if she just did not care. But it didn't happen. Her tent stood, zipped up and mute and indifferent, like a person keeping a secret. For the first time, I got the shiver-up-my-spine feeling that Daphne might not be inside that tent at all.

Finally Kate shrugged and said, "Daphne."

Jare scanned the group with his scalding gaze. Then he hissed, through gritted teeth, "Get her."

Everyone looked at Randolph, whose eyes grew big as silver dollars. He shook his head. *Henchman,* I thought. *Remora. Coward.*

Because no one moved, I sighed, walked over to Daphne's tent, and yanked up the zipper. Inside: nothing. No backpack, no sleeping bag, no Daphne. Even though, in general, I was a firm believer in the philosophy that no Daphne was always better than Daphne, another shiver ran through me. As I gazed into the empty space where she was supposed to be, Daphne seemed more than missing. She seemed truly and utterly *gone.*

I flashed to the evening before: Daphne's slap; the cold, hard rage in Jare's eyes. Slowly I turned around to look at Jare.

"Let's get this show on the road," roared Jare, smacking his hands together. "Who's on breakfast duty?"

People shuffled their feet, glanced nervously at Jare and at each other, but no one made a single move to get the show on the road.

"She's gone," I said, thinking maybe he hadn't seen that the tent was empty.

It could have been the morning sun playing tricks, but I

swear that just for a second, I saw Jare smile. Then he said, "Whatever. I'm not worried about it."

Everyone else probably thought he didn't mean it, that he was just acting tough, playing it cool, lying to cover up embarrassment or anger or concern. But I saw right away that he was telling the truth. His honesty was as stark and clear and unmistakable as the mountains behind him. A fourteen-year-old camper under his care—if you could call it "care"—had vanished overnight into the thin, dry desert air, and Jare *wasn't worried*, not even a little. As I considered why this might be true, icy fear ran up my spine, and for the third time that morning, I shivered.

Louis and I had dish duty. It wasn't an easy job for Louis for a lot of reasons—the smell of the creosote leaves, the texture of the creosote leaves, the sound of the creosote leaves against the aluminum bowls, the gluiness of the oatmeal. But he did it anyway. While we scrubbed away at not sixteen but *fifteen* bowls and spoons, we discussed the Daphne situation. It had been nearly an hour since we'd discovered her gone.

"And who knows what time she left last night?" I said. "She may have been gone for as long as eight hours at this point. And not that I miss her or anything, but wouldn't a normal camp director be doing something? Looking for her himself? Setting up a search party? Something?"

"Maybe he called the ranger station? He's been in his tent awhile. According to the camp brochure, there's no cell service here, but he must have some way to communicate with the outside world, right? A satellite telephone, maybe?"

"Maybe, but I doubt he used it."

"Are you *sure* he wasn't lying?"

That morning, in a rushed breakfast conversation, I'd filled Louis and Kate in on my unsuperpower. Louis had said, "Cool!" but Kate had said, "Yeah, cool, but I can also see how it could have a big downside," and if we'd had time, I might have hugged her for understanding that. Instead I went on to tell them that I knew Jare was telling the truth when he said he wasn't worried about Daphne.

"Absolutely sure. I am never wrong about lying. Ever. And believe me, there are definitely times when I wish I were."

"You think the reason he's not worried about her disappearing is that he's the one who disappeared her?" asked Louis.

"I don't want to think that, but she did send him into a rage and then slapped him across the face."

Louis winced, probably imagining what it would feel like to be slapped. A minute or two later, he set down the bowl he was scrubbing and said in a pained voice, "Okay, now my brain is going a mile a minute, thinking up all these terrible things he might have done."

"Sorry about that."

"Not your fault. You had to tell us. And most of the things I'm thinking are ridiculous, way worse than anything that could really happen."

"Probably so. Even if he were involved, it could have been an accident. Maybe he didn't mean to hurt her."

Louis nodded, then blurted out, "I mean, one of the scenarios in my head involves a swarm of specially trained, genetically modified killer bees, which is crazy, right?"

I smiled. "Right. I think we can rule that one out."

A few seconds later, he said, "Vicious javelinas? Drone bombers? Telekinesis?"

"Not a chance." I sighed. "Try not to worry, Louis. We'll just keep an eye on Jare and wait to see what happens next. I could be wrong about the whole thing."

Louis nodded and picked up the bowl. A minute later, he dropped it again.

"There could be a totally reasonable explanation for why he's not worried, right?" he said.

"Sure."

"Well, maybe someone should just ask him, so we can all stop imagining Jare sneaking rabid jackrabbits into Daphne's tent in the dead of night."

I hesitated. I really wasn't up for a chat with Jare, but Louis's eyes were dilated with terror.

"Okay, I'll go," I said.

Louis swiveled his head in my direction, hope dawning on his face. But then it faded.

"No," he said resolutely. "You can't. What if he did do something awful to Daphne? He might go all homicidal maniac on you if you ask him any questions. You're right; we'll just keep an eye on him for now."

"Okay," I said. "Look, we're almost finished here. Why don't you go sit under that tree and relax? We don't want you overbreathing or anything. I'll put this stuff away."

Louis nodded and shambled unsteadily in the direction of a nearby cottonwood, which is why when, after I'd finished cleaning up and gone to check on him, I was surprised to find him gone. Kate was collecting firewood nearby.

"Have you seen Louis?" I asked her.

"A few minutes ago, he was sitting on that rock over there, doing the breathing thing with his finger on his nose. He said he was fine, and after a while, he walked that way." Kate pointed. "I figured he needed some time alone. This Daphne thing has freaked him out."

I looked in the direction she'd pointed.

"There's nothing really over there," I said.

"Except Jare's tent," said Aaron.

I stared at him and then sat down hard on the same rock Louis had been sitting on. "Oh, no."

"What?" asked Kate.

Quickly I told them about my plate-scrubbing conversation with Louis.

"He went to ask Jare himself," said Aaron. "Wow."

"Wow is right," said Kate, wide-eyed. "Louis, taking the bull by the horns. Bearding the lion in his den. Where does that phrase even come from? Do lions have beards?"

She and I looked at Aaron, who immediately got the expression he always got when he was rifling through his memory. Then he shrugged.

"Well?" I asked.

"Lions have manes," said Aaron.

Kate and I said, "Thanks, Aaron," in exactly the same sarcastic tone at exactly the same time.

"But the point is," said Aaron, "that Louis is being insanely brave."

Louis was being brave, and Aaron was figuring out the point. I smiled. "Yes, he is," I agreed.

"I just hope Jare doesn't start screaming at Louis," said Kate. "You know how he can't stand loud noises."

In a few minutes, during which no screams of any kind issued from the direction of Jare's tent, Louis was back. He didn't look traumatized. In fact, he looked pretty proud of himself, and that was a very nice sight to see.

"So maybe it's not so bad after all," he said excitedly, sitting down on the ground next to us, without even scrupulously checking it for scorpions or pointy rocks or whatever it was he usually checked for first. The instant he was settled, the story poured out of him. "I started by asking Jare if he wanted me to take down Daphne's tent, and he said no, and I said why, and he said because he figures she's just trying to throw off our schedule or scare everyone because she's mad at him and that she's probably nearby, just sitting someplace, laughing her head off, and he thinks it's just a matter of time before she gets hungry or thirsty or bored and comes moseying on back, and then she can take down her own darn tent."

We sat for a moment, letting this sink in.

"Oh," I said. "So you think that's why he wasn't worried?"

"It seems plausible," said Aaron.

"All of that sounds like something Daphne would do," said Kate.

I had to admit it did. Privately, I still wasn't totally ruling out that Jare had had something to do with Daphne's disappearance. Maybe he hadn't murdered her, but he could have killed her by accident in a fit of rage. Or maybe he'd been trying to scare her, teach her a lesson, and she'd gotten lost, or something else had gone wrong. But there didn't seem to be any point in bringing up these possibilities right then, and, honestly, looking at the relief on Louis's face, I just didn't have the heart.

"Louis," said Kate, "you went to talk to Jare all by yourself, even though he might have screamed at you. That took guts."

"Not really," said Louis. "I know my brain. It wouldn't have stopped, ever. It would have thought up horrible things Jare might have done to Daphne, each one scarier than the one before, until it had terrified me into a coma. I had to do something."

"So you're saying that you terrified yourself into being brave?" Aaron asked.

"Yep," said Louis. "I was too scared to chicken out."

"That's not exactly how it happened," I said. "Because you could have let me go talk to him, but you were afraid he'd go all homicidal maniac on me. He could have done the same to you. You risked your life, Louis."

Louis's cheeks went red, and he waved a hand in the air dismissively. "No, Jare already despises me so much that if he were going to kill me off, he would have already done it. Since he hasn't, he must have decided that I'm just not worth it. I was safe."

Because it was clear that we could spend the rest of

the day trying to convince Louis he'd committed an act of courage and get nowhere, I let it drop and said, "So now we wait for Daphne to get back, I guess."

"I guess so," said Louis. "Although there's no rule that we can't enjoy her absence in the meantime, right?"

Aaron looked sheepish. "I'd be lying if I said I hadn't been enjoying it this whole time."

"You'd be lying, and I'd know you were lying," I said.

"Ain't that the truth," said Kate, and the four of us looked at each other and grinned.

Lunch came and went, and there was still no sign of Daphne.

Jare had given us all the job of scrubbing out our water bottles and food containers and repacking our bags, the usual busywork. Kate, Aaron, Louis, and I sat in a huddle, scrubbing and talking. Louis was still glowing faintly from his act of heroism, and the others all seemed to accept that Jare hadn't had a hand in Daphne's disappearance. I wasn't so sure. I couldn't stop thinking about that slap, and about Jare's crying—*crying*—in front of all of us.

"You know what's weird about Jare?" I said suddenly.

"He's a psycho?" asked Aaron.

"He's got the biggest feet in the world and still manages to find hiking boots to fit him?" asked Kate.

"He's really, really, really loud?" asked Louis.

"Yes. And also . . . he loves this place," I said.

They looked at me doubtfully.

"That seems somewhat less weird than the size of his feet," said Kate. "I mean, he works here, and it's kind of a cool place, right?"

"Plus he's made himself king of it," said Louis. "It's his personal domain, and he gets to make the rules and push everyone around. He's like an overgrown playground bully, and this is his playground. Bullies love their playgrounds."

"I know, I know," I said. "But did you see him yesterday with the old man hoodoo? All that crying? How often do you think a guy like Jare cries *in public*?"

After a moment, Louis said, "You know, he said something about a church. Maybe this place is sacred to Jare."

Aaron said, "Maybe this place is Jare's white chickens."

"Right," I said. "White chickens. But maybe it's even more. He acted like Daphne hadn't just destroyed an ancient and extremely interesting rock formation with wise, grandpalike qualities, which is a rotten thing to do all by itself. He acted like she'd killed a real old man, one Jare loved. Like she'd killed his actual grandpa."

"This place is his family," said Kate softly, pressing her hands together and lowering her eyes. "And it's beautiful, but it's not easy. It stings. It's hard and dry. It's not like a garden or a beach. It's like a family that's hard to love, but you do it anyway. And—" She stopped and looked up and waited for someone to finish.

"The anyway is the whole point," I said quietly.

We sat and thought about this. Then I said, "People will do anything to defend their families. I hope Daphne is out there, laughing at all of us right now. She probably is, but I just want us to remember that when it comes to what they really love, people will do anything."

"I really hope that if he did something, he didn't do it on purpose," said Kate. "Like he might have gotten mad and just shoved her harder than he meant to because he was all worked up. Or something."

"Either way, we should probably keep an eye on Jare," said Louis. "Watch what he does next. He has to do something soon, right?"

"Right," said Aaron. "Even if he—he knows where she is, he'll need to at least *pretend* to try to find her, soon."

"Look," said Kate, lifting her head to see something over Louis's shoulder.

Jare strode toward us holding a map, all unfolded, big and white and catching wind like a sail. An image popped into my head of his catcher's-mitt hands wrapped around

Daphne's neck, but I pushed it away.

"Here we go," I murmured.

Jare told us we'd wasted enough time being patient with Daphne's little stunt. Now, he said, it was time to flush her out. He assigned each group a territory to search and gave us instructions on how to fan out and cover as much ground as possible. We'd divide each group into people who would search the ground for clues and people who would keep their heads up, scanning the horizon, the treetops, hills, and boulders. He gave our group the search area—a big square of dry, stony desert—farthest from what he, very importantly, called the P.L.S., or Point Last Seen.

"We got the worst area," grumbled Kate. "It'll take an hour just to hike out to it. But on the bright side, at least it's a scorching hot day."

As we all got busy gathering supplies and putting on sunscreen and doing all the other PHWSS stuff, Jare noticed that Randolph was sitting on his pack, doing nothing. Well, not nothing, exactly, because he was whistling. Randolph was either tone-deaf or just a horrendous whistler. He had his hands clasped behind his head and his eyes closed, like a person taking a nap, except that he was sitting up straight and whistling like a demented sparrow, which, in my experience, people taking naps rarely did.

"Randolph!" bellowed Jare.

Because he'd obviously been waiting for Jare to do exactly that, Randolph didn't jump. He just opened his eyes and glared.

"What?"

"We've already lost precious hiking time because of your pathetic, attention-seeking friend. Get hopping!"

Randolph sneered, but I'd seen his eyes light up when Jare had said "friend."

"Not going," said Randolph.

"Oh, for the love of Pete," murmured Louis, his hands hovering around his ears.

"What did you say?" asked Jare, narrowing his eyes.

"Not going."

"And why would you consider yourself exempt from this activity?" said Jare, his face beginning its puff-up-turn-purple routine.

"I don't need to search for Daphne," said Randolph, "because I know where she went."

Lie.

"Like fun you do!" spat Jare.

"Who says that?" whispered Kate, suddenly at my side. "'Like fun'?"

"No one," I whispered back. "But Randolph *is* lying."

Kate's eyes widened. "Seriously?"

"Oh, but I do," said Randolph to Jare.

"How?" asked Jare. His tone was as belligerent as ever, but I saw something odd in his face. For the first time since Daphne had gone missing, Jare was nervous.

"Duh," said Randolph. "She told me."

The "me" squeaked like a mouse when it sees a cat. Another lie.

"No, she didn't," I whispered to Kate, but it came out louder than I intended.

Randolph jumped up, wheeled around, and yelled at me, "Yes! She! Did!"

I shook my head. "You're lying. You lie all the time, and you're lying now."

"Shut up!" shouted Randolph. He took a couple of steps toward me, and out of the corner of my eye, I saw Kate and then Aaron both take a couple of steps toward him. Randolph's jaw was working as if he were grinding his teeth together, which he probably was, but then he said, "You guys don't know jack," and turned back to Jare.

"Maybe you don't either," said Jare.

"I do! Daphne tells me everything!" said Randolph. He crossed his muscle-bound arms over his muscle-bound chest. "But you are out of your stupid mind if you think I'm gonna tell you."

Jare smiled. He stood there, his eyes locked on Randolph's. Then he waved his arm in the air and said,

"Move out, people! Report back here in four hours on the dot—or before, if you find something!"

We moved out—all but Randolph, who sat back down on his pack, a confused and disappointed expression on his face, as if his bombshell hadn't made quite the splat he'd intended. Either Jare had believed me or he had seen for himself that Randolph was lying—because, unsurprisingly, Randolph wasn't the slickest liar in the world—or he was planning to torture information out of him as soon as the rest of us were out of earshot. As the four of us hiked toward our search area, Kate said dryly, "If Randolph disappears next, we'll know Jare's a homicidal maniac."

"Are you sure Randolph was lying?" Louis asked me, and then he caught himself. "Never mind. I know you're sure."

"Positive," I said. "But what I wonder is—why? Why would he pretend to know where Daphne is? Just to get Jare all riled up?"

"Why? Well, that's obvious, isn't it?" said Kate.

I hiked a few more steps before I got what she meant. "Oh, right," I said. "Because he's a liar, and liars lie."

"Uh, no, Audrey," said Kate. "I mean, maybe some people lie because they're liars, but mostly they lie for a reason."

"Well, yeah. They lie to get something they couldn't get any other way," I said. "Lying is like stealing, sort of. But what I don't understand is why Randolph would lie about knowing where Daphne went, when all a lie like that was going to get him was trouble."

Kate laid a hand on my arm, and I stopped hiking.

"What?"

"I thought you were an expert on lying," Kate said, puzzled.

"Yeah, so did I," said Louis.

"Same here," said Aaron.

"Wait," I said, pointing at Aaron. "*You* know why Randolph lied?"

"I think so," said Aaron.

"*Sometimes* people lie because they're liars. *Sometimes* people lie to get something," said Kate. "But a lot of times, they lie because of how they feel. Randolph lied because he was sad."

"Sad?" I said. "I'm having trouble picturing Randolph being anything as deep as sad."

"I'm basically an expert on sad," said Kate, "and Randolph is sad a lot."

"But why is he sad now?" I asked. "Because Daphne is gone?"

Kate looked at me like I'd just said one plus one was four.

"Because he *wishes* Daphne had told him where she was going . . . ," began Kate.

"Because he *wishes* Daphne trusted him . . . ," continued Louis.

"Because he *wishes* Daphne were his friend. But she's not," finished Aaron. "So he made up a lie."

"That doesn't make sense," I said.

"Yes, it does," said Kate. "Think about it."

I started hiking again, turning over and over inside my head the possibility that people lied not only to get something or to get out of something or to get back at someone or just because they were bad people, but because they were something as simple as sad.

"Maybe you're right," I said finally, my voice coming out smaller than I meant for it to.

I felt flustered, off-kilter. I wasn't used to being the only person in a group who didn't know something. In fact, I was used to being the person in the group who knew things other people didn't, things like when someone was lying. Now that I thought about it, though, I realized I hadn't spent much time thinking about *why* people lied. And as I hiked along, with the afternoon sun in my face, sweat starting to slide down the back of my neck, I suddenly remembered Janie in the doorway of her house, the wild anger in her eyes, when she told me, "You think you're so smart. You think you see right into people! But you know what? You don't see anything!"

Because I didn't want to think about that horrible moment, and because I wanted to feel, once again, like a person who knew things, I said, "Do you notice where we're going?"

"Where?" asked everyone, and I thought, *That's more like it.*

"Straight into the heart of the desert, which is the last place Daphne would head," I said.

"It would be the last place anyone would head," said Louis, eyeing an especially large lizard skittering into the shadow of a prickly pear with a shudder.

"Unless it was by accident," said Kate.

Then Aaron said, in a remarkably good imitation of Daphne's voice, "'Please. This is like my fourth wilderness camp. They're all alike.'"

"Exactly, Aaron," I said. "Daphne was experienced. She'd head toward water or toward the hills or one of those abandoned buildings we've passed during our hikes. She wouldn't come this way."

"She didn't even bring a tent," said Kate.

"Which raises the question of why Jare would send our group—the group that he must know is better at figuring things out than all the others because, technically, we won both of the challenges—to the search area where Daphne is least likely to be," I said.

"Because he doesn't want her to be found," said Kate.

"What should we do?" asked Louis, looking at me. "Quit?"

"We're two thirds of the way finished. We may as well get it done, just in case," I said.

"I bet you're right, though," said Aaron. "We won't find anything."

"Because there is nothing to find," I said, and even though Janie's terrible words and all that stuff about lying and feelings and sadness were still there, in the back of my mind, I felt steady again, capable, more like myself.

But then, twenty minutes later, the doubt came back. Because eagle-eyed Louis, who, along with Aaron, was in charge of searching the ground for clues, found one. In the shade of an unusually large cottonwood tree, caught under a rock, was a black bandanna with tiny skulls all over it. I'd only ever seen that bandanna on one person, who tied it around her head underneath her hat to keep her chopped-off, ketchup-colored hair out of her eyes.

We all leaned over to examine the bandanna. It was

still knotted, and there was even a ketchup-colored hair caught in the knot.

"So she did come out here," said Kate. "But why?"

None of us had an answer. A little while later, when we were even deeper into the wildest part of the wilderness and Louis found an empty plastic Baggie with the broken-off end of an almond in it, we were more mystified—and, with the sun beating relentlessly down and no water source in sight, more afraid for Daphne—than ever.

CHAPTER TWELVE

Aaron Archer

El Viaje a la Confianza

BY THE TIME WE GOT back to our rendezvous point, Audrey, Kate, Louis, and I had decided we had to tell Jare what we'd found. Sure, we thought he might be a maniac, but we weren't positive. If we knew something that might save Daphne and didn't share it and then something happened to her—well, none of us wanted *that* on our consciences. So the team elected me to fill Jare in on the two clues.

Jare was already talking when we arrived. "Every year, somebody can't measure up," he was saying to the other search parties, who had gotten back before us and found spots on the ground in the blazing sun to collapse. "Every year somebody gets discouraged. Every year somebody quits. It's part of the el Viaje mystique."

"Daphne measured up!" cried Randolph truculently.

"I'm afraid I have to disagree with you, Captain

Knucklehead," replied Jare disdainfully. "Daphne *didn't* measure up. Daphne was—is—a girl with serious shortcomings." Randolph stuck his bottom lip out and seethed.

"Whatever was going on with Daphne," observed Kate, "she didn't seem discouraged."

"She seemed *mad*," said Enod.

"At you," added Audrey.

"Plus she was actually pretty good at hiking and camping, even if she was a total jerk," tossed in Kevin.

"And since, every year, somebody runs off across the desert, usually in the most nonsensical direction possible," continued Jare, ignoring as many of us as he could, "there is a standard procedure for the event of a self-initiated camper disappearance. That is the procedure we are now following, and will continue to follow, in order to establish last known direction of travel."

"Tell him!" Audrey mouthed silently. She was right. This was as good a time as any to tell Jare what we'd found, since, even though none of us was sure we trusted him, we couldn't keep the bandanna and the trail-mix bag a secret forever, and the longer we stayed quiet, the madder he would be when we finally told him.

"We found her bandanna," I said. "And on the way back, we found her trash."

“So. When were you planning to tell me?” asked Jare, studying our team with an expression I couldn’t figure out. I glanced at Audrey. She shrugged. She couldn’t figure out what Jare was thinking either.

“I . . . just . . . you were talking . . . ,” I began. “We didn’t want to interrupt. We were going to tell you.”

“Did you bother to keep track of *where* you found all this?” asked Jare dismissively. He glanced at his watch.

“We left everything where it was,” said Kate.

“Like on *Law and Order*,” said Louis. “We didn’t think we were supposed to disturb evidence.”

Jare just shrugged. “Probably the smart play, all things considered,” he said. “Come on, Sherlock Holmes. Show me the clues. Everybody on your feet. I need all eyes for this.”

But Randolph was already on his feet and headed into the desert. “I’m *definitely* going to find her now!” he crowed. He was so busy enjoying visions of his own heroism that he stepped right in the middle of a fire ant colony. “Ow ow ow ow,” he cried.

“That’s gonna hurt later,” observed Jare. “Now stop clowning around and get going.”

As we hiked back to the spot where we’d found the trail-mix bag, Jare got talkative, even for Jare. He told us there was a lesson in all this: if you face challenges with a can-do attitude and a will to win, you will turn adversity to account. For example, Jare said, we should consider him. We should consider the time he was quarterback of his high school team, the Hillsdale, Montana, Grizzlies, and he noticed a three-hundred-pound linebacker charging full speed through the line toward his star halfback. To meet this challenge, Jare had manned up and gotten his can-do attitude in gear, and he had charged right back *at* that linebacker, with no regard for his own personal safety, and despite the fact that quarterbacks almost never do this kind of thing, he had laid a crack-back block on him that basically saved his teammate's life, probably, Jare was pretty sure. Now *that* was turning adversity to account. Got him a full ride to a Big Ten school too, when the scouts saw it on video. Small-town boy makes good. Ha ha ha.

Or, Jare continued, consider the fourth quarter of the 2007 Bowl Championship Series title game, when his favorite receiver, Terrell Brandeis, had suffered a concussion with two seconds left to play, and his team was behind by four points. Jare called a play where *he* ran the ball in for the score, winning the game and the championship and saving Terrell from getting hit in the head and bruising his brain any more than he had to, all because Jare had made the decision to turn adversity to account and meet this formidable challenge head-on. Literally. Ha ha ha.

"Ha ha ha," muttered Kate.

As Jare told us of these exploits, and others, I noticed Audrey's expression growing puzzled. "Wait," I whispered to her. "Is he telling the tr—"

"If you were so great in college," Audrey burst out before I could finish asking, "then how come you never played in the NFL?"

"I wasn't one of those guys who wanted to devote my entire life to tossing an oblate spheroid around an Astroturf field," Jare said. "I wanted more."

I couldn't help noticing he'd already delivered this line during the speech he gave on our first day on el Viaje. I also couldn't help noticing that he'd gotten the shape of the football wrong that time too. And even though I'd learned enough by now to keep my mouth shut about things like this, Jare must've noticed the expression on my face, because he glared at me and said, "Not a word, Memory Boy. Not a stinking word."

We came to the Baggie impaled on the agave spine. "There it is," Kate told Jare.

"Already?" he replied, glancing at his watch, and then at the sun. "That was quick."

Jare snatched the plastic bag off the agave. He looked it over. "Definitely her litter, though. Look, everybody. Even got an almond in it." He held the Baggie up for us all to see. "Definite clue." He jammed it into his pocket. "Now where's the bandanna?"

I pointed to the cottonwood tree out in the desert.

"Had skulls on it and everything, just like Daphne's?" he mused.

"Right," Kate said. "Daphne's. Who else is wandering around out here dropping pretentious fashion statements?"

"Good point, Little Miss Sunshine," said Jare. "It's probably Daphne's." He glanced at his watch. He checked the sky again. "Let's go see." We went.

Once Jare had the second clue in his pocket, he checked his watch again and said, "Outstanding. But here's the thing. We need one more clue."

"Aww," said Randolph. "What? Why?"

"Because, Mr. Einstein, two coordinates don't necessarily tell us which way she's headed," said Jare. "She could be zigzagging, walking in a circle, anything. If we can find one more clue, and it lines up with what we've already got, then we'll have a direction I can trust. Now let's see. How do I want to do this?" He spread out his crinkly new map.

"Randolph, you and your grumpy pals head down this

old mine trail," he instructed. "Audrey's team, take that sector over there." Once again, he directed us into the emptiest, flattest, driest, hottest part of the countryside. "And if there's anything to find, you better find it. And if I come along behind you and find there was something to find, and you didn't find it, then there's not gonna be anything left of *you* to find."

"Jare has *such* a way with words," muttered Audrey as soon as we'd worked our way out of his earshot.

"Why'd Jare send us out here?" wondered Louis, scanning the emptiness all around. "There's no way Daphne came in this direction. She'd have to be crazy. I'll bet you a night in the presidential suite at the El Paso Doubletree that she took off down that mine trail he sent Randolph to search."

"You know," Kate said, "it *would* make Randolph's day—"

"Week."

"Year."

"—if he were actually the one to rescue Daphne."

"So maybe Jare hopes it'll make him easier to live with," concluded Kate.

We searched in silence for a while, and Louis spotted a roadrunner nest and I found a tangle of barbed wire left over from somebody's old cattle ranch. Louis found the skeleton of a mountain lion, fangs and all.

"Wow. Jare wasn't kidding," I said. "Mastodons to mountain lions."

Kate spotted a brass button.

"You know what I can't figure out?" asked Audrey finally.

"What Randolph does with all his T-shirt sleeves after he cuts them off?" asked Louis.

"Ha ha ha. I can't figure out why Jare would lie about his reason for not playing in the NFL," said Audrey.

"Yeah, why does he have to keep saying he had better things to do?" asked Kate. "What football player has better things to do than the NFL?"

"Hold on," I said. Because as soon as Audrey brought up Jare and the NFL again, I scanned a few pages of the old NFL record book where I used to find facts to amuse Hardy Gillooly. "Jare isn't lying about his *reasons*."

"He's not?" said Audrey. She sounded dubious. "He sure looks like it to me."

"He's lying about *playing*," I said. "Because actually, he *didn't* skip the NFL. He got drafted by the Cleveland Browns, and he started at quarterback the first game of his rookie season!"

"Then why does he keep telling us he didn't play?" asked Louis.

"Because," I said, turning the page of the record book in my head, "he was the worst quarterback ever to suit up in the National Football League."

"How can somebody be the *worst* quarterback?" asked Kate.

"You have to be really special. Especially bad. Like Jare. He holds the all-time record for single-game futility," I replied. It was all there at the bottom of the last page of the chapter on quarterbacks. I'd never noticed it before. I guess I'd never looked. Because what fun would records like this have been for Hardy Gillooly? Hardy was all about winners. He wouldn't have wanted to hear about Jare. "During his first and only NFL appearance, Jared Eastbrook threw a total of four passes. Each was intercepted and two were returned for touchdowns, all in the first half. Eastbrook was benched before the start of the third quarter and did not take the field again. Eastbrook sustained an unsubstantiated toe injury in practice the following week, and subsequently never played football again."

"Wow," said Louis quietly. "Poor Jare."

"Yeah," I agreed. "It's almost enough to make you feel sorry for him."

"Almost," said Kate.

"But not quite," threw in Audrey.

"He's not actually one of the all-time winners. He's one

of the all-time losers," observed Louis.

"Maybe that explains a few things about Jare," I said.

"How?" asked Audrey.

"This is his playground, right?" I asked.

"Yeah," said Kate. "Like we talked about when Daphne knocked over the hoodoo. This is his playground, and he's the bully."

"So why do people turn into playground bullies?" I asked.

"Because they're losers!" said Louis. "They hate themselves, they hate their lives, and they take over the playground and act like the king."

"And the bigger the loser, the bigger the bully, and the bigger the bully, the meaner the king," continued Kate.

"Plus," added Audrey, "if the desert really *is* Jare's kingdom, the point of his weird, lonely life is to protect it. And Daphne is a barbarian trying to destroy it."

"Which is why Jare totally flamed out on her," said Louis. "Yeah. All this does explain a few things about him. . . . Hey," he said, spotting something on the ground in the distance. "What's that?" Slowly he made his way through the clumps of desiccated bunchgrass to stand beside a tiny barrel cactus with enormous yellow flowers. Kate followed him and reached down to pluck off the fingerless black glove impaled on the spines.

"Don't!" Louis reminded her. "We have to leave it for Jare. Let's go get him."

"Let's just yell," said Kate. "Nobody's very far away yet. Plug your ears, Louis."

"Hey! Over here!" shouted Audrey into the distance. "Jare! Everybody!"

For half a mile around, we could see glimpses of searchers turning in the brush to head in our direction.

"What?" said Jare to Audrey as he arrived. Audrey pointed at the glove on the cactus. "Now that," he said, "is definitely Daphne's. Nobody else would be stupid enough to wear gloves while making her desert getaway." He stuffed it in his pocket and glanced at the dropping sun. "Who's making our dinner tonight?" he asked.

"Me," said Edie in a small voice, "and . . . Daphne?"

"Figures," grumbled Jare. "You," he said, pointing at Audrey, "are pinch cooking. Get going."

As Edie and Audrey made their way back to camp, Jare spread out his map on the ground, weighting the corners with stones. Then he used jagged pebbles to mark the three places we'd found Daphne memorabilia. "Look. All you have to do is connect the dots. She was walking in a straight line." He traced a trail between pebbles. "She went on for a while, got hot, and found herself a nice bush to crawl under, not far from where we're standing." He tapped our location on the map and glanced around, as if he expected to see Daphne crouched under a creosote plant nearby.

"Then we hafta—let's go—now we can find her!" spluttered Randolph, gesturing helplessly in the direction Daphne had been walking.

"Nope. Time to head back," said Jare, smacking his hands together briskly.

"What?" shrieked Randolph. "We're not going to go get her? You just said we know for sure which way she's headed! She's under a bush! She's not far! Let's find her!" Jare had to grab Randolph's belt to keep him from running off across the desert.

"Keep your pants on, Slick," said Jare. "I don't need the rest of you tearing out there getting lost too."

"But . . . this doesn't make any sense!" cried Randolph. "You just had us wandering all over the place looking for Daphne's trail—and we found it. So now why can't we just go find her?"

As much as I hated to admit it, Randolph had a point. Jare's thinking didn't really add up.

But Jare carefully ignored Randolph's point. He checked the sun. It was dropping toward the horizon. He glanced around like he was memorizing the spot. "We'll give her another night," he muttered, almost to himself. "Tomorrow, if I have to call the sheriff, I'll know right where to send him."

CHAPTER THIRTEEN

Audrey Alcott

El Viaje a la Confianza

THAT NIGHT, I DREAMED THAT a grizzly bear in a football helmet was charging toward me down a steep hill, and I stood petrified, my brain whirring like an eggbeater in a desperate attempt to remember what you're supposed to do when a bear comes after you (Run? Scream? Curl up in a ball? Climb a tree? Punch it on the nose?). And just before the bear attacked, when I could see its glittering black eyes and its four long, white, needle-sharp canines, the bear stopped, stood on its hind legs, and said, in Jare's arrogant voice, "Hillsdale, Montana, Grizzlies," and then another voice, one I recognized but couldn't place, came from all around me, loud and echoing. "Montana, Montana, Montana," it said.

I woke up still hearing it inside my head, that unidentifiable voice saying that single word, and then, suddenly, the voice wasn't unidentifiable at all, and even though it was the middle of the night and even though I'd just been sound asleep, inside my head it was broad daylight and I was so awake, I tingled. I knew. I *knew.* And I had to tell someone right that second.

As quietly as I could, my heart galloping, my fingers shaking, I unzipped my tent and was just starting to climb out when I saw them: directly in front of me and not three feet away, a pair of hiking boots, big ones, and I was just thinking how weird it was that someone had left boots outside my tent when I saw the boots were on feet, connected to legs, and my galloping heart seemed to stop dead. *Oh, no, oh, no, oh, help, it's him!* I thought, and threw myself backward into my tent, my fingers fumbling to zip the flap of it back up, as if there were a hope in the world that that flimsy barrier could save me.

It wasn't until I heard a voice whisper, "Audrey! It's me!" that I realized the legs attached to those feet inside those boots were far too skinny to be Jare's, and a flood of relief washed through me. In a flash, I was out of my tent, telling Aaron, "You've got some really big feet, do you know that?" and, Aaron looking every bit as startled as I'd just felt, was saying, "Yes."

"What are you doing out here?" I demanded. "I was just coming to get you."

"I remembered something," he said breathlessly. "Something important."

His face was vivid and sharp, and maybe it was just the moonlight falling on him, but he seemed to shine with excitement.

Astonished, I said, "Same here!" I started to say more when Aaron put a hand on my arm to stop me.

"Wait," he said. "Let's get Kate and have a meeting in Louis's tent."

We woke up Kate with ease, and then the three of us argued in whispers over how best to awaken the earplugged Louis without his screaming bloody murder and rousing the entire camp. Finally Kate just said, "Enough. Leave it to me," unzipped Louis's tent, and climbed in. Aaron and I hovered outside, watching. Louis was sound asleep. He looked peaceful in a way that he never did when he was awake, a sign that his air mattress was working the exact kind of magic we'd hoped it would. Very, very gently, Kate touched one fingertip to Louis's left arm, and as soon as he stirred, she whispered, almost inaudibly, a tiny, velvet sound: "It's Kate." Maybe because she was so small or so still or because she just had a knack for making people feel safe, Louis didn't scream. He sat up fast, blinked hard a few times, and pulled out his earplugs.

"Oh, hi," he said, smoothing down his hair, which

really sort of needed it. Louis had told us that he hated having long hair because he was terrified of things getting caught in it, like burrs or flying grasshoppers or bats, but that he hated haircuts more. "All that tugging and touching and the sound of the scissors, like swords clashing right next to my ears," he'd said, shuddering.

Once we were all settled in, I looked at Aaron, who said, "You first."

I was so eager to tell what I'd figured out that I didn't even bother to be polite and say he should go first. "Thanks," I said. "Okay. Do you happen to have a map of Montana inside your head?"

"Well, sure, along with all the other states," said Aaron. "There was a really good U.S. map in my fifth-grade classroom. I looked at it a lot. I especially liked the names of the rivers. There's the Tugaloo, the Passagassawakeag, the Scuppernong, the—"

"Aaron!" I said.

"Sorry."

"Where's Hillsdale, Montana?" I asked.

"Why is that name familiar?" asked Kate, knitting her brows.

I held up a finger, signaling her to wait.

"It's in the northern part of the state," said Aaron. "So far up it's almost in—"

"Canada!" I finished triumphantly.

"Well, I was going to say Grasslands National Park, Saskatchewan," said Aaron smugly. "But I guess Canada works." Then his eyes lit up, and I could tell he had just realized what I was getting at. "Oh!"

"What?" asked Louis.

"It can't be a coincidence," I said to Aaron.

"What?" asked Kate.

"Time for your Daphne imitation, Aaron," I said.

" 'My witch mom hired some fancy lawyer who tricked my dad into giving up custody of me. But as soon as he can work it out, he's totally taking me back. We'll go live in this amazing little town in Montana where he grew up. It's so far north that it's practically Canada. Which means I'll never see my mom again, thank god. She hates the cold—' " He stopped.

I realized my jaw had dropped a little. It happened a lot: just when I thought I was getting used to Aaron's memory, he'd throw me for a loop. "You know, that really is amazing."

Aaron's face fell, just the tiniest bit. "Thanks."

Quickly I said, "It's not even close to the coolest thing about you, but I can see how Hardy Giloolly might have gotten that impression."

Aaron shrugged again, but this time he looked happy.

"So," said Kate slowly, "you're saying that Jare might have known Daphne's dad?"

"Yes!" I said. "I mean, what are the chances that Jare and Daphne's dad, who must be about the same age, both just happened to grow up in small towns in northern Montana, right near the Canadian border?"

We all looked at Aaron.

"Well, out of the fifty states, Montana *is* one of the least populous. It's ranked forty-fourth, and the majority of Montanans live in cities like Billings, Bozeman, Butte, and Helena, and while I don't know the population of Hillsdale, I do know that some parts of Montana have a population density of fewer than four people per square mile, so . . ."

"It's *very* unlikely!" I finished. "Which means that Jare must have planned the entire thing."

"Planned to do . . . *something* to Daphne?" asked Louis, wincing.

"What's Daphne's last name?" I asked.

"Pepin," said Aaron. "It's written in magic marker on her backpack."

"Well, I'm guessing that this Pepin was an enemy of Jare's from back home, and when he figured out that Daphne was Pepin's daughter, he decided to make Pepin pay," I said.

"By killing Daphne?" asked Louis. He winced again,

and at the word "killing," the rest of us winced right along with him.

"Look, I agree that it's hard to imagine Jare as a murderer, but maybe that's just because it's hard to imagine any real person you know as a murderer," I said. "Maybe he was just trying to scare her and left her in the desert alone, or maybe he's hiding her someplace for a while to scare Pepin. Or maybe Pepin's rich, and Jare's planning to hold Daphne for ransom. I don't know. I just can't believe there's not a connection between Jare and Daphne's dad, and if there is, I think whatever happened wasn't a spur-of-the-moment thing. It was planned. And if it was planned, well, that makes it much more creepy."

"It *was* planned," said Aaron. "Definitely."

"You sound so sure," said Kate, surprised.

"I am sure. Remember when Jare put those pebbles down on the map, one for each piece of evidence we'd found that Daphne had been there?"

"Yes. They made a straight line," I said.

"After we went to bed, I couldn't fall asleep because I kept thinking about those three pebbles, and I kept telling myself to connect the dots, connect the dots. Then, out of nowhere, I remembered where I'd seen them before!" said Aaron.

"The pebbles?" asked Louis.

"Not pebbles. Back then, they were dots, in purple colored pencil, marking those same three locations," said Aaron.

"Back when?" I asked.

"Back when Enod baked his knees. Remember when Jare ran up over that arroyo and dropped all his maps? I picked them up, and the one on top was folded exactly to the part of the desert where Jare sent us to search for Daphne, and there were the purple dots."

We all sat, letting this sink in.

"That was well over a week ago," I said, and one of those now-familiar shivers went up my spine.

"Gosh, you were right, Audrey," said Kate somberly. "Whatever happened to Daphne, Jare did plan it."

"He planted those clues to make it look like she'd run away," said Louis. "And he chose our team for that search area because he knew we were the best at finding stuff."

"Daphne was never at any of those places," said Kate in a small, scared voice. "Right now, it feels like she isn't anywhere at all."

"And Jare had her stuff," said Louis. I could tell he was trying to keep his breathing in check.

"Daphne wore that bandanna all the time," said Kate. "She hated Jare. She wouldn't have just given him her stuff."

"Which means he took it," said Aaron. "Either he stole

the glove and bandanna or he took them by force. Or—" He stopped.

"He took them after she was in no position to resist," I said grimly.

We stared at each other, horror dawning on all our faces.

"We need to tell someone," said Aaron. "Now. Today."

"Even though there's no cell phone service here, Jare couldn't spend six weeks in the wilderness with no way of communicating with the outside world," I said. "He must have some kind of phone. We just need to find it."

"Whatever we do, though, we can't let Jare know we know," said Louis, his breath getting shallow. "He'll disappear us too."

"He might try, but even Jare can't make *fifteen* people disappear," I said.

"He can't?" asked Louis hopefully.

"Fifteen?" asked Kate.

I leaned in. "Listen. I have a plan."

We stayed in Louis's tent with the flap open until the sky turned from black to that soft mouse gray that means the sun is about to rise, and then—as Louis tiptoed to the far end of the campsite to keep an eye on Jare—Aaron, Kate, and I began to wake the other campers, all but Randolph.

Staying calm and matter-of-fact, we told them about our theory that Jare had disappeared Daphne—either permanently or temporarily—and we also told them our evidence: the three purple dots, the Montana connection. No one freaked out completely, although a girl named Frankie started to cry and Kevin Larkspur looked like he might throw up. Edie and Cyrus weren't surprised; they said they'd both had a gut feeling that Jare had done it—whatever "it" was.

"We need the two of you for the next part of our plan," I told them. "Are you okay with that?"

"Sure," said Cyrus. He nodded so hard, the springy black curls all over his head danced.

"Definitely," said Edie. "I mean, it's not like I've missed being called E-death, but a grown man can't go around killing kids."

"Good," said Aaron and I together.

"Let me ask you something, Edie," I said. "I hope it doesn't come to this, but what if you got one of those shots you had when you ate the Worcestershire sauce when you weren't actually having an allergic reaction?"

Edie gave me a funny look, but she said, "Nothing too bad, I don't think. I'd probably just get jittery. If that's what I need to do to help, I'll do it."

"I think you could pretty easily convince him that you

didn't need it, but just in case, I wanted to ask," I said, and Aaron and I told them the plan.

After about fifteen minutes, Louis came jogging back.

"He was already up when I got there," he said. "Acting kind of weird. Pacing around like a lion in the zoo."

"Cage stereotypy," said Aaron. "Abnormal, repetitive motor behaviors often exhibited by animals in captivity and thought to be a result of stress and insufficiently complex environments."

"Aaron," I said sternly.

"I know, I know," said Aaron, scratching his head. "All right. Jare's not in a cage, but maybe he's . . . stressed? Anxious? Worried?"

"It sounds that way," I said. "I just wish we knew what he was worried about."

Louis gulped. "Uh, you think he suspects that we know?"

"How could he? Maybe he feels guilty. Or maybe something went wrong with his plan. But we can't think about that now," I said. "Look, everyone's in on it, the whole camp, except for Randolph, who just can't be trusted. Jare can't fight off all of us, can he?"

"Nope," said Kate, shoving up her sleeves. Her black eyes glinted.

"Fight?" said Louis, in a quavering voice. "You mean—fight-fight?"

"I sincerely hope not," I said.

"Edie and Cyrus are on board with the plan," said Aaron. "Now we just wait until everyone's eating breakfast."

I took a deep breath. One by one, I met each person's eyes. Kate's were fierce and black; Louis's were wide, scared, and desert-sky blue; Aaron's were as bright brown and hopeful as ever.

"Are we ready?" I asked them.

Kate put out her hand; without a hesitation or a flinch, Louis placed his on top of hers; Aaron laid his on top of Louis's. I lifted my hand but let it hover for a moment. *This isn't friendship,* I reassured myself. *This is teamwork. Teamwork is different.* I set my hand firmly down on top of Aaron's, and before I realized I was doing it, I squeezed, then he squeezed Louis's, and suddenly, we were all holding on.

"The Fearless Four," said Kate fiercely. "All for one, and one for all."

"There's no I in team," declared Aaron.

"Except in Spanish," I added.

We all smiled.

“Dudes, we got this!” said Louis, and for the first time since we’d woken him up, his voice wasn’t shaking at all.

After we were all settled in eating oatmeal with dried fruit, Jare went back to his tent the way he always did, possibly to devour a spectacular breakfast created from his private stash of food, possibly to wear a new gully in the ground with more cage-stereotypy pacing. I wondered if Jare was like the guilt-ridden guy in the Edgar Allan Poe story who was plagued by the sound of his murder victim’s heart; then I wondered if Daphne even had a heart; then I felt instantly bad about wondering this. When Daphne was around, almost nobody could stand her, but now that she was gone, the other campers and I felt a kind of solidarity with her. Like, sure, she was an evil, cold-blooded bully, but she was *our* evil, cold-blooded bully. And no matter who she was, she didn’t deserve to be disappeared.

As we’d planned, Aaron and I sat at the far edge of the group, as close to Jare’s tent as we could without obviously invading his space. Cyrus and Edie sat at the opposite end of camp, while Kate and Louis were stationed at different points in between. When we’d all been eating for about five minutes, I signaled Kate, who signaled Cyrus, who ran across the campsite toward Jare’s tent. As he passed us, he shut one of his licorice-black eyes in a conspiratorial wink, and Aaron and I gave him a quick thumbs-up.

"Jare, Jare!" cried Cyrus as he ran. "Something's wrong with Edie!"

In a couple of minutes, Cyrus reappeared with Jare. As they walked, Cyrus hovered around Jare like a dragonfly, talking a mile a minute. Jare wasn't exactly rushing, but I also noticed that he was moving a lot faster than he had the last time Edie had been in trouble.

"She didn't want me to tell you," said Cyrus, wiping at his eyes as he and Jare passed us, "because she wasn't sure how bad it was going to be, and she didn't want to inconvenience you for nothing. But I'm really worried!"

He gave a convincing sob, but after they'd passed, he darted a mischievous look at us over his shoulder. Louis watched until Jare and Cyrus were all the way on the other side of the campsite and then nodded at us. Casually, we set down our plates and slipped away.

Jare's tent was big enough for us to stand inside, and the rain cap was off, so plenty of sunlight filtered through the side mesh. Luckily, it appeared that Jare hadn't repacked his backpack yet. Sitting outside the pack were some smaller sacks, a few boxlike containers, and what looked like a tiny plastic suitcase, but that was it. As big as he was, Jare could carry more than the rest of us, but not a lot more.

"You start on that side, and I'll start over here," I told Aaron.

"We need to move fast," said Aaron, already opening up one of the bags. "And listen for Kate's whistle."

"You're sure you don't know what a satellite phone looks like?" I asked.

"Nope. Sorry."

I opened a metal box with a strong latch that looked like a miniature version of the bear-proof food containers we'd seen at the various campsites. The latch was complicated, and my nervous fingers struggled clumsily with it for what felt like an excruciatingly long time before the box popped open. When I saw what was inside, I stifled a laugh. There was some fresh fruit, but mostly the box was full of Twinkies, honeybuns, and single-serving boxes of Froot Loops.

"You found something?" asked Aaron.

"Just Jare's secret junk-food stash," I said. "Would it be wrong to steal a Twinkie?"

"Definitely," said Aaron.

For several more minutes, we frantically searched.

"There's nothing in the stuff on my side of the tent that looks like a phone," said Aaron.

"Same here," I said.

Then I opened the tiny plastic suitcase, and it was not

just a phone but what looked like a mini communication station.

“Found it!” I said.

“Okay, let’s get out of here and call!” said Aaron.

Our campsite was at the base of a steep hill, and at the bottom of it, in back of Jare’s tent, sat a big boulder that appeared to have rolled down a long time before. Aaron and I crouched behind it and opened the satellite phone case again. It seemed oddly old-fashioned and complex, but in a not-high-tech way. There was a compass-looking gadget, switches, buttons, and some antenna-type pieces that unfolded.

“This looks like it’s from the Revolutionary War or something,” I whispered in exasperation, and then I snapped, “And, no, you don’t have to tell me that the phone wasn’t yet invented during the Revolutionary War era.”

“I wasn’t going to,” said Aaron.

“Sorry. Rushing makes me grumpy.”

“This sure doesn’t look like any phone I’ve ever seen,” said Aaron.

He picked up the handset, held it to his ear, and shook his head. He pushed some buttons. “Nothing. There must be an on switch somewhere or something.”

I started messing with the buttons and switches on the phone, desperately trying to make it work. “Ack! He’s going to show up any minute!" I hissed.

And that's when a voice from above said, "I'm already here."

Aaron and I both jerked our heads back to look, and instantly I felt like I'd been punched in the stomach. There was Randolph, standing with his hands on his hips and smiling the nastiest smile I'd ever seen.

"You guys are *so busted*," he said through his smile. "I can't wait to see what Jare does when he finds out you were trying to steal his stuff."

Aaron stood up. "You don't understand," he said.

Randolph's smile vanished. "Shut up. You think I'm stupid? You think I don't understand?"

"That's not what he meant," I said. I stayed crouched by the phone. "Work!" I told it. "Just work!"

"Get up, dumb girl," said Randolph.

"No," I said. "I need to figure this out."

Just then, a high, piercing whistle sliced the air. Kate. Jare was on his way!

"Listen. Please," I said, looking up at Randolph. "You can't tell Jare."

Randolph gave a snide chuckle and put his hands on the sides of his mouth, as if to yell.

"Audrey, we have to tell him what's going on," said Aaron, talking fast and seeming to catch sight of something over Randolph's head. "Jare's coming, and he's mad. Really mad. I can tell by the way he's walking."

"You don't have to tell me nothing," said Randolph. "I already know what's going on."

"Yes, tell him!" I said, banging on the phone in frustration.

Aaron blurted it out: "We think Jare killed Daphne. We're trying to call 911."

Randolph grabbed Aaron by the front of his shirt and yanked him closer. "What? Liar! Daphne ran away!"

Aaron said, "Oh, shoot. Jare sees us. He *sees us.* Take the phone and run, Audrey!"

I slammed the tiny suitcase shut. There was no time to latch it. I jumped to my feet, getting a glimpse of Jare striding toward us, kicking up dust, looking like a mad bull—or a herd of mad bulls—and I tucked the suitcase under my arm like a football and took off running in the only direction there was to run: straight uphill.

"Hey!" I heard Jare yell, his voice terrifyingly close. "What the heck is going on?"

I glanced over my shoulder and saw Aaron tug himself free from Randolph.

"Don't look back!" he shouted, waving me onward. "I'm right behind you! Just go, go, go!"

Adrenaline surged through me like electricity. It was

punishing terrain, but I realized that being smaller and nimbler than Jare, I had a better chance of outrunning him on a stony, uneven uphill than I would have on the flat desert floor. It occurred to me that I had no plan, no direction, no idea what I would do even if I could manage to lose Jare. It also occurred to me that I was literally running for my life. But I shoved those thoughts away and tried to make my body into a machine whose only job was upward, upward, upward.

I could hear footfalls behind me, and I prayed that they were Aaron's, not Jare's. Aaron had gotten a pretty good head start, but Jare was so big, so strong, so angry. Sweat trickled into my eyes and burned them, and once I fell and felt the sharp rocks cut my one free palm, but I kept going. When I got to the top of the hill, I was so relieved that I pitched forward and almost landed flat on my face. But I scrambled up and allowed myself one glance behind me. Aaron was about twenty yards back, and Jare wasn't far behind.

"He's getting closer!" I screamed.

"Keep going!" shouted Aaron.

"Stop!" bellowed Jare.

My breathing was loud and raucous in my ears, and I was bone tired. For a moment, I considered just letting Jare catch me, because at least I'd get a rest before he did—but then I thought of my parents, how much they loved me, and suddenly it was like all of home was inside my head: Janie and the hallways at school and Dean Amory and the cool, green woods. And I understood that I liked my life, that I wasn't anywhere close to done with it, and I felt this knowledge flow like strength into my legs and arms and back, and before I even knew I'd gotten up, I was running, running across the flat mesa at the top of the hill, my legs pumping, my ponytail swinging, the phone still safely under my arm.

But then a terrible, unexpected thing happened: the mesa ended. I skidded to a stop just inches from the edge and gazed desolately down. It wasn't a cliff, exactly, but it was such a steep, drastic drop and so pitted and stony that I knew there was no way I could ever run down it without breaking my neck.

"Audrey, keep running!"

I spun around to see Aaron tearing across the mesa, with Jare so close—no more than twenty feet—behind him.

"I can't! It's too steep!" I cried. I swiveled my head crazily from side to side, looking for an escape route that just wasn't there. I could have taken off in another direction, but I knew that running around the top of the hill made no sense. Jare would catch me in the end.

"Aaron, he's right behind you!" I screamed.

Then Aaron did an amazing thing. He stopped. And spun around. He ducked his head and, in a low crouch, ran *toward* Jare instead of away from him, toward the furious, charging animal Jare had become, and he threw all of his gangly weight against the center of Jare's wide chest. I saw the shock on Jare's face at impact, but he didn't fall, just staggered backward. Aaron was the one who fell, flopped sideways like a rag doll, and lay still, and I was afraid his neck was broken and wanted to watch for him to move or get up, but there was Jare, not running now, but striding toward me, wild-eyed, unstoppable.

"Everyone knows!" I shouted. "We told everyone in the camp what you did! Even if you kill me, you won't get away with it."

"Give me the phone!" boomed Jare. His hands were clenched into huge fists at his sides.

"It's over! Use the phone to turn yourself in!"

Jare was close now, close enough to push me over the edge. Emptied of hope, I just stood my ground and waited for the shove. But the shove didn't come. Jare reached out and yanked the phone away from me.

"Stupid kids!" he spat, and just like that, all my fear vanished. It was replaced by a cold fury.

"Yeah, we're kids," I said. "Look at yourself. A big guy

like you, going around hurting kids. You're pathetic."

Jare narrowed his eyes. "What?"

"Is that what Pepin thought too?" I asked him. "Back in high school? Is that why you hated him so much?"

Jare's face changed. "Pepin? George Pepin?"

I heard a shout come from the other end of the mesa, but my eyes stayed locked on Jare's.

"Did he call you a coward?" I said. "Humiliate you? Is that why you killed his daughter?"

Confusion clouded Jare's eyes. He shook his head. "What? No. You don't understand."

"What did Pepin do to make you hate him so much?"

Jare straightened and said, "George Pepin is my best friend. I would never hurt him or his kid."

Truth. *Truth.* It hit me so hard I gasped. Even though what he was saying made no sense at all, it was stone-cold true.

Jare slumped and rubbed his forehead. "I was trying to help. I was only trying to help."

It happened so fast. The words were barely out of Jare's mouth before: pounding footsteps, Randolph hurtling headlong across the mesa, howling, "You! Killed! Her! You! Killed! Her!" He was unhinged, clawing the air as he ran, a human torpedo, headed straight for Jare, who didn't even have time to turn around to see what was coming.

"No!" I screamed.

But it was too late. Randolph hit Jare squarely between the shoulder blades. The phone flew over the edge first; then, with a long, awful, drawn-out "Ahhh!" Jare fell too. I thought Randolph would roll down next, but he landed with a thud at my feet, and everything in the world went dead still and wretchedly silent. I covered my face with my hands, scared to look, and eventually felt someone standing next to me. I uncovered my eyes to see Aaron, his lip bleeding, his terrified eyes trained on the downward slope. I was so glad he was alive that I put my arms around him and buried my face in his shoulder. He didn't move, just stood as if frozen, staring down the hill.

"Is it bad?" I asked.

In a hoarse whisper, Aaron said, "Bad."

I looked. Scattered along the side of the hill were pieces of the satellite phone, and at the bottom, his body oddly twisted and motionless, the kind of motionless that looks permanent, lay Jare.

CHAPTER FOURTEEN

Aaron Archer

El Viaje a la Confianza

IT TOOK LESS THAN THREE seconds for the desert to shatter Jare. At first I was afraid it had killed him. But after we scrambled down the slope, I saw his chest rising and falling and I could feel his pulse, and as Audrey crouched next to me, his eyelids fluttered open. "I can't walk," he whispered. I could tell he was in agony from the way the skin around his eyes had gone white under his tan. He glanced over my shoulder. "Somebody make Louis sit before he falls down," he gasped, pointing at Louis, who'd staggered down the hill behind us.

Louis did his best not to collapse at the spectacle of Jare's leg, which protruded at an angle it had no natural right to protrude at. The rest of the campers, who must've gotten curious about the shouting, began to trickle over the edge of the embankment. Randolph had disappeared.

Edie handed Louis her water bottle and sat him on the nearest rock.

"Who," Jare said, "thinks they are tough?"

We all glanced at each other. Since Jare had made it crystal clear that he didn't think any of us were tough, it seemed like sort of a weird question. "I know," said Jare softly. "That's kind of a weird question. But I need help. And it's gonna take somebody tough."

"I'm tough," Kate volunteered.

"Kate *is* tough," agreed Enod.

"Enod," said Jare, "run back to camp for the first-aid kit." Jare turned to Kate. "Okay, Little Miss Sun—okay, Kate," he said, his eyes fluttering upward in agony as he dug a Swiss Army knife out of his pocket. "Ready?"

Kate nodded.

"I'm pretty sure it's a compound fracture," said Jare. "'Cause of all the blood. So could you please slice off my jeans above the knee? We need to have a look." Kate did it. She tried to not hurt him. What she slowly uncovered brought tears to her eyes, but she resolutely sawed through the fabric and dropped the shredded pieces of blue jean in the dust beside her, and when she was done, she waited for instructions.

Unfortunately, Jare had passed out from the pain.

"What do we do?" asked Kate, keeping her eyes off Jare's leg.

I'd once read part of a Red Cross first-aid manual while recovering in the lifeguard shack at Splashview Swim Club after one of the guards had to "rescue" me because I did such a wicked belly flop, I ran into a little trouble swimming to the ladder. The pictures of compound fractures were so horrible I could barely look at them, because a compound fracture happens when not only is your leg broken so crazily it bends like you have an extra, sideways knee, but also the jagged pieces of bone stab through your muscle and rip a gash in your skin from the inside. Like Jare's. The lifeguard, who was a little peeved at me anyway because I'd made him jump in and ruin his hair, saw what I was staring at and took the manual away, but not before he turned green.

"I don't know," I said. "We have to wait for Jare to wake up."

Enod called down from the lip of the drop and tossed the first-aid kit to us.

Slowly Jare stirred. "Take this," whispered Jare, handing Kate a huge gauze square from the kit. "Press on the gash as hard as you can. Keep mashing until I stop bleeding. I might pass out again. Actually, I kinda hope I do. But keep on it. Only . . . your hands are sort of small. You're gonna need help."

"I'll help," said Kevin Larkspur. "I want to be a doctor when I grow up."

This was another thing Jare would've scoffed at ordinarily, but things were not ordinary. "Good man," murmured Jare as they pressed the gauze against the break. "Hoo. That hurts." As they squeezed, he closed his eyes and fell silent, but he stayed conscious. After a while, the bleeding slowed, and Jare handed Kate another square of gauze, a tube of antiseptic, and a roll of adhesive tape. "Wrap that baby on there tight, and maybe we can keep enough germs out to stop gangrene from setting in," he said.

"Gangrene?" cried Kate. "We have to get you out of here. Quick."

"We have to get us *all* out of here," rasped Jare. "Quick."

"How are we going to do that?" asked Audrey.

"*You* are going to do that," replied Jare. "By applying the lessons you've learned along el Viaje a la Confianza." Maybe we didn't look like we thought this would be a real game changer. "Oh, come on," he cried, gritting his teeth as he propped his leg on a rock made of sea-snail fossils. "Just because I'm a loser and a blowhard doesn't mean I haven't taught you anything!"

I guess I looked surprised when he called himself a

loser. "Aaron. Come on. With a brain like yours, you've gotta remember my statistics. Dontcha? Then you know. It's okay to say it. I'm a loser."

"You're a loser!" piped up Cyrus.

"I didn't mean say it right this second," muttered Jare.

"Sorry," said Cyrus.

"I hope you guys realize something. You're fortunate. Blessed in a way I never was," Jare went on. "Things are hard for you. All the time. You're lucky."

"Then I guess *I've* had about all the luck one guy can stand," cracked Louis.

Jare started to laugh, and then he froze and turned green. And decided not to laugh. "Sadly," he wheezed, "I always had it easy. Easy in Hillside, Montana. Easy in Ann Arbor, Michigan. And then one day in Cleveland, Ohio, when things got tough, it took me less than half an hour to become professional football's all-time loser. You guys, though, you've been up against it your whole lives. You had it rough back home, and once you got here, I made sure to keep the problems coming. This might be hard to believe, but even when I was acting like a colossal jerk, I was teaching you something: not to fold in the clutch. And I guess today is when we find out if you absorbed my lesson."

"Whoa, Jare. You were a good guy all along?" called Randolph, gazing down from the precipice. "This is blowing my mind." Smashing Jare's leg hadn't exactly transformed him into a model camper. In fact, he seemed like more of a jerk than ever.

"The flatulence of an underfed gnat," called back Jare, "would blow your mind." He started to laugh again, and grimaced, and turned white. "Note to self. Laughing. Really hurts." Shifting to find a position he could bear, Jare spread out a map. "Audrey and Aaron, you're going for help. There's a ranch twelve miles up the trail with two cowhands living in it. It'll be a slog, but all you've got to do is stick to the path and keep walking. Two good people should make it before sundown. The rest of you are going to strike camp and bring it down here, since I can't go back up that hill. And we'll all hold the fort until Audrey and Aaron send help."

"But what if Audrey and Aaron don't make it in time?" asked Edie. "We've barely got enough water for the rest of today."

"I know," said Jare. "I was planning for us all to be at the ranch by tonight. Our next supply cache is there."

After a pause that gave me a chance to think about how far we were from help, and how tired, hungry, thirsty, and puny we were in a land that had been bone-dry and full of rocks hot enough to kill mastodons and mountain lions for millions of years, Jare said, "I think we've got a high likelihood of survival. But we can't make even one more mistake. And by 'we,' I mean myself. I definitely made a mistake or two."

"Does one of your mistakes explain where Daphne is?" asked Audrey.

Jare sighed. The last of the bluster leaked out of him as he slumped against the rocky bluff. "I was trying to *help* Daphne. And her dad. He's my old buddy George Pepin. George had a close call this spring. Barrier Reef. Unruly sharks. Caused him to turn over a new leaf. Felt bad about how he'd handed over custody of Daphne all those years ago without a fight, regretted the way he'd neglected her ever since. Wanted to make amends, treat her to a summer of adventure. And of course, that mother of hers wasn't gonna let it happen.

"So we hatched a plan where Daphne could rendezvous with him from here, make it look like she ran off. I faked the trail in the wrong direction in case the authorities decided to get involved, and I made sure you guys discovered it. Meanwhile, Daphne was gonna hike the other way on an old sheep path. Her dad planned to kayak down the river to meet her at the trailhead by an abandoned farm, and then, right before they vamoosed to Mexico, they were gonna call me on George's satellite phone. I thought our plan was pure gold."

"Except for one little detail: it was a felony. Kidnapping. Her dad doesn't have custody," I pointed out.

"I know Daphne's mom. She'd never prosecute George, because even if she thinks he's a loser, she knows Daphne loves him. If he went to prison, it would break Daphne's heart," replied Jare.

"And another little detail," threw in Enod. "It didn't work."

"There *is* that," allowed Jare.

"So how long ago were you expecting their call?" asked Audrey.

For the first time ever, Jare's voice was so quiet, I could hardly hear it. "About twenty-four hours ago."

"Something happened to Daphne," said Louis.

"She must not have made it to the rendezvous point," Jare added wearily.

"How do you know something didn't happen to her *dad*?" asked Cyrus. "Maybe *he* never made it."

"Dude kayaked the length of the Amazon. Twice. Once in each direction," said Jare. "He's solid."

"So why didn't he call when Daphne didn't show?" I asked.

"Good question," replied Jare, but he didn't really seem to think there was anything good about it. "I think she must've gotten behind schedule. But guess what: the Terminator up there smashed my phone, so there's no way to tell." He pointed to Randolph, squatting on his rocky perch.

"What if George got to the meeting point, and when Daphne wasn't there, he went looking for her?" asked Audrey. "And got lost? What if they're *both* in trouble?"

"Why are you asking all these questions?" shot back Jare.

"Because *we're* going to find Daphne," I said. "And her dad too, if he's lost with her." Audrey nodded.

"Our whole team," added Kate.

"Right," agreed Louis.

"Then who's going to the ranch?" asked Jare.

"Enod and Kevin," Audrey replied. "You said two good people can make it to the ranch by midnight. Enod and Kevin are better than good. They're great."

"Thanks, Audrey," said Enod.

"Don't get all mushy on me, Enod," said Audrey.

"Sorry," said Enod.

"I can't let you guys go after Daphne," said Jare. "I already lost one camper. I can't lose four more."

"We're going," I said.

"No," said Jare.

"How are you going to stop us?" wondered Louis.

"That's a conundrum, all right," admitted Jare, gazing at his leg. "I could order the other campers to band together and detain you." He gazed around at Cyrus, Edie, and the rest, who stared back at him with wide, round eyes. "Or not. Okay. If you gotta go, you gotta go."

We inventoried the water left in camp. Six and a half gallons: three to share among the ten people staying behind, a gallon and a half for Kevin and Enod, and two gallons for Audrey, Kate, Louis, and me. We figured this was fair.

"Enod," said Jare. "You and your buddy keep your brains in gear, and this time tomorrow, everybody will be enjoying a nice tall glass of ice water delivered by law-enforcement helicopter."

He turned to Audrey, Louis, Kate, and me. From his front pocket, he dug a tattered map. "This isn't much good," he said. "All it shows is where Daphne is supposed to be. Which, as we know, is actually where she isn't. But it's better than nothing. Now be careful. I really couldn't stand it if I lost any more of you. And Kate, you can leave the railroad spike here."

"Thanks, Jare," said Kate. "You're turning into a big softy."

"Searing pain will do that to you," replied Jare.

As we slowly crossed the dusty pan in the direction Daphne had taken, searching for some sign of her, I could feel the ground rise a tiny bit to the left and to the right, as if, out there somewhere so far away I couldn't even see it, the desert was shrugging its shoulders. And as we pushed on, I realized our route was leading us into a vast downward funnel as big as an entire county back in Pennsylvania. Soon I could see stony hills miles and miles away to the east and west, rising higher and closing in on us as we made our way south. And above the hilltops to our right, I spied a puffy white cloud.

"That's the first cloud I've seen since we got here," observed Louis.

I knew all these things added up to something, even if I didn't know what it was. And I could sense by the way Audrey, Kate, and Louis scoured the landscape that they knew something waited out there too. I knew now not to go digging in a file cabinet in my brain for a bunch of facts that would give everybody the illusion I had it all figured out. I knew to stay quiet and keep watching, walking, and thinking, because I realized there was no shortcut to the answers we were after. But I knew the Fearless Four would figure out everything we needed to know when the time came.

Two hours into our rescue effort, as the sun really began to beat on us, Louis spotted one of Daphne's unbelievably red hairs snagged on a yucca, undulating like a tiny pennant on the rising heat waves. He stopped and plucked it off the greeny wooden spray of spines. "Hers," he said.

Kate shrugged out of her pack straps. "Anybody want an orange?" she asked.

"You've got oranges?" marveled Audrey.

"Jare gave me a bag from his secret stash," she said. "He told me not to tell you until we were on the trail."

"You are the Queen of the Fearless Four!" declared Audrey. "Now don't be a stingy queen! Give me an orange!" Kate bestowed one upon her. *"Mmmmmmm,"* Audrey moaned as she bit in and orange juice spritzed through the hot, bright morning.

"I hereby proclaim the orange," said Kate, "the official fruit of the Fearless Four!"

While the taste of tropical Florida trickled down my throat, I inked another X on the map in my head, marking the spot where we'd found Daphne's hair. It was smack on the path she'd been supposed to follow. Which meant that wherever she'd run into trouble, it was still ahead of us. A breeze kicked up from the direction of the western hills, and I felt, at that moment, like the Fearless Four were unbeatable. We were smart. We were on the right track. And we had oranges.

The breeze died and heat began shimmering from the desert floor as we stowed our water bottles and reshouldered our packs. Louis wound Daphne's hair around his finger. It looked too red. It tried too hard, just like Daphne, and it was impossible not to think of her and wonder, even though she seemed as hard-shelled as a fossilized trilobite, how many things could have happened to her out here under a sky as wide, blue, and unconcerned as the one above our heads. If her water bottle had cracked . . . if she'd wandered off course . . . if she'd slipped, or stumbled, or fallen, or gotten bitten by a rattler . . .

Even the terrible Daphne, when you got down to it, was just a teenage girl alone in an immensity that didn't care whether she lived or died.

We found one of her giant boot prints in a swath of dust blown across the trail.

After another hour, I still had total faith in the Fearless Four, but a certain fact had become too plain to ignore.

"We've drunk half our water," said Louis as we took a breather under a lonely cottonwood tree in a patch of shade we shared with the bones of a longhorn steer. "So if we want to get back to camp, we should turn around here."

"Except there's hardly any water in camp," I reminded him.

"And we haven't found Daphne yet," Audrey added.

"So we're not turning around," Kate decreed. "Remember, I'm the queen."

"How could we forget, Your Majesty?" said Louis.

"Straighten up, or no more oranges," ordered Kate.

It was hotter than it'd ever been on el Viaje, so hot that my eyes refused to focus on objects in the distance, objects like mountains and clouds. I checked my watch. Turned out my eyes wouldn't focus on things that *weren't* in the distance, either. "What time is it?" I asked Louis, holding up my wrist.

"Nearly noon," he said.

As he spoke, the heat grew so strong I could hear it thrumming like a freight train in my ears.

"Should we stop?" I asked.

"We can't. Daphne is out in this," said Kate.

"The river is only a few hours away," I said, squinting at the map in my head. "On the other side of those cliffs," I added, pointing ahead to where the hills converged to form a rock wall smack in our path.

"Then we'll keep going," said Louis resolutely. "To the river. We'll find Daphne on the way and have all the water we need."

We pushed on. My mouth felt like I'd eaten the cotton batting out of my mom's sofa. My eyes glued themselves into their sockets. My muscles began to feel fluffy with exhaustion, and every individual one of my bones ached.

I saw Kate stumble over a pebble no bigger than a pea, and I knew she felt the same way. We all did.

"What's that!" hissed Louis fifteen minutes later.

"What's what?" I asked, slowing down to let him catch up.

"That smell! It's horrible! Is it a javelina? A skunk? A composting facility, tucked away in the desert?" he said, frantically glancing around.

"I don't smell anything," I said. "Oh. Wait. I do. Hold on. I think it's—"

"Hatchet aftershave," said Kate from a few feet ahead, rolling her eyes. "Spectacular."

Crashing through the yucca and the creosote came Randolph, wild-eyed and delirious, oblivious to the desert spines and spears. How he'd caught up with us I did not know. He'd probably run the whole way, visions of Daphne dancing in his lime-sized brain.

"Hey, everybody!" Randolph yodeled. "I'm here!" He staggered in three small circles like a drunk, bodybuilding ballerina, and collapsed in a heap.

"Dizzy," I observed. As hot as it was, I noticed that his skin was perfectly dry. "Unable to perspire." I pinched Randolph's forearm. I was taking a chance, I knew, because ordinarily, he'd have dealt me a black eye for touching him, but Randolph just giggled. "Ha ha ha! That tickles!" The skin stayed pinched after I let go, like he was made of Play-Doh.

"Inelastic skin," I recited from the Splashview first-aid manual. "Symptomatic of severe dehydration."

"What do we do?" asked Kate in a voice more tinged with pity than disgust.

"Pour water down him," I said. "Right now."

"We don't have a lot," said Audrey.

"Then we have to give him what we've got," I said. "At least most of it. Because if we don't, he might die."

And of course, when it came down to it, no matter what we might've said back at camp when he was acting like the world's biggest jackass, nobody wanted Randolph to die.

"What are *we* going to drink?" asked Audrey.

"Whatever is left," I said. "Bottoms up, Randolph," I said, carefully emptying my bottle down his gullet. I didn't want him to chuck it right back up. That would've been a waste.

"MMMMM!" cried Randolph happily. Kate handed over her bottle next. He slurped it down, and almost immediately he seemed a little less befuddled, which was only a relative improvement, since this was Randolph.

"Now what do we do with him?" asked Louis. "We can't leave him here. Can we?" Louis sounded slightly hopeful.

But I was afraid that as soon as our water revived him, Randolph would hop up and do something else stupid. When I mentioned this, everybody agreed. Especially Randolph. "Got that right, Memory Boy!" he cried cheerfully. "So whatcha gonna do?"

"Bring you," I said. "Can you drink a little? And walk a little? Until you feel better?"

"Drink a little. Walk a little. Drink a little. Walk a little. Cheep, cheep, cheep! I'm a creep, I'm an ishkabibble," sang Randolph, doing a pretty good job riffing on the classic musical, for a delirious dehydration victim with almost no singing ability to begin with.

"Ishkabibble?'" said Kate.

"Ish Kabibble was a comedian and cornet player, born Merwyn Bogue in North East, Pennsylvania, in 1908," I said.

"Exactly!" cried Randolph.

"If we didn't have so much else to worry about," commented Audrey, "I'd be very concerned that you both know that."

"See ya!" cried Randolph. With that, he stood up and

took off running for Mexico. And fell flat on his face.

Audrey, Kate, and I all three turned to Louis at exactly the same time.

Louis took a deep breath, grabbed Randolph's ankles with one hand, snatched his wrists with the other, and slung the poor bonehead over his shoulders. For a second, it looked like Louis might pass out from the trauma of Randolph's entire skeevy body draped across him.

But Louis squeezed his eyes shut, gritted his teeth, and started walking.

"Is he heavy?" asked Kate.

"Yes," wheezed Louis. "But I'll make it."

"You're strong," Kate observed.

"I used to think the universe was playing a joke on me," said Louis, "making me as big as a truck driver but scared of my own shadow." He hefted Randolph to a more comfortable position and glanced to see, beside his ear, Randolph, suddenly wide-awake, grinning at him like a maniac. "And now I'm *sure* the universe is playing a joke on me."

CHAPTER FIFTEEN

Audrey Alcott

The Desert

WE HIKED AND HIKED. MY throat was coated with sandpaper, and whenever I opened my mouth to speak, the corners of it felt like they were cracking, but apart from the occasional cloud passing in front of the sun, conversation was our only relief.

We talked about everything and nothing. I told them about my woods. Louis discussed his lifelong hatred of sandboxes. Kate told us a funny story about her grandmother yelling at the mailman, threatening to sic her dog on him because he knocked on the door during her favorite soap opera, even though she didn't have a dog, and we all croaked with laughter like a group of frogs. We weren't finding any signs of Daphne, but things were going pretty well otherwise, when Aaron said, "After this is over, we have to get together."

I felt a flutter of nervousness start in my chest.

"A Fearless Four reunion!" said Louis. "Only instead of life-threatening heat, insane ex-jocks, and lost campers, how about if we have lemonade, Popsicles, ice cream, watermelon, a tree-shaded swimming pool, and an aerial trapeze? Everybody can come to my house!"

The flutter intensified.

"Wait," said Kate. "*You* have an aerial trapeze?"

"Are you crazy?" replied Louis. "Of course not. Those things are terrifying. I just threw it in to make sure everyone was paying attention."

"Or everyone could come to my house," said Aaron. "I have super-high-speed internet and a prime subscription to the Library of Congress online special collections."

"Yeah, right," said Kate. "Another trick to be sure we're really listening."

"No," said Aaron. "I really do."

The flutter became a whole flock of birds, startled ones, flapping their wings in a frenzy. I felt like I did once in New York City, when I almost walked out in front of a taxi—that rush of air, the streak of yellow just inches away, the blast of a horn—before my father, at the very last second, tugged me back by the hood of my coat. Because as soon as Aaron said that about "after this is over," I realized I'd almost done it: I'd almost forgotten my vow. In the tumble of events, the search, the conversation, the *team-work*, I'd come *this* close to letting myself get sucked into friendship. As the other three bantered about our potential get-together, I pulled back. I reminded myself that for me, there could be no "after this." But, wow, it was hard. I liked Kate, Aaron, and Louis so much, and they seemed different from other people, truer. I'd trusted them enough to tell them about my gift; it was tempting to trust them all the way. But I forced my mind back to Janie's porch, the icy-wave slap of her lie in my face.

"No," I mumbled. "I can't."

No one heard me. And the reason that no one heard me was that Kate was saying this: "Well, I *would* invite you to my house, but my mom is having our kitchen, um, totally remodeled, and, when I left, there was sawdust everywhere, and I'm sure it's only going to get worse, so you know, Aaron's or Louis's would probably be better. . . ." She trailed off.

I didn't look up to see her scratch her elbow. I didn't have to. I knew she'd done it, Poison Ivy Liar that she was. And unlike the last time she'd lied—about how long her mom stayed sad after her grandmother died—Kate didn't jump in right away to tell the truth, so that her lie hardly even counted. She let the lie stand. The funny thing is that I should have felt happy. Right when I most needed reminding that everyone you trust eventually lies, she'd gone and done just that. But for some reason, I felt sad instead.

In a low voice, I said, "Count me out."

"What?" said Aaron. "You have to come!"

"Yeah," said Louis, stopping in his tracks. "What's the Fearless Four without, you know, *four*?"

"I can't," I said.

"Why not?" asked Aaron.

I felt so weighed down with sadness that I stopped walking. Maybe because it looked like this conversation might take a while, Louis carefully laid Randolph down on the ground. He, Kate, and Aaron stared at me expectantly. I tried to take a deep breath, but all it did was parch my throat more. I wanted to look up, to meet the three pairs of eyes that were staring at me, but somehow, that was more than I could stand. I kept my gaze on the stony, chalk-dusty path at my feet.

"Because getting together after this is over is what friends do, and we—" I drew in another chestful of hot air. "We aren't friends."

A smothering, smoke-thick silence swallowed us. Finally Aaron said, in a voice so confused it hurt my heart, "Audrey?"

"It's nothing personal," I said softly.

"What does that mean?" said Louis. "Because it feels pretty personal to me." It was the closest I'd ever heard him come to sounding mad.

"I just promised myself that I wouldn't have friends. At least not for a really long time."

"But why?" asked Kate.

With effort, I lifted my head and looked into her black eyes. "Because if you don't have any friends, then your friends can't lie to you the way my former best friend Janie did a few weeks ago. And the way you did, just now."

Kate stared at me, stunned, and I realized that when she'd said what she'd said about the kitchen renovation, she'd forgotten that I would know she was lying. Her eyes filled with tears.

"Oh!" she said, and pressed her hand to her mouth. Then, with short, quick, stiff-legged steps, she charged far ahead of us, her head down, her hands clenched into fists. We all watched her go.

"Audrey," said Aaron, "Kate's been having a hard time, remember? Did you really have to say that to her?"

I stared at him. "But—"

"Even if you don't want her to be a friend to *you*," Louis hissed, "you might have considered being a friend to *her*!"

There was no mistaking his anger now.

"But why did she have to say her house was full of sawdust?" I said. "Why?"

Louis leaned in and spoke to me slowly, like I was either incredibly dense or about five years old. "Maybe because it's not about *sawdust*. Maybe it's about grief and anger and arguments with her parents. Maybe she didn't want us to see *that* in her house."

"She still didn't have to lie!" I said.

"Remember Randolph?" said Aaron. "How he lied about knowing where Daphne was because of how he was feeling?"

"But that was Randolph. This is Kate!"

"Well, at least you know that much," said Louis coldly. "For a second there, it seemed a lot like you forgot who she was."

Aaron and Louis exchanged a look; then Louis bent over and heaved Randolph onto his shoulders, and the two of them turned around and started after Kate.

I was right. I *was*. Lying was wrong, and lying to a friend was doubly wrong. I *knew* I was right. Nothing could be more obvious: it was better not to have friends, because nothing felt worse than the moment—and it always came—when the person you trusted lied.

Except that now, something *did* feel worse. As I was walking alone, far behind Aaron, Kate, and Louis (and Randolph, who, being mostly unconscious and also being Randolph, didn't count), I felt worse than I ever had.

I remembered the night Aaron had handed me his flashlight and I'd played connect the dots with the stars. As I trudged through the desert, I thought and thought about that moment, and everything became so clear: how the four of us had been a constellation, shining, connected, complete. How had I not seen it before? Even today, marching over the stony, stinging land, the sun pounding on us like a hammer, thirsty, tired, looking for a girl none of us even liked and probably wouldn't find, had been good, true, and right because we were doing it together. And I had ruined it. Aaron, Kate, and Louis were a three-star constellation now, Orion's belt, and I was all alone, a lost star, falling and sputtering and about to flicker out entirely.

I thought about how, before I'd come to camp, I had wanted to leave civilization and live alone with nature, like Henry David Thoreau. But what I understood now was that even though nature was pure and never lied, it never laughed at your jokes or listened to your stories either. It didn't pull cactus spines out of your hand or watch sunsets with you or laugh at itself for being scared of dodgeball. And it didn't spin around and run headfirst into a giant, angry man to try to stop him from chasing you across a desert mesa. Nature could be beautiful and harsh and inspiring, but one thing it never did was love you back. Or love you anyway.

I wanted to flop down on the desert floor and cry.

But instead, after several false starts, I scraped together every bit of courage I could find, sucked some breath into my chest, and ran to catch up with them. When they heard my footsteps, they didn't turn around, just stopped, waited for me to step into place, *my* place, and then we started walking again. For a long time, no one said much of anything, although Louis did a fair amount of grunting, as he shifted Randolph around like the sack of wormy potatoes he was, and every now and then, we stopped to scour the ground for Daphne's footprints or to eye places where the scrub might have been disturbed, searching for anything that might show where Daphne had left the trail, gone astray. But we never found a single clue. I could tell that everything wasn't really okay between me and the others, but every time I opened my mouth to speak, it was like all the words I could think of to say turned to dust on my tongue. But at least I was there.

Finally Aaron said, in a creepily accurate imitation of Jare, "'Unruly sharks. Caused him to turn over a new leaf. Felt bad about how he'd given up custody of Daphne all those years ago without a fight, regretted the way he'd neglected her ever since. Wanted to make amends, treat her to a summer of adventure.'"

"Sharks'll do that, I guess," said Louis, managing to shudder at the thought of sharks, despite the dead weight of Randolph on his shoulders.

"It's weird, though, right, Audrey?" asked Aaron.

I was so startled and grateful to hear him say my name that it took me a second to realize what else he'd said.

"Weird?" I asked.

"Remember the night we spied on them? By the fire?"

I flashed back to Daphne's and Randolph's faces in the orange glow, to their voices shot through with the usual anger. But not just anger—hope, a clear bell tone of hope rising up out of Daphne's usual growl.

"She said she was going to live with her dad in Montana, just as soon as he could get custody of her," I said.

"Right," said Aaron, "but think about what she said right before that."

"Why? Why can't you just tell me?"

"Come on, Audrey," said Aaron gently. "Just try."

I sighed. "Okay, fine."

The landscape around me blurred as I tried to send myself backward, further into the moment when we crouched in the bushes, listening. Then I had it.

"She said her mom had hired fancy lawyers who tricked her dad into giving up custody!" I said triumphantly.

"But Jare said he gave it up without a fight," said Kate, speaking for the first time since I'd rejoined them. "And why would Pepin have told him that, if it wasn't true? I mean, giving up your kid, that's not exactly something to brag about."

"No, it's not," said Aaron. "Audrey, when Daphne said that about the lawyer, was she lying to Randolph?"

"Definitely not," I said. "She believed it."

"Probably that's what her dad told her," said Louis, "to save face."

"Maybe," said Aaron. "But Audrey, remember what Jare said when I brought up the fact that what they were plotting was kidnapping? A felony?"

The other two didn't answer, as if they were leaving it to me. Slowly I said, "He said her mother would never press charges because if her dad went to prison, it would break Daphne's heart. He said her mom knows Daphne loves her dad."

For at least two minutes, there was no sound but the *crunch, crunch, crunch* of the dirt under our boots. I pondered Daphne, her mom, her dad, trying as hard as I'd ever tried to connect the dots. *Daphne's mom doesn't want to hurt Daphne. Daphne's mom knows Daphne loves her dad. Daphne's mom wouldn't tell on Daphne's dad, even if he did something really bad, because she wants Daphne to have her dad in her life.* Dot, dot, dot, dot.

"I bet her mom lied too, about the custody thing," I said in a breathless rush. "Or at least she went along with the story about the fancy lawyers tricking Daphne's dad. Her mom could have told her the truth, probably could have proven to her that her dad didn't want her, but she didn't do that because she didn't want Daphne to know that her dad didn't want her."

"Imagine thinking that your own dad didn't want you," said Louis quietly. "I drive my parents up the wall, as you can probably imagine, but they still like me. They still want me around."

"Mine too," said Kate.

"And mine," said Aaron.

"Same here," I said. "But now Daphne hates her mom and thinks her dad is the greatest thing in the world. Why would her mom lie if it made Daphne hate her?"

Crunch, crunch, crunch.

"I don't know about you," said Aaron, "but I can only think of one reason."

After a few seconds, so could I.

"Because she loves her," I said. I considered that: lying out of love. Lying even if it made the person you loved resent you forever. Could lying be noble? Generous? Right?

"No," I said.

"No, what?" asked Aaron.

"I just don't think lying is ever the right choice."

"Probably not," said Kate glumly.

"But maybe," I said carefully, "maybe sometimes it's an understandable choice. Maybe sometimes it doesn't mean the person telling the lie is bad. Maybe not all lies are created equal."

Crunch, crunch, crunch.

Kate cleared her throat and, with her eyes trained on the ground, said, "Maybe sometimes, for example, a person will lie about sawdust because she's worried that ever since her grandmother died, her family doesn't get along so well, and her house isn't a very nice place to visit."

Even though I would have sworn there wasn't a drop of extra liquid left in my body, my eyes filled with tears. I reached over, took Kate's hand, squeezed it, and let it go. She raised her dark eyes to me and smiled.

"And maybe," I said, "a person will lie and say she isn't friends with her friends because she's scared of being hurt, and she's been telling herself that same lie for so long that she almost—but not quite—believes it, and then, afterward, she'll realize she would give anything if she could just take the lie back."

I held my breath.

"It sounds to me like she just did," said Louis.

I shook my head. "No. I lied to you guys. I did. Nothing can change that."

Kate, Aaron, and Louis all looked at me.

"What I'm hoping," I said, "is that you'll stay friends with me anyway."

They exchanged glances with each other, smiles dawning on all their faces. On mine too.

"Well, sure," said Aaron. "Definitely. Because—" He paused.

The four of us said it at the same time: "The anyway is the whole point."

For a second, even with my backpack straps digging into my shoulders, I felt light as air, like I might float right off that gritty trail.

"Ishkabbible! Pishkabbible! Mishkabbible!" Randolph sang in his sleep.

We all laughed. When we finished, we kept hiking.

"Kate?" said Aaron after a minute or two.

"Yeah?"

"I'm just wondering. I mean, you're so good at walking in other people's shoes, right?"

"I guess."

"Well, I'm wondering if you've ever tried to walk in

your mom's, to try to figure out why she acts like she's not sad about her own mom dying. Because I bet there's a reason."

"I bet so too," I said.

Kate walked a few steps, her face soft with thought. Then she nodded. "Maybe I will," she said. She nodded again. "I will."

A cloud covered the sun, and in unison, Aaron, Kate, Louis, and I stopped hiking and lifted our faces to the sudden coolness. We stood there together, soaking up the sunlessness, until the cloud slid away, and then we started hiking again.

An hour later, the seamless rock wall we seemed to be hiking smack into stopped being seamless. When we shielded our eyes with our hands, we could just make out the slot canyon, a mere crack in the towering sandstone face. According to the map inside Aaron's head, on the other side of the canyon was the river, the point where Daphne was supposed to meet her father, the spot at which she'd never arrived. In less than an hour, we'd be at the mouth of the slot canyon, and not only had we not found Daphne, we hadn't found any trace of her since the boot print hours ago. And now, with the mountains rising up steeply on either side of us, it seemed less likely than ever that she'd accidentally strayed from the trail. Who would leave a perfectly good trail and head straight up a near-vertical incline? And why?

We were taking a break. The four of us sat in a circle, with Randolph lying a little ways away. With a sigh, Kate had poured the last of our water down him, and we'd left him lying in the meager shadow—all the shadow we'd been able to find—of a creosote bush.

"This doesn't make sense," groaned Kate. "If she'd gotten hurt or run out of water, we would have found her. If she'd gotten delirious or lost in the dark and wandered off the trail, we would have found her or some trace of her. If her father had found her, he would've called Jare. If he'd come to find her and gotten hurt or dehydrated, we would've found him or both of them. She isn't on the trail and she isn't off the trail. Where could she have gone?"

"Ugh. I just wish I could climb inside her head," I said.

"Really?" said Louis, wide-eyed. "That could be a pretty scary place."

"Can you, Kate?" asked Aaron.

Kate stopped and shut her eyes, trying to imagine what it was like to be Daphne, but then she shook her head and opened them.

"I just didn't know her well enough," she said, then caught herself. "I mean *don't* know her well enough."

"None of us really knew her very well," I said. "I mean *know* her very well."

"Yeah, she wasn't what you'd call approachable," said Louis. "I mean *isn't*."

"I kind of hate to suggest this," said Kate, "but maybe it's time we talked to the only person around here who did know her. I mean *does*. He seems to be getting perkier."

We all turned to look at Randolph, who was sitting up, scowling in a familiar way, and not singing a nonsense song. As we watched, he reached out to the creosote bush that had been sharing its puddle of shade with him, yanked off a handful of it, threw the handful on the ground, and eyed it with satisfaction.

"Randomly tormenting the innocent," observed Louis.

"Yep," I said grimly. "He appears to be back to normal."

"If only he could spend his entire life in a state of life-threatening dehydration, he'd be a much nicer guy," said Kate. "Weird and with a really bad singing voice, but nicer."

Reluctantly, we all lugged ourselves to our feet and started toward Randolph. When he saw us, he yelled, "Hey! I'm thirsty. Which one of you morons is hogging all the water?"

I saw Kate tense up, but I said quietly, "I know, I know, but hold off. Remember we want his help."

When we got to Randolph, Aaron said, in his cheerful

way, "It looks like you're feeling better."

"Fit as a fizzle," said Randolph, thumping himself on the chest.

"Fiddle," mumbled Kate.

"What was that?" growled Randolph.

"'Fit as a fiddle' is an idiom that dates from the early 1600s. Originally it was used to describe suitability or appropriateness rather than health, and while its exact origins are unknown, some speculate that it refers to the way a violin fits snugly under the chin," said Aaron. I glanced at him, his tired face and anxious eyes. I knew he was doing his best. He'd dialed way back on the info-spouting lately, but when he got stressed, the facts just seemed to pop out on their own.

Before Randolph could throw something at Aaron, I jumped in. "Randolph, we were hoping you'd help us," I said.

"Ha! Like that's ever gonna happen."

"Not us," said Kate. "Daphne."

It was exactly the right thing to say. I could practically see the storm cloud over Randolph's head dissolve.

"Oh," he said.

"You know her better than anyone," I said, following Kate's lead. "We think you're her best hope."

Heaven help me—and Daphne—this wasn't a lie.

Randolph dropped his sneer and, for a few seconds, looked almost human, blinking and flattered and about seven years old. Then he smirked and said, "More like her only hope. You guys are obviously clueless. Okay. What?"

"Well, she was supposed to meet her father, but it seems like she never did, and she doesn't seem to have run into any trouble along the trail. So we were wondering if you have any idea about where she might have gone instead."

"The answer to that is a big fat nowhere," said Randolph. "She never would've stood up her dad." After a second, he added, "That girl thinks he's the greatest thing since sliced bread."

"In 1928, Iowan Otto Frederick Rohwedder perfected the first loaf-at-a-time—" began Aaron, but before I could even send him a warning glance, he stopped, which was good because it meant that I never had to take my eyes off Randolph, so I caught the expression that flickered over his face right after Aaron said the Otto Frederick Rohwedder thing. It was an expression I had never seen Randolph make before and, until that moment, would've bet wasn't even something his face could convey: pity. Randolph felt sorry for Daphne.

"She thinks he's great," I said. "But you don't, do you?"

He stuck out his jaw. "Yeah, I do! The guy is like the

coolest dad in the world. Anyone would kill to have a dad like that."

Lie. Lie. Lie.

"Do you really think so?" I asked.

"Most definitely!" said Randolph.

Lie. But I knew that if I called him on his lying, he'd get mad and clam up. No matter how irritating Randolph was, if we wanted his help, I had to tread lightly.

"I know Daphne confided in you. Why don't you tell us what you know about him?" I asked. "It might help."

Randolph punched his thighs with his fists, not hard, but not that lightly either. He was thinking. He stopped punching and looked up.

"Okay, so there was this one Christmas break when he invited Daphne to go snowboarding in, like, one of those awesome places in Colorado where movie stars and whatnot go. He bought her a business-class ticket and everything. He got to the place a couple days ahead of her, and get this, he met Vaughan Gray!"

"Who's Vaughan Gray?" asked Louis.

"X Games? Snowboarder? Only the best in the whole entire freaking world?" said Randolph disgustedly.

"Oh."

"Anyway, Vaughan and a bunch of his X Games buds

were taking off for this other really amazing resort in, like, Park City, Utah, and *they invited Daphne's dad to come with them*."

"Wow," I said, doing my best to sound impressed. I'd never been a snowboarding fan and honestly only knew Vaughan Gray because he starred in some funny soap commercials that Janie loved, but it seemed like a bad idea to tell Randolph that.

"Did he go?" asked Aaron.

"Duh. Of course he went," said Randolph. "Do you know how many people would kill to hang with guys like Vaughan Gray? Like, millions."

He stopped and squinted up at the sky.

"Go on," Kate said. "Please."

Randolph shrugged. "That's it."

Lie.

"Really?" said Kate gently. "Because it seemed like there was more you wanted to say. To, you know, help Daphne."

At the sound of Daphne's name, Randolph's face got serious.

"Okay. A couple days later, Daphne's dad texted her all these awesome pictures of him with the X Gamers. Obviously, she was blown away. She printed a bunch out and hung them on her bulletin board, after she got home."

Randolph dropped his eyes as he said this, but not before I saw the pity flare in them again.

"Home from where?" I asked.

Randolph kicked the clump of leaves and branches he'd broken off the creosote bush. "Well, the really hilarious thing is that she got the pictures while she was waiting at the airport," he said.

"Which airport?" asked Aaron. "Was she about to get on the plane to go to Colorado?"

"No. The airport *in* Colorado, stupid," said Randolph. "She was in baggage claim. Had been there for a while, I guess."

"How long?" asked Louis.

"Why does it matter?" snapped Randolph.

"It might," I said simply.

"Whatever. All day. I mean, I think that's what she said. Like the place was practically deserted. The janitors were mopping and whatnot."

"So hold on," said Aaron, frowning. "He left town and forgot to pick up his daughter at the airport? She waited there for *hours and hours*?"

Randolph glared at her. "Dude! It was the chance of a lifetime to snowboard with those guys! In his position, I would've done the same thing."

Lie.

"Anyway, it was fine. She got a cab to this fancy hotel, ordered room service, took a bath in a tub as big as a swimming pool. She had a blast. And he came to get her late the next night, so she got to spend a full twenty-four hours in the hotel. By the time he got there, they only had a day left before Daphne had to go home, so they never actually went snowboarding, but that was cool because the hotel was awesome."

"He didn't come get her until the next night?" I asked. "He didn't rush back? So, what? There was a snowboarder party that day he didn't want to miss?"

I was so horrified by Daphne's dad that I had forgotten to tread lightly. I braced myself, waiting for Randolph to lash out at me, get defensive. But the odd thing was, he didn't.

He looked straight at me and said, "I guess the snow conditions were especially dandy. He brought her a T-shirt from that other resort, though, signed by Vaughan Gray. So it was all good."

His tone was hard, quiet but bitter. You didn't have to have a lie-detecting unsuperpower to know that Randolph didn't think there was anything "all good" about any of it.

After a while, Kate said, "I don't buy it. No one could really forget his own kid like that."

We looked at her, surprised.

"I guess Daphne's dad could," said Louis.

"He admitted to it," said Randolph defensively. "That's totally what happened!"

"Forgetting your kid doesn't exactly make you look good," said Aaron. "Why would anyone lie about that? Kate? What do you think?"

Kate lifted her chin. She looked furious. "Yeah, forgetting your kid is bad. I can only think of one thing worse."

Aaron, Louis, and I exchanged puzzled looks.

"Oh!" I said, suddenly understanding. "The only thing worse is if he remembered and still didn't pick her up."

"Yeah! Just left her there because he chickened out, couldn't handle the parent-child alone-time thing," blurted out Randolph angrily. Quickly he collected himself. "Not that that's what happened. It would just be kind of a typical dad thing to do."

We all stared at Randolph. Deserting your kid because you were scared to hang out with her was a typical dad thing to do?

"Okay, but if her dad had let her down like that before," I said, "why would she have agreed to this plan, the one we're in the middle of? Why would she ever trust him again?"

Louis shook his head, baffled. "No idea."

"It doesn't make sense," said Aaron.

"Kate?" I asked.

Kate shook her head. "I don't know. She'd have to be stupid, and Daphne is a lot of things, but she's not stupid."

There was a scuffle, and Randolph was on his feet, jabbing his finger at us. "You're the stupid ones!" he said. "Your dads probably—what? Go to your dopey little soccer games? Take you out for ice cream afterward? Sit in the audience at your stupid band concerts to hear you play the stupid flute? Give you high-fives when you ace your special little math tests?"

Randolph's voice was dripping with sarcasm, but he'd actually just given a pretty accurate description of my dad. From the looks on the others' faces, I imagined they were thinking more or less the same thing.

"Tuba, actually," said Kate.

"You want to know why Daphne would trust him to show up this time, brainiacs?" said Randolph. "Because he's her *dad*. I bet there are even kids out there whose dads left when they were five and never called or wrote and probably don't even know where their kids live, especially because they spend a lot of time in foster care, whenever their moms decide to be 'unfit,' but every single time the dumb doorbell rings, the kids think, *I bet that's him.* That's just how it works, morons."

He turned his back and stomped away, kicking up clouds of dust as he went.

I didn't like Randolph. I wasn't sure I had it in me to ever like him. But right then, I was blindsided by this huge wish that one day, someone would like him. No, it was more than that. I wished someone would love him, all-out love, the way my parents loved me. The wish burned my eyes and tickled my throat, and it took everything I had not to cry on the spot.

After what seemed like a long time, Aaron said tentatively, "You know where Daphne just might be?"

We all nodded, except Randolph, who had found another, much smaller creosote bush fifty yards away, and appeared to be trying to kick it to death. I turned around and pointed to the jagged cleft in the rock face.

"On the other side of that slot canyon, at the edge of the Rio Grande, waiting for her dad," I said.

"Who forgot to come," said Louis.

"Or didn't forget," said Aaron.

"Let's go get her," said Kate, starting to walk toward our heap of backpacks.

"Wait. We can't leave without Randolph," said Aaron.

He was right. We couldn't. Kate heaved a sigh and walked back to where we stood.

"I meant let's go get her," she said wearily, "just as soon as Randolph is finished murdering the local shrubbery."

"Randolph, the herbicidal maniac. Does he really need to come with us?" said Louis. But before anyone could answer, he shouted, "Hey, Randolph, let's go get Daphne!"

CHAPTER SIXTEEN

Aaron Archer

The Desert

NOW THAT WE KNEW DAPHNE had stuck to her plan, all we had to do was hike to the end of the path. No wondering. No wandering. No worrying we'd missed her, or the place she'd gotten lost, or hurt, or whatever had happened to her. Clouds drifted overhead. Our trail led through the remains of an abandoned farm. Not much was left. A rusty windmill. A ramshackle house. A tilting fence. A collapsing barn. And—

"Hey, Aaron!" said Audrey. "A red wheelbarrow!"

It was still in pretty good shape too, propped against a gnarled locust tree. Not a white chicken in sight, though. And of course, no rainwater. This was the desert.

As we left the decrepit farm behind, the trail dropped into a sandy streambed lined with cottonwood trees. It felt like we were walking down a green tunnel. The wind swirled, ruffling the leaves around us so their silver backs flashed. Dusk began to darken the sky to the west, although it felt too early for nightfall.

I realized we'd done it. We'd solved the puzzle. Audrey, Louis, Kate, and me. Even Randolph, behind us, stomping the occasional cactus pad to keep himself occupied, had helped. Soon we'd have Daphne. We'd have water—and all we'd need to do to drink it would be to drop in a couple of iodine pills.

We'd hike back to camp. Enod and Kevin would bring the sheriff to rescue all of us, and if they didn't, well, I knew we'd figure out what to do about that too. We were the Fearless Four, Plus Randolph.

A blast of wind roiled the cottonwood leaves. They heaved like a green wave. Above us, the sky had dimmed almost to black. One last shaft of sunlight stabbed out of nowhere, and in it, I could see the streambed loop around a half-buried stone in the trail and disappear into the gash in the cliff.

"That," murmured Louis, his face turning white, "is way deeper than the last one."

"But at least, if there are any bats," I said encouragingly, "they're probably gone for the night."

"I'm not going to let my imagination run away with me," vowed Louis, strapping on his headlamp. The rest of us dug ours out of our packs too.

"I haven't *got* a light," complained Randolph.

"Then stay here," suggested Audrey.

"No way," said Randolph. "I'm coming with you! To see Daphne! I'll step where you step."

"Swell," muttered Audrey.

I remembered the canyon's name from Jare's map: Gage Cut. Its mouth flared like a trumpet, buffed by ten million years of swirling water, sculpted like the entrance to a spectacular, spooky cathedral. The sand of the streambed sifted a few yards into the gap, and then the floor became polished stone.

"Look," said Louis, pointing at shapes in the sand. "Daphne's big clodhopper bootprints."

"How did this place even get here?" wondered Randolph, gazing at the dips, channels, pools, and grooves carved into the floor of the passageway as we hiked.

"Erosion," Kate said.

"Nuh-uh," said Randolph smugly. "You've got to have rainwater for that. And it never rains in the desert, stupid."

Which was all it took. As soon as Randolph finished calling Kate stupid, the first drop hit.

"Oh, no," I said, slowing to a stop on the trail in the depths of the canyon.

I realized I might actually have done it: killed us all.

In the slit at the top of the canyon, a green streak of lightning snaked across the sky, unlike anything I'd ever seen, as thick as a school bus. By its glare, I checked my watch. Five thirty p.m. It wasn't nighttime at all.

And for us, time ground to a halt. Compared to the storm, engulfing us with astounding speed, we could only move in slow motion.

"Turn around! Go back!" I cried.

Louis and Audrey jostled into each other. Randolph tripped over Audrey and fell to his knees, blocking the way out.

It wasn't nighttime. The sky was just black.

Dusk doesn't fall in the west.

Dusk falls in the east.

That wasn't twilight darkening the sky.

It was a storm cloud larger than any I'd ever seen, so big it had filled the entire horizon, so colossal I hadn't recognized it until now.

"Hurry! Get up!" I cried. "Get up, Randolph! Run!"

The thunder from the lightning bolt dropped into the canyon and hit like a sledgehammer. Audrey reached out to steady herself against the stone wall. Louis dragged Randolph to his feet.

Another bolt of lightning flared, a spiderweb of white

arcs as bright as day. In the flash, I saw all my friends' faces, frozen in astonishment. A hiss sounded, softly at first, like a drop of water in a skillet, growing until it sounded like the roar of a NASA rocket lifting off. Hot, sizzling thunder. And then the rain began. It came in buckets. It came in sheets. It came in cascades down the stone walls.

Like Randolph said. It never rains in the desert.

It pours. And when it pours, more water can fall in one hour than in an entire year. Or in two, or four.

"Get out!" I cried. "Run!"

But it was already too late. I felt it, flowing around my toes—a tongue of water surging down the passageway, sucking at our feet, tugging at our ankles. In seconds it had reached our shins and we could barely stand up in it. This was the first trickle of the flash flood that would soon rage down the canyon.

More lightning, this time an orange bolt striking the rim. When the clap of thunder came, it was like being smacked in the head with a board.

Everything I thought I'd been right about, I'd been wrong about. The map, the trail, the endless baking sheet we'd trekked across that day, everything leading to this spot, drawing all the paths together, ours, Randolph's, Daphne's, the storm's—I hadn't understood it. And because I hadn't understood it, I'd put us all in harm's way.

The water rose to our knees. It rose to our thighs. And began to rage.

We weren't the Fearless Four, Plus Randolph, in the perfect spot at the perfect time. We were in the most awful spot we could be in. We were going to drown in the desert.

Every bit of rain that had fallen or was falling or was going to fall for twenty miles around, every drop to come out of this storm, was now rushing toward us. The colossal forces that had carved this canyon—billions of gallons of water, tons of gravel and boulders and stones—were all in motion and couldn't be stopped.

Then the water rose another foot. The tempo of the lightning quickened. White, yellow, blue, green. Cracks, explosions, thuds, bangs, crashes, until the noises ran together into a shriek like a fighter jet blasting down Gage Cut over our heads, and the walls and floor around us were lit up like morning. Skeletal ocotillo arms and yucca stalks eddied crazily past us. Fence posts. Rusty windmill blades. We held on to each other for support.

The flood grew stronger. And higher. Up to our waists. All we could do was try to stay on our feet. When the rising water swirled or rippled or crested, I felt it heave me around like a doll. It was a thousand times stronger than any of us. A million. It had carved through fifty feet of rock. And this was only the beginning. There was much, much more to come. Enough, I was sure, to fill the canyon to the brim, and overflow.

"I hope Daphne made it out the other side before this started!" Audrey cried into the swirling wind.

Lightning. Thunder. Beside me, I saw Kate stagger, and the current swept her away. Audrey stumbled next. I tried to reach her, but the water wrenched her out of my grasp, and she was gone. Randolph cried, "Oh, man!" and disappeared beneath the flood. Louis was the only one strong enough to stand, and the last thing I remember before I lost my footing was the sight of him behind me, terrified, his hands over his ears, fighting the water, and slowly losing. A blue bolt of lightning, the biggest one yet, forked in two and struck both edges of the canyon above him. A thousand tons of stone exploded into rubble and began crashing down the cut straight at Louis.

"Dive, Louis! Dive!" I cried, and then I felt the current tumble me head over heels, and after that, I didn't know which way was up. I didn't know where anybody was. I could only hope Louis had plunged into the flood ahead of the avalanche. I heard a distant noise through the bubbles and the foam . . . somebody calling my name . . . and then all four of my friends and I were lying in a dazed pile, and the floodwater was gone.

"What . . . hap—pened?" cried Kate, climbing to her feet. A rill of storm water trickled past our feet, and the storm still raged above us, but the torrent had subsided.

I looked up the canyon the way we'd come. The rock slide caused by the lightning strike had crashed into Gage Cut and stuffed it shut like a plug.

"The flood is dammed up on the other side of the avalanche!" I cried above the thunder. "For now!" But I knew, as the storm water accumulated, the entire flooded desert would rise against the other side like a flood from the Bible, and blast the whole thing loose like a colossal champagne cork. And we really didn't want to be standing underneath it when that happened.

I heard the stones groaning against one another. Small fountains of floodwater began to spray from the cracks in the bottom.

"What do we do?" cried Kate.

"Run," I said.

We ran like crazy. We ran like Usain Bolt and Indiana Jones rolled into one. The canyon floor was wet, and slick, and full of flood-scoured holes. We tripped. We bruised our elbows and knees. Randolph split his chin. It began to bleed.

"So what?" He shrugged. "Not the first time."

We pulled each other back up and kept running.

The rain fell harder and cascaded down the canyon wall in sheets. Behind us, the rock slide shifted as the water pressed harder and harder against its far side, rumbles and moans echoing down the stone corridor between thunderbolts.

Hailstones began rattling down the walls and rolling beneath our feet like marbles.

We stumbled and slid and skidded down in a pile.

And looked up to see the canyon mouth fifteen feet away.

"Hurry," said Kate, leaping to her feet.

We all felt, along the backs of our necks, that soon the inundation would come crashing down upon us.

We ran out into the open and found ourselves standing on a broad sandbar beside the Rio Grande.

"What are you doing?" demanded Daphne, who stood glaring at us like a bedraggled Siamese cat in a sopping black sweater.

"Daphne!" cried Randolph through the roar of the rain. "You're safe! We came to rescue you!"

"Of course I'm safe, you dolt!" retorted Daphne. "Which means I don't need anybody rescuing me!"

"What do we do now?" panted Audrey, glancing warily at the canyon mouth behind us.

"Get off my sandbar!" snapped Daphne, glancing

upriver, soaked to the skin and furious. I noticed she had a whole campsite set up. She'd been here awhile. "That's what! Leave! My dad's going to be here any second. If he sees you, he's going to be furious! Nobody's supposed to know about our plan!"

The rain still beat down, but it was slowing.

"Your dad's not coming," said Louis.

Daphne slapped him. Louis quivered, but he kept his eyes on hers. "You have to face it," he said. Daphne made a fist and drew that back too. But before she could land her punch, we heard the rumble of the flood, the real flood, the whole deluge gathered and towering, thundering down Gage Cut, about to empty from the gap in the cliff a few feet from us. The rock-slide dam had given way. We had a few seconds before it hit. But not much more.

"Run!" I cried. Everybody did. Except, of course, Daphne. She had no idea what kind of calamity was blasting down that canyon. And even if she did, I think she was ready to wait for her dad until doomsday. Literally.

Louis, Audrey, and Kate didn't see her; they sprinted upriver on the sandbar as fast and far as they could go.

But Daphne dug in her heels. Literally.

Randolph dithered back and forth, not knowing whether to try one more time to rescue Daphne or to save himself.

"Go, Randolph!" I shouted.

And I grabbed Daphne, and I carried her. She was bony, thin, and delicate under her soaking clothes, much more fragile than I'd ever have guessed. She tried to slug me, but I had her over my shoulder with her head facing backward, so she only managed to punch my tailbone, which must've hurt her more than it hurt me.

The sandbar stretched far enough to let us run maybe half a football field upstream from the notch in the cliff where the water would burst. It wasn't nearly far enough. I set Daphne down. "You—" she screeched.

The flood exploded out of the canyon, a wall of water as tall as Dolley Madison Middle School, inundating the spot where she'd just been standing in the rain, waiting for her dad. Daphne's anger evaporated. She looked at me with a look I'd never witnessed, not on her face, at least.

The girl who'd seen everything was surprised.

"I'd be dead if you—" she began to say. But now the flood was coming for us. As it crashed into the river, the crest broke, and it began to spread out in a semicircle. The water wall dropped lower and lower, thirty feet, twenty-five feet, twenty. But still awfully high. Still deadly.

"What do we do?" cried Kate.

I tried to think. I thought of Roger Woodward who, when he was seven years old, survived the drop over

Niagara Falls. I though of General John Wesley Powell washing down three miles of the Colorado River at the bottom of the Grand Canyon after he fell out of his boat in 1869. I thought . . . I thought—

And I quit thinking.

"We take the plunge," I said. "I think it'll be small enough by the time it gets here." I eyed the surge that still loomed fifteen feet above our heads, and would hit us in seconds.

"Small enough to what?" asked Daphne.

"Surf!" I cried.

"I can't surf!" cried Daphne. "I can't even swim!"

Louis grabbed Daphne and swung her onto his back.

"Dive, everybody!" cried Kate.

We did. And shot the curling flood wave like we were riding a breaker at the beach.

The last thing I remember was the sight of my friends sliding down the front of the swell, like it was a roller at the shore, if the roller were fifteen feet high and spiked with flood debris. But just when it seemed like we might all actually make it to safety upstream from the flooded canyon, an undertow grabbed me.

The current of the Rio Grande still flowed beneath the water pouring from Gage Cut, and it had sucked me down. And might pull me, I realized, a hundred miles, to Langtry,

Texas. Two hundred, to Del Rio. Maybe eight hundred, to the Atlantic Ocean. And that was longer than I could hold my breath. I fought toward the surface, but I couldn't be sure where the surface was, and besides, the Rio Grande was stronger than I was.

So I went down. Everything faded into a kind of dream. I imagined I was turning into a fish, and would soon have gills, and be able to breathe water, which seemed strange, and hard to believe, but then, what choice did I have? As I was about to draw my first and last lungful of water, I dreamed that a pair of hands appeared in the murk and grabbed me by my hair. They were big hands. Strong hands. I dreamed that one of the hands let go of me and started paddling—I could see the froth it made under the water, but the other hand kept a firm grip on my hair. In the dream, it really hurt. When my head broke the surface, I started to think maybe I wasn't dreaming after all. My hair still hurt. I heard Louis shout, "Hold on to my shirt. I'll pull you in."

"This is not a dream?" I called back.

"Nope," Louis replied, and started swimming.

All I remember from there to the shore was that even though Louis seemed to be cruising through the water like an aircraft carrier, he barely made a splash. He didn't move his arms fast, or kick much. He didn't even breathe very often. But every time he took a stroke, he grabbed a giant handful of water and shot ahead. He could've taught that Splashview lifeguard a thing or two.

Soon I found myself sitting on the sand. The surface of the river slid slowly away from my toes, dropping back into the riverbed where it belonged. The last of the flood trickled out of Gage Cut, a quarter mile downstream.

"Louis!" gasped Audrey in amazement.

"He saved all of us, didn't he?" I asked when I could talk.

Kate, Daphne, and Audrey nodded. Randolph made some kind of grunt that sounded appreciative.

"He pulled you in last," Kate added.

"Well, I'm sure he got to me as soon as he could," I said diplomatically.

"Where did the hero stuff come from, Louis?" asked Kate. "No offense, but how can someone who can't deal with a haircut and has to wear elastic waistbands swim like that?"

"The one thing I *can* stand is water," Louis said. "I'm no Michael Phelps, but I'm pretty good."

"No kidding," said Audrey.

We were sitting on a sandy bank tucked under the cliff at the river's edge.

The rain slowed. It stopped. Above us, as the pitch-black

storm cloud scuttled away, I saw blue sky peek over the river bluff. Amazing. The sun hadn't even set yet.

We'd made it. We were safe. Once we'd caught our collective breath, the Fearless Four would put our heads together and figure out how to find our way back to el Viaje a la Confianza and, from there, sooner or later, to civilization. But for now, I just wanted to take the moment to appreciate being alive. "You've got to be kidding," I said.

"About what?" asked Audrey.

I pointed. Half buried in the sand was—

"A wheelbarrow," Audrey said.

"The red one. From the farm at the other end of the canyon. It must've washed down here in the flood," I surmised.

"It's glazed with rainwater," Kate observed.

"Unfortunately, still no chickens," said Louis.

"That's okay," I said.

"Are *you* okay?" asked Audrey. "You nearly drowned."

"I'm perfect," I answered.

"Me too," replied Audrey, Louis, and Kate all at once. And then we fell into silence, which was also perfect.

I remembered the question Mrs. Dunaway had asked after the Quiz Bowl Catastrophe—I felt like she'd asked it in another lifetime, and like she'd asked another me: How much depends upon a red wheelbarrow?

In a flash, I realized everything that'd happened on el Viaje a la Confianza had been leading me to the answer. I finally understood what William Carlos Williams meant: things aren't always just plain things. They aren't simply objects and facts and details you can memorize. His wheelbarrow was more than just paint and iron and wooden handles and a rubber tire, because sometimes what you experience adds up something bigger, brighter, more important than yourself, and once in a while something becomes so much yours, you know you'll carry it with you always.

A shiny wheelbarrow.

A rinsed-clean sky with friends gathered under it.

We'd all get up soon and make our way back to camp, but this moment would last forever. And how much depended on it? Everything.

In the meantime, in the sunlight after the storm, the red wheelbarrow from the abandoned farm looked beautiful. As beautiful as I felt. "I get it, Mrs. Dunaway," I murmured. "I really do."

Daphne stared up the river, the way she'd probably been staring for two days, hoping for a kayak to appear. "I waited," she murmured. "I almost drowned."

"It's not your fault if you wait and your dad doesn't come," Randolph said to comfort her. "Believe me. I know."

Daphne turned to me. "I almost killed all of you," she said.

I thought about the lie Daphne had believed for so long about her dad. I also thought about the truth she would have to face now. The shattered look in her eyes made me think she'd already started to see it. Out of everything that'd happened, this felt like the worst thing of all. Because nobody could fix it.

I knew that President Barack Obama, President Bill Clinton, and Olympic medalist Michael Phelps grew up without their fathers. And after age eleven, George Washington didn't have one either.

I also knew that telling Daphne these facts wouldn't change a thing. Sometimes facts help. But they can't tell the whole story. Sometimes, facts are no help at all.

"He never came," said Daphne.

"But we did," Audrey answered.

"But you don't even like me," said Daphne.

"It's not that we don't like you," I began. Audrey turned her head and gave me a look.

"Okay," I said, sighing. "We haven't liked you all that much so far."

"But you came anyway," said Daphne.

I shrugged. "Yeah, we came anyway."

Then Daphne smiled and said, "Thanks."

* * *

After we got ourselves together, and dried our socks, and filled our bottles, and dropped in the water-purifying pills, we hiked back to camp through the remnants of the flood, just a few harmless trickles in the bottom of Gage Cut. The rock slide had been blasted to oblivion. Not even a shard of gravel remained on that trail. It was as clean as a whistle.

We crossed the desert as darkness grew deeper and deeper around us, and then receded again, as the moon rose and soon shone so brilliantly, we could see one anothers' faces, sharp and white.

Nobody talked. Not because we were unhappy. It was the opposite. We felt like we'd won a victory that would last a long time.

Above us, as we hiked, the stars of the Milky Way brightened until they joined into a solid streak of light, and finally Audrey spoke the only words of the night. She stopped in the trail, barely half a mile from camp, and turned her face toward the blazing sky. "Look," she whispered, pointing at the Milky Way. "They're all one star."

In camp the next morning, we explained as much as we could to the rangers Enod and Kevin had fetched. We didn't lie, although I admit we did leave some things out. We told them that Daphne had taken off on her own, and because Jare got hurt, the five of us had gone to save her. We didn't see Jare again, because he'd already been airlifted to a hospital in El Paso, but none of the rangers mentioned that Jare was being charged with kidnapping, so we figured he must have done some leaving out of his own. Even so, it was pretty clear that he'd have to find another line of work. Stick a fork in el Viaje a la Confianza. It was done.

When we got back to the camp headquarters, some of the parents were already there. Daphne's dad was nowhere to be found, but there was a woman waiting for Daphne who must've been her mother, because, except for her regular brown hair and regular mom clothes, she looked exactly like her. You could tell from the woman's eyes that she'd spent at least an entire plane ride crying, but when she saw Daphne, her face lit up like a skyful of stars, and when Daphne ran over to her and hugged her, Audrey, Kate, Louis, Randolph, and I watched as she hung on just the way we'd all held on to Louis when he was saving us from drowning.

A few days after I flew home, Hardy Gillooly and I went to hang out at Splashview Pool so I could tell him about the whole thing. When I was finished, I also told Hardy I wanted to start a wilderness club at school.

"Good idea," said Hardy. "I'll join up. And next year? Why don't we just skip Quiz Masters?" He was trying to be nice. To let me off the hook after last spring.

I told him no. I wanted to start a wilderness club, but I still wanted to do Quiz Masters. Because being captain of the Quiz Masters team was still part of who I was, and now that el Viaje a la Confianza had taught me how important it is to trust your friends, I knew I could do a much better job.

"What if there's another, um—" began Hardy.

"Catastrophe?" I asked. "So what? I'm still doing it."

Hardy looked a little doubtful.

"I'm doing it *anyway*!" I said.

"Anyway?" repeated Hardy.

I said, "When my friend Audrey visits, we'll tell you all about the anyway. You're gonna like Audrey."

EPILOGUE

Audrey Alcott

Greenwood, Delaware

JANIE'S PARENTS WERE GETTING A divorce. By the time she told me this, I'd already figured it out. It takes a long time to fly from Texas to the Philadelphia airport, which was the closest one to my house in Delaware, but I needed every minute because, while I was a natural at knowing when people were lying, I was brand-new at understanding the reasons they might have for doing it.

All the dots were there for my connecting: Janie's quietness; her absences from school; her undone homework; her tired, February-looking face; the flowerpots her dad had left unfilled; the stolen bracelet; how when her mother stood in the doorway with her arm around Janie and lied to me, her words had said she'd picked the bracelet out of a catalog for Janie to buy, but her voice and eyes had said something more like *Audrey, please just let this drop, I'm begging you.*

As soon as the plane wheels hit the tarmac in Philly, I was texting Janie, asking her to meet me the following day in the woods between our neighborhood and the school, which I knew was a good place to be alone but thought would be an even better place to talk to your best friend for the first time in much too long, the perfect place to tell the truth, the perfect place to say "I'm sorry." Because I was so sorry.

I started this way: "When it comes to friendship, the anyway is the whole point." And I hoped harder than I'd ever hoped for anything before that Janie would agree.

She did.

Later, we went back to Janie's house, and I told her about my unsuperpower because she was my best friend and I trusted her. Besides, if I was ever going to accept it as just another part of myself, like Aaron had suggested, I was going to need all the help I could get, especially at school.

Afterward, the two of us boxed up the bracelet and sent it back, and even though I told her she didn't have to, Janie wrote a note to Lyza explaining what had really happened, all of it. The day before she'd stolen the bracelet, her dad had moved out of their house and into an apartment.

All I could think was that I hadn't seen my mom smile in so long. That's no excuse, though, for what I did to you and to Audrey, and I've felt terrible about it ever since. Whatever the consequences will be, I'm ready to take them.

She did take them too—two days later, when Lyza and her mom showed up at her front door. Lyza's mom brought a casserole. Lyza brought Boo-Dog on a leash and asked Janie if she wanted to go for a walk. They picked me up along the way.

Yes, good people can lie and still be good people. But when they tell the truth, it gives all of us the chance to be amazing.

The minute I got home from that walk, I texted Aaron, Louis, and Kate to tell them about it because without them, it never would have happened.

Aaron, Kate, Louis, and I agreed: the hardest part of camp wasn't almost drowning in a flash flood. It wasn't brutal heat or desperate thirst, cactus spines, bats, or hailstones. It wasn't late-night crying or gluey oatmeal or being chased by a giant, possibly homicidal ex-football player or body-slammed by Randolph. It wasn't even getting a millipede down your shirt, although Louis said that was a close second. No, in the end, the hardest part was saying good-bye.

Of the Fearless Four, I was the first to leave for the airport, and as I was saying good-bye to each of my friends in turn, I laughed through my tears and said, "Sheesh, this is like the end of *The Wizard of Oz*."

I didn't just mean the tears and the hugs and the going home. I meant, also, that we were all leaving with gifts, ones we'd given each other, not medals or diplomas or watches shaped like hearts like in the movie, but new ways of being who we were. Although I guess they weren't really new; they'd been there all along, but we'd needed each other in order to see them.

When I got to Aaron, he smiled and said, "Did you notice how I didn't even mention that the Cowardly Lion's costume was made from real lion pelts or that the Tin Man's oil was actually chocolate sauce?"

Aaron Archer, I think I'll miss you most of all.

"Don't forget! My house in three weeks!" said Louis. "That'll give me plenty of time to install the trapeze and get really good at it."

It had turned out that we all lived within a couple of hours of each other, and even though "a couple of hours" wasn't the same as "a few tents away," we would take it. I'm pretty sure that Louis was joking about the trapeze. But I'm not positive.

When we'd gotten to camp, we'd been Louis the

Scared, Kate the Sad, Aaron the Memory Boy, and Audrey the Hermit. We left it Louis the Brave, Kate the Protector, Aaron the Kind, and Audrey the—well, by the time I got home, I was so many Audreys: the Confused, the Understanding, the Liar, the Loyal, the Trusting, the Friend. I'd gone from being a human polygraph test to just plain human.

And all of this in just two and a half weeks. Next summer, at whatever camp we decide on, we'll have the whole six.

Just imagine what could happen.

ACKNOWLEDGMENTS

PROFOUNDEST THANKS TO: our awesome agent, Jennifer Carlson, who is great when times are great, tough when times are tough, and gracious always;

our spectacular editors, Alice Jerman and Kari Sutherland, who kindly allowed us to wander into the wilderness and skillfully guided us back;

everyone who loves the desert as much as we do, especially James Barnes, Mark Caughey, Susan Davis, Todd Lancaster, Kym Pinder, Erik Ryberg, Kristina de los Santos, Andrew Teague, and Charles Teague;

our avid early readers, Andrew Avila, Annabel Teague, and Julie Heaney;

and finally, David thanks Marisa for seeing the desert so vividly, and Marisa thanks David for showing it to her.